W9-BNN-389

SPIRITS REVIVED

SPIRITS REVIVED

ALICE DUNCAN

FIVE STAR
A part of Gale, Cengage Learning

Detroit • New York • San Francisco • New Haven, Conn • Waterville, Maine • London

GALE
CENGAGE Learning®

LIBRARY OF CONGRESS CATALOGING-IN-PUBLICATION DATA

Duncan, Alice, 1945–
    Spirits revived : spirits, featuring Daisy Gumm Majesty / Alice Duncan.
        pages cm.
        ISBN 978-1-4328-2798-4 (hardcover) — ISBN 1-4328-2798-7 (hardcover)
    1. Majesty, Daisy Gumm (Fictitious character)—Fiction. 2. Spiritualists—Fiction. 3. Motion pictures—Production and direction—Fiction. 4. Pasadena (Calif.)—Fiction. I. Title.
PS3554.U463394S65 2014
813'.54—dc23   2013041054

First Edition. First Printing: March 2014
Find us on Facebook– https://www.facebook.com/FiveStarCengage
Visit our website– http://www.gale.cengage.com/fivestar/
Contact Five Star™ Publishing at FiveStar@cengage.com

Printed in Mexico
1 2 3 4 5 6 7 18 17 16 15 14

ACKNOWLEDGMENTS

I couldn't have written this book without input from Mimi Riser, who, not for the first time, gave me the main plot line when we were chatting on the phone one day.

And to Lynne Welch and Sue Krekeler, who very bravely offered to be beta readers for me, I offer my vast and unfettered appreciation. Covered in chocolate. This past year (2012) has been heck for me, what with three surgeries and approximately ten million jaunts from Roswell to Albuquerque (a four-hundred-mile round trip) to visit doctors and have medical procedures, and without them, I'd never have finished the darned thing. Thank you both so very, *very* much!

By the way, the Keiji in this story was named for my late son-in-law, Keiji Oshita, who died far too young.

CHAPTER ONE

June 15, 1923. A year to the day since my husband, Billy Majesty, was laid to rest in Morningside Cemetery in Altadena, California.

The sun shone down upon the lovely spread of green grass and majestic trees as if bestowing a benediction on the day. The weather was as perfect as it had been a year prior, and again this year I felt betrayed by it. How could the sun still shine and my hometown still be beautiful with my darling Billy gone? No answer came from above—or anywhere else. Again.

Today I'd come to the cemetery with Spike, Billy's wonderful and well-loved, black-and-tan dachshund. I'm pretty sure dogs aren't allowed in the cemetery, but I drove us in our lovely self-starting Chevrolet, and nobody saw us. At least nobody stopped us. I kept Spike on the leash as I walked him to Billy's grave.

This wasn't the first time, by far, I'd visited my husband's last resting place, but it was the first time I'd brought Spike and flowers both. It was also the first time I aimed to have a long chat with Billy.

Not that I can communicate with the dead, in spite of how I make my living, which is as a spiritualist medium for people with more money than brains in the Pasadena/Altadena area. There were lots of them. I don't mean to sound cynical, and I truly liked most of the people for whom I performed séances and worked the Ouija board and read tarot cards. But really. Anybody with an ounce of common sense knows better than to believe in communication from the Other Side. Whatever that is. According to our Methodist minister, the Other Side is heaven. Guess I'd find out for myself one day.

At any rate, that day I felt like talking, so talk I did, while Spike wandered close by, sniffing up a storm. I'd taken him to dog obedience classes at Brookside Park a year or so ago, and he was expertly trained. Those folks at the obedience club really knew their stuff. They trained people to train their dogs like nobody's business, and neither Spike nor I had forgotten our lessons.

I laid the dozen red roses, purchased at a nearby florist's shop for a fortune, on Billy's grave near the headstone, and sat beside it. Spending the money didn't bother me, nor did it cause a hardship. As I said, I had a large and wealthy clientele. I'd worn a simple day dress of blue-checked gingham, since I'd anticipated grass stains. Naturally, I'd made the dress myself because I was a crackerjack seamstress.

The headstone, by the way, had been installed on the site about three months after Billy's interment. It was a lovely gray color, not tall, but with a pretty filigree pattern surrounding the words: "Sacred to the memory of William Anthony Majesty. Beloved husband of Daisy. July 12, 1897–June 10, 1922. Rest now as you could not in life. *The Good Die First.*" That last part is from Wordsworth. I must have spent a week and a half in the library, going through their copy of *Bartlett's Familiar Quotations,* before I settled on it. My family didn't like the "Rest now" part, but I insisted upon it because it was the truth. And, since I paid for both the headstone and the engraving, I got what I wanted. At the time he died, Billy didn't have any family except me, so I only had to argue with my mother and father and aunt.

"I miss you, Billy," I said, and instantly started crying. Stupid, emotional me. But I'd loved him practically since I could walk, so I think I deserved a good cry or fifty. After blotting my tears with my hankie, I went on.

"If you can really see what's going on down here on earth, you probably know I went through a rough time after you left me. That was bosh you wrote in that note, by the way, about wanting to die in the summertime because it wasn't around any major holidays, so we wouldn't connect your death with Thanksgiving or Christmas or New Year's Day or Easter or whatever. We missed you like fire on all those days and on every other day in the year since you left us, and we would have, no matter when you'd died."

Billy had killed himself. I know that sounds stark and bald and probably unchristian, but you need to know that Billy was a casualty of the Great War. I know, I know. When he finally drank all the morphine syrup he'd stored up, the war had been over for five years. But Billy had been shot and gassed by the forever-cursed Germans, and had been a shell-shocked wreck of himself almost since he first set foot on European soil. He existed in constant pain, could hardly breathe, and hated living the way he lived. Everyone who knew us knew that Billy was doomed to die early. He'd just taken matters into his own hands when life got too much for him. I don't blame him, really, but I still think it was stupid to write that we wouldn't miss him because he'd died during the summertime. Silly Billy.

"Anyhow, that's beside the point. If you can see what's going on down here"—I refused to believe a just God would deny Billy entry into heaven merely because he'd ended his own shattered life—"you know that Harold took me on a trip to Egypt last August. It was too darned hot, and we spent most of our time in Turkey, and I was sick as a dog the whole time. Well, not the *whole* time, but you know what I mean."

Neither Billy nor Sam Rotondo (Billy's best friend) cared for Harold Kincaid, son of Mrs. Pinkerton (my best client) and one of my dearest friends, because he . . . oh, bother. This is always so difficult to explain. You see, Harold Kincaid is one of those men who don't care for the ladies. He and his friend, Delray Farrington, had been together for years. Kind of like Billy and me, only they're two men. If you see what I mean.

"The really galling part about our trip to Egypt was that King Tutankhamen's tomb was discovered in November, a mere three months after we left the place. Well, you already know life isn't fair."

I heaved a deep sigh. "I renewed your subscription to *National Geographic* because Pa and I like to read it. They've had lots of interesting articles about the discovery of the tomb lately. The pictures they've printed have been fascinating. I only wish they could show us the colors of the objects. I guess King Tut was a minor pharaoh, but he's sure interesting, and the discovery of his tomb has been a real eye-opener."

Deciding a cheery note would not come amiss, I said, "Flossie and Johnny had a bouncing baby boy last October. They named him William, in honor of you." I swallowed another bout of sobs and tried to sound happy. "I thought that was so sweet of them. They said if the baby had been a girl, they were going to name her Daisy, so it's a good thing Flossie had a boy."

Johnny Buckingham, by the way, was a captain in the Salvation Army, and Flossie was his wife. They've always credited me with bringing them together, and I guess they're right. I was actually attempting to pry Flossie away from her mean-tempered bully of a mobster gentleman friend at the time. No matter how or why they met, Flossie and Johnny seemed perfect together.

As for the Daisy thing, I'd never been awfully fond of my name. That's one of the reasons I'd selected Desdemona as the name of my spiritualist persona when I was ten years old and discovered I had a knack for spiritualistic matters. If I'd been a bit older or had been forced to read *Othello* when I was a mere child, I'd probably have chosen something other than the name of a world-famous murderee, but what can you expect from a ten-year-old? I was stuck with Desdemona now.

The next part of the message I wanted to convey to Billy was difficult. "Um, I heard you tell Sam to please take care of me after you were gone a couple of weeks before you did the deed, Billy. I figured you were up to something then, although I hoped I was wrong." Another huge sigh from me made Spike turn from sniffing the trunk of a gigantic oak tree and give a soft whine.

"It's all right, Spike. I'm fine."

That was a lie, but Spike didn't need to know it. "Anyway, Sam's been as good as his word. He's always coming over to play rummy with Pa and eat dinner with us."

Sam Rotondo was a Pasadena police detective and, as I've already said, he'd been Billy's very best friend. Sam occasionally drove me nuts, but he was a good man. It had taken me a couple of years to admit it, mainly because Sam was always blaming me for things that weren't my fault. I mean, could *I* have made Stacy Kincaid, daughter of Mrs. Pinkerton, behave herself when even her mother couldn't? Was it *my* fault Mrs. Pinkerton had begged me to conduct a séance in a speakeasy that managed to get itself raided the very night I did so? And could *I* be faulted for a couple of crooks crashing my cooking class at the Salvation Army? No, darn it. Not to mention that me teaching a cooking class was akin to having Jack the Ripper teach Sunday School. Well, maybe not quite *that* bad. But close. I could, literally, burn water. Very well, I hadn't actually burned the water itself, but we'd had to throw the saucepan out because I'd left it on the stove long after the water had evaporated, and the house smelled like smoke for a week or more. But that was beside the point.

"Um . . . Sam followed us to Turkey because he thought I

was too stupid to take care of myself, and he didn't trust Harold to do it.

"But," I added in staunch defense of my buddy Harold, "when push came to shove and Sam was kidnapped, Harold pulled through like a champ. He even shot one of the villains." He'd fainted immediately after he'd done it, but he'd stopped the crook. Anyway, there was no reason to tell Billy about Harold fainting. If Billy really was in heaven looking down upon us mortals struggling away on this mortal coil, he'd already know it. And if there was nothing to go to after death, in spite of what my lifetime of Methodist training had taught me, it didn't matter anyway.

There was one other thing I wanted to tell Billy, but it was difficult, so I'd been putting it off. I sucked in a deep breath. "But the important thing is that after we rescued Sam, he told me he loved me." I said it in kind of a hurry, and my words stumbled together. "Not that he's said a single word about his feelings since, or that we've done anything except eat dinner together at our house. Well, and he's taken the whole family out to the flickers a couple of times."

Sam's confession had shocked me speechless. That was probably a good thing, since we'd been arguing rather fiercely at the time. But honestly, how could I have known that all his fussing and fuming about what I did and how I did it stemmed from love? In truth, I'm pretty sure it didn't, at least at first. He was an excellent friend to Billy, but at first Sam had seen me merely as somebody who got into trouble and worked at an unsuitable job. Billy had thought so, too. He'd even gone so far as to say that what I did to put bread on the table was wicked.

Nuts to that. I made scads more money as a phony spiritualist than I would have as an elevator operator or a clerk in Nash's Department Store or anything like that. In fact, my income went to support the entire family. My father had been unable to work since having a heart attack a few years earlier. My aunt Viola worked as Mrs. Pinkerton's cook, and my mother worked as chief bookkeeper at the Hotel Marengo. So, all things considered, and also considering that women made a good deal less than men in the world of work, our family had it pretty good. The country had been in an economic slump ever since the war ended.

It's frightening to think that war is good for business, but I guess it is. For the manufacturing magnates, anyhow. Wars aren't the tiniest bit good for the soldiers who fight in them. And don't tell me the Great War was a noble conflict, either. It was a waste of time, money, and life, it took my husband from me, and I'll hate it forever.

Anyhow, I'd figured Sam to be Billy's friend and my worst nightmare until Harold whisked me away to Egypt on a trip I didn't want to take. Then Sam and I began corresponding, and I discovered I missed him. That came as a gigantic surprise, believe me.

"But I want you to know, Billy," I went on, "that I'm still working as a spiritualist. I know you hated my line of work, but if you'd been honest, you'd have admitted I made more money doing that than anything else." I didn't say what we both had known since the war: that Billy was unable to support even the two of us because of his grievous injuries. That's why we lived with my folks in our bungalow on South Marengo Avenue. I suspect that's also why Billy groused about my spiritualist work. He felt bad that he couldn't support us.

"We still walk to church every Sunday, and I still sing in the choir. And—oh! I almost forgot to tell you that Lucy Spinks is seeing a very nice man!"

Very well, so Billy probably didn't care about that. I did, because Lucy had been soft on Sam at one time, and had been disappointed when he didn't return her affections. I had no idea, of course, that Sam was in love with me, which was perhaps why he didn't appreciate Lucy as she ought to be appreciated. Not that Lucy was a great beauty. In fact, she was tall and thin and kind of rabbity, but she had a gorgeous soprano voice. Besides, the truth was that so many young men had been killed or otherwise ruined by the Great War, young men were slim on the ground for single women our age, which was twenty-two. Maybe Lucy was twenty-three or -four, but still . . .

"Anyhow, a fellow named Albert Zollinger began attending First Methodist about a year ago. He's a widower from Michigan or somewhere like that, and he and Lucy recently began stepping out." Not that I considered Albert such a great catch, being a good deal older than Lucy, bald, not awfully handsome, and a widower, but the times being what they were, I guess Lucy'd decided to take what she could get. I didn't say that to Billy.

I was about to expound on the Lucy-Albert situation because, while it was inconsequential to Billy, it was easier than talking about Sam and me, when Spike set up his "Oh, goody, a friend is coming to visit" bark. I looked up quickly and was surprised—that's putting it mildly—when I beheld Sam Rotondo himself standing a few feet away from me, greeting Spike.

In a jiffy, I jumped to my feet and brushed down my skirt, hoping my eyes weren't red and swollen and I hadn't picked up too many grass stains.

"Sam! What are you doing here?" Once the words were out, I wished I'd rephrased my question because it sounded rude.

He glanced up and rose slowly from patting the dog. Spike continued to bounce around his feet. Once, when Spike was a puppy, he'd peed on one of Sam's shoes, and I'd been glad of it. Today I was glad to see Spike happy to see Sam. My, how times change.

"I came here to visit my wife's grave," he said. "And I thought

I'd visit Billy's, too. I didn't know you'd be here, although I don't know why, this being the fifteenth and all."

He looked a little abashed. Sam Rotondo. Big, rugged detective, whom I'd seldom seen discomposed, much less shy. Well, except for after he'd told me he loved me, and that had only lasted a second before he got mad again. I sighed.

"I didn't know your Margaret was buried here in Morningside, Sam."

"Yeah. She's over there." He pointed over his shoulder. "Under that sycamore tree."

"This is a beautiful place," I said inanely. I mean, it was a cemetery. How beautiful could it be?

Actually, it was beautiful—but it contained so much grief, its beauty was marred somehow, at least for me.

"Um . . . would you like a little time alone with Billy?" I asked, still being inane.

"No, that's all right. I'll just . . ." He shrugged as his voice trailed off.

Hmm. All right, so neither one of us knew what to say now that we were alone together except for Spike. Ergo, I decided to take matters into my own two competent hands. "May I see Margaret's gravesite, Sam? I'd like to see it."

"You would?" He seemed surprised, which vaguely irked me.

Unfortunately, Sam almost always irked me. That was probably my fault. After all, I'd not treated him especially well in times past. He probably expected a tongue-lashing every time we met.

"Yes," I said, suppressing my annoyance. "I'd like to see where she is. She's not too far away from Billy, is she?"

"No, she's not." He glanced down at Spike, who had begun leaping upon his trousers.

"Spike. Down," I said, recalling my manners and those of my dog.

Spike lay at Sam's feet. See what I mean about that obedience class? Even in his ecstasy, Spike obeyed me. Would that people did the same.

"Well, come along then," said Sam, as ungracious as ever.

I let his surly comment go. No use provoking the beast. Sam, I mean. Not Spike. "Thanks, Sam."

He hooked his elbow for me to take, I placed my hand on his arm, and we set off for that sycamore tree a mere several yards from Billy's grave.

"Spike, heel," said I as we started off.

Spike, brilliant dog that he was—he'd placed first in his obedience class—heeled.

CHAPTER TWO

We didn't speak as we walked to Sam's late wife's final resting place. Our silence wasn't at all uncomfortable, as so many of our conversations had been. I no longer considered Sam the enemy. For sure, Spike didn't. He was so happy to be there on this glorious day with the two of us, he pranced at heel alongside us as if he were dancing.

Sam stopped in front of another gravestone, less elaborate than Billy's, although it too had a filigree design on top. On it was written: "Margaret Mary Rotondo. b. 1893. d. 1918." She'd been only twenty-five years old. The same age my Billy would have been last year if he'd lived until July. But I didn't want to think about that.

"That's it? You didn't want them to say anything else about her?" I asked Sam, thinking somebody involved in her burial had lacked imagination. I suspected Sam.

I felt him shrug. "Didn't know what else to say. I was . . . upset at the time, and there was nobody else around to help. Her family was gone, and mine was in New York."

After a pause, I said, "I can understand that."

"But you wrote a nice thing for Billy," Sam said.

Inwardly I preened a little. "I had to dig for that quotation for a long time."

"Which one? The one about him resting or the one about the good dying first?"

Oh, Lord. I guess Sam didn't read poetry on a regular basis.

"I made up the one about him resting. The good dying first one was written by William Wordsworth."

"Hmm. Wasn't he a poet or something?"

Merciful heavens. "Yes, Sam, he was a poet. A famous one. The complete quotation is, 'The good die first, and they whose hearts are dry as summer dust, burn to the socket.' "

His brow furrowed and he frowned. "What the heck does that mean?"

"Sam Rotondo, if you aren't the most—"

"Don't get mad. I'm serious. What does that mean, 'the good die first'? And that 'burn to the socket' part. What does that mean?"

"Well, I guess it means that life isn't fair. That good people die young, and lots of bad—or less good—people live forever and wear out when they're ninety-five or something like that."

"Kind of like, 'Only the good die young'?"

"Kind of, I suppose. I think that one's from Euripides. He said something like, 'whom the gods love die young.' Which doesn't make any sense to me. If any god ever loved Billy, he sure put him through hell before he let him die." I pondered some of those pronouns, but I needn't have. Sam understood.

"Yeah. I agree. Like Margaret. She was good, and she got tuberculosis. What kind of reward is that for being good? Like Billy got shot all to hell and gassed. I can't see a reasonable god allowing stuff like that to happen."

I was beginning to feel blasphemous, so I fell back on one of my Methodist fundamentals. With a shrug, I said, "God gives us the earth and everything on it, and it's up to us to do with it what we will. Neither you nor I began that stupid war or created consumption. The fact that neither Margaret nor Billy deserved their fate is a man-made thing, not God's fault."

"Huh. In Billy's case, maybe. People didn't create the tuberculosis bacillus."

I sighed. "Too true. I don't know what the answer is, Sam."

"I'm beginning to think there isn't one."

How depressing. "I'm afraid you may be right."

Spike took that moment to break his training and make a running leap at a dawdling bird. Fortunately for all of us (except Spike) he missed the bird. He'd actually snapped a sparrow out of the air once, in our back yard. Shocked everyone, especially the bird, which didn't survive the experience, poor thing.

But at least he broke the melancholy mood pervading Sam and me. "Spike! Come!"

As much as he didn't want to, Spike came. I knelt down. "Good boy. What a good boy you are!" Effusive praise for an erring pet, but that was part of the training. If I were trying to teach him a new behavior, I'd give him a treat for his compliance, but in this case Spike was happy with praise. Dogs are so much better able to deal with life than we humans. I mean, if a dog is sick or unhappy, he goes and lies down somewhere and rests. He doesn't dwell on the evils of life or how crummy he feels.

Mind you, I don't know that for a certified fact, but I'd noticed that if Spike couldn't eat something or play with it, he'd just ignore it and go do something else. We humans like to brood over our grievances and suffer and moan and groan. Heck, after Billy died, I'd nearly starved myself to death. Not on purpose. But I couldn't seem to eat. Harold told me I looked skeletal. Me! Daisy Gumm Majesty, who has deplored my unseemly curves ever since the "lean and boyish" look for women became fashionable.

A year later, I'd regained some of the weight I'd lost, but not all of it. I suppose that was a good thing, since I have to look ethereal for my job, and makeup and somber clothing can only do so much. Nobody wants a robust spiritualist, after all. The only problem with my weight loss was that most of my clothes had to be altered, but as I'm so good with a sewing machine, even that wasn't much of a big deal.

Sam broke the silence that had settled over us after Spike had made his break and come back. "I'm glad we didn't have kids, Margaret and me."

I looked up at him sharply. "You didn't want children?" I'd always envisioned Billy and me with three children. Two boys and a girl, and the boys would protect the little girl and make sure nobody ever hurt her. I'd had an older brother and an older sister, and neither one of them had protected me, but a girl can dream, can't she? Besides, my dream didn't last past the first year of my marriage to Billy.

With one of his characteristic shrugs, Sam said, "Well, sure, I'd have liked to have kids, but I sure wouldn't want to rear them all by myself. My job takes all my time. I'd probably have had to send them to my parents in New York City, and how nice would that have been? My parents don't need to raise any more kids, and my kids and I wouldn't even know each other."

"Yes," I said thoughtfully. "I'd hate to have someone else rear my children. I don't know about your folks, but mine have enough to do without raising a brood of other people's children."

"Mine, too. My dad still works as a jeweler. And my mother has a ton of grandchildren at the house all the time. My sisters' kids. I have three sisters."

I'm not sure, but I think Sam shuddered slightly. I almost laughed. "Three sisters must have been a strain on you."

"You have no idea."

"I remember you told us your father was a jeweler. Somehow, I always think of Italians as owning restaurants and Jewish people owning the jewelry stores. Stereotypes don't always work out, do they?"

"There are plenty of Jewish jewelers in New York City. But other folks get in on the business, too. And all sorts of people have restaurants. Have you ever heard of Delmonico's?"

"Yes. I've read about it in books. The *National Geographic* said Delmonico's changed the way America eats, and that everything before it opened was either boiled or fried. But now, thanks to Delmonico's, we've expanded our taste buds, or something like that."

"Delmonico's was opened by a couple of Swiss brothers."

"Really? I guess I missed that in the article. The name sounds Italian."

"It might be Italian, but the Delmonico brothers were Swiss." I heard the scorn in Sam's voice.

"Well, how should I know?" I asked, feeling defensive. "I don't know very many Swiss people. Or Italians, either, for that matter."

A year and a half or so ago, I'd met a German woman who was trying to pass herself off as a Swiss, but I'd found her out. I was going to have her deported, what's more, because I generally loathe all things German because of the war. But the poor girl hadn't started the stupid war any more than I had, and she'd suffered from it, too. I ended up calling upon a very rich friend, and we managed to get Hilda Schwartz and another German boy asylum in the good old US of A. Another case of stereotypes toppling, I suppose. I shook my head, thinking you couldn't depend on anything anymore.

"Why are you shaking your head?" Sam asked, as if he thought I doubted him. "It's the truth. The Delmonico brothers were from Switzerland."

"I believe you. I was just thinking about . . . something else." Sam didn't approve of anyone circumventing the law, even for a just cause. One more reason we often clashed.

"Huh. You were thinking about that German girl in your cooking class, I'll bet."

Startled, I said, "How could you know about Hilda?"

"I don't know about Hilda. I know about you."

"Oh."

"Always trying to save the world. That's you. The world isn't worth saving, if you ask me."

"Don't be so cynical. The world is just the world. It's the people on it who do all the good and evil things. Neither Hilda nor you nor Billy nor I were in any way responsible for that reprehensible war. The blasted so-called leaders of our various nations were the ones who started it. And that guy who shot the Archduke Ferdinand, but I think he was only an excuse. I think the Kaiser and his cohorts were just *looking* for an excuse to take over the world. Stupid Kaiser."

"Yeah. Well, it didn't work."

"They'll try again."

"Now who's sounding cynical?"

I heaved another sigh. "You're right. War sure changes everything, doesn't it? Look at all the young folks now, the ones who are left, I mean: not believing in anything, drinking and smoking and dancing and thinking 'what's the use?' It makes me sad. And mad."

A lopsided smile creased Sam's face. "I've heard you rant about F. Scott Fitzgerald before."

"Right. All the bright young things with too much money and no goals, going to parties and contributing nothing. Like Stacy Kincaid." I felt like spitting as I spoke her name. "The rest of us have to work for a living."

"Well, she's still doing good works for the Salvation Army now, so you can't kick about her any longer."

"Huh," I said, borrowing a grunt from Sam. "I bet it won't last. It didn't last before."

Stacy had actually joined the Salvation Army before this latest foray into doing good works. Her conversion that time had lasted long enough for her to recruit me to teach that wretched cooking class. Then she'd slid back into her evil ways, got picked up in a raid on a speakeasy, hit one copper and kicked another one, and actually had to serve time in jail. During her first stint in the Salvation Army, her mother had been appalled. Didn't think the Salvation Army was right for her pampered daughter. If she'd been saved by an Episcopalian, Mrs. Pinkerton would have approved, I'm sure.

However, after Stacy's last fall from grace, poor Mrs. Pinkerton was willing to do anything to help her daughter stay on the straight and narrow path. My personal opinion on that score was that if Mrs. P. had smacked Stacy's hind end several times when she'd misbehaved as a child, she wouldn't be such a pain in the neck today. By the time of the cop-slapping incident, it was far too late for such reasonable measures as childhood discipline.

"You sound like you don't want Stacy to be a good girl."

"She's *not* a good girl. She's a pill. I feel sorry for her mother."

"Her mother is half her problem."

Exactly what I'd been thinking. I gave in with good grace. "I know. But Mrs. Pinkerton is such an . . ." Shoot, it sounded crass to call my best customer an idiot. "Well, she's not a very effective parent."

Sam let out a shout of laughter that probably had the inhabitants of the Morningside Cemetery turning in their graves.

"Sam! This is a graveyard, for Pete's sake!"

"So what? You think the residents are going to object? Margaret loved a good joke as much as anyone, and Billy would have laughed harder than I did if he'd heard you say that." His attitude sobered. "If he could have laughed at all."

There it was again. The damned German mustard gas that had ruined my husband's lungs.

I said, "You're right," and had to grab a hankie.

"Please don't cry, Daisy. I didn't mean to make you cry."

Shaking my head, I said, "It's all right, Sam. I've been crying ever since Spike and I got here today. Can't help it. Billy's life and death just seem so . . . unjust. You know what I mean?"

"I know exactly what you mean." He hesitated for a minute. "Say, Daisy, would you like to go out to dinner with me one of these days? I'd like to take you to that new restaurant in town. The Japanese one."

"There's another Japanese restaurant in town?" I sniffled and tried to wipe my tears away with my hankie. I felt like a fool, crying in front of Sam, although, God knew, I'd done it before.

"Miyaki's, or something like that. It's on South Los Robles."

I blinked a couple of times to get the world back in focus. Then it was I remembered Sam's declaration of love almost a year earlier, and began feeling shy. In front of Sam Rotondo, of all people. I swear.

"I . . . I . . ."

Sam rolled his eyes, another characteristic gesture of his when in my presence, and one that invariably irked me. "I'm not planning to ravish you, for God's sake. I just thought you might like to have dinner with me one evening. That's all. Hell, I'll take the whole family if that'll make you feel better. God knows, they feed me often enough."

That was true. "I didn't mean . . . I mean, I didn't think . . . Um, what do Japanese people eat, anyway?"

I thought I heard Sam mumble "Christ," under his breath, but I'm not sure. "Rice, I think. And probably lots of other stuff. Some of the guys at the station have eaten there, and they claim it's good."

"Well . . . sure, I'd like that, Sam." Then I started feeling guilty because I'd be enjoying a new cuisine and leaving the rest of my family home alone to dine on Aunt Vi's fare. Not that Aunt Vi isn't the world's best cook. It's just that . . . Oh, nuts. It's just that I'm crazy, I suppose.

Sam heaved one of the huger sighs I'd ever heard. "I'm going to invite your whole family, Daisy. Just so you won't feel guilty. Is that better?"

I squinted at Sam. "How'd you know what I was thinking?"

"I know you, Daisy Majesty. Believe me, I know you."

Well . . . maybe he did, at that.

CHAPTER THREE

We couldn't dine out at the Japanese restaurant (which was, indeed, called Miyaki's) the next day, which was Saturday, because I had to conduct a séance at Mrs. Bissel's house that evening. Mrs. Bissel is the woman who gave me Spike when I rid her basement of a ghost.

I know, I know. I wouldn't believe me either if I heard me say that. And in truth, the invader of her basement wasn't a real ghost—if there is such a thing—but merely an errant girl. But Mrs. Bissel didn't have to know that, and anyhow, the job garnered me not merely a big bonus, but also Spike. Mrs. Bissel, you see, breeds and raises dachshunds. Her primary goal in life is to have one of her dogs entered at the Westminster Kennel Club Dog Show in New York City one day. She's rich, of course. The goal most of the rest of us have is to survive from day to day, but to each her own.

At any rate, Sam came to dinner (again) on Friday night after we met in the cemetery, and he propounded the Japanese dinner as a treat for the whole family. Naturally, I then felt guilty about spending more of Sam's money than he'd originally intended. Some days I felt guilty about living. Maybe everyone does.

"A Japanese restaurant?" Aunt Vi said. She aimed an interested glance at me. "You didn't have any Japanese food when you went on that trip with Harold, did you, Daisy?"

I'd brought Vi back a Turkish cookbook, and every now and

again she actually prepared something from the book. Although it sounds impossible, since Vi is an expert cook and, if she were a man, would be called a chef and make a heap more money than she did, her attempts at Turkish cookery sometimes didn't live up to the original. Perhaps that's because she couldn't get all the proper ingredients or something.

"Nope. We had French food, Egyptian food, English food, and Turkish food, but no Japanese food."

"What do they eat in Japan?" asked my mother, whose name is Peggy, should anyone want to know.

Sam shrugged. "I'm not sure. Lots of rice. And something called . . . um . . . terra-something. Some of the guys at the station have eaten there, and they liked the terra-whatever-it-is. Oh, and they really liked the fried vegetables."

"Fried vegetables?" asked Vi, looking skeptical. "You mean they fry green peas instead of boiling them or something like that?"

"Interesting," muttered my father, whose name is Joe, forking up some buttered peas as he did so.

"Not like that," said Sam, whose brow furrowed in concentration. "I wish I'd paid more attention, but from what I gather, they dip the vegetables in some kind of batter and then fry them. Then you pick 'em up with your fingers and dip them into some kind of sauce."

Vi's eyes went round. "They eat with their *fingers*?" Vi, who was very strict about table manners—mine in particular—seemed shocked.

"No," said Sam. "*They* eat with chopsticks, like Chinese people do. The guys at the station ate with their fingers because they couldn't handle the chopsticks."

"Now *that* makes sense," said Pa, patting his mouth with a napkin.

"How interesting," said Ma, who was the least adventurous

of my whole family when it came to comestibles. I could tell she was prepared to endure dining at a Japanese restaurant, but she didn't plan on enjoying it. But she'd enjoyed Mexican food when we'd eaten at a wonderful Mexican restaurant in town, and she'd liked the Chop Suey Palace on Fair Oaks when we'd gone there.

We didn't dine out very often, mainly because folks like us just didn't. We could neither afford to do so, nor was it necessary. This was especially true since we had Vi. For instance, this evening, she'd prepared a simply delicious meal of pork chops, potatoes thinly sliced and baked in a pan with butter and milk—I think Vi called them scalloped potatoes, but I'm not sure—the aforementioned buttered peas, and some of her feather-light dinner rolls. I'm pretty sure she'd made extra rolls at Mrs. Pinkerton's house and brought them home for us. In effect, Vi had two jobs: cooking for Mrs. Pinkerton and her family, and cooking for us. I'd have felt sorry for her if she didn't seem to enjoy her work so much. You can bet we enjoyed it, too.

"I don't know," I said after a pause and a bite of pork chop. "I might like to try using chopsticks, if somebody would teach me how to."

"Don't look at me," said Sam, frowning. "I don't know how to use 'em. Anyhow, if the Chinese and Japanese are so smart, how come *they* didn't invent forks and spoons?"

"Evidently," I said somewhat stiffly, "they didn't need them because *they* can use chopsticks."

Sam rolled his eyes again, and I bridled.

"Don't roll your eyes at me, Sam Rotondo. Mrs. Bissel has a Japanese houseboy, and I'm going to ask him if he'll teach me how to eat with chopsticks. I'll show you."

"Daisy," said my mother in *that* voice. I felt like doing some eye-rolling of my own.

"I'm not arguing," I said, in hopes of mollifying her, although

28

this ploy seldom worked. "I'm just curious to see why it seems so hard for everyone who isn't Chinese or Japanese to eat with chopsticks."

"It probably isn't, if you know the trick," said Pa, always easygoing and sensible.

"You're probably right," said Sam.

"Well," said I, "if I can get Keiji to teach me the trick, I'll be happy to pass along the method."

"Thanks," said Sam.

I could tell he didn't mean it. In spite of Sam, we decided that our trek to Miyaki's would commence the following week on Saturday evening. Sam said he'd pick us all up at six o'clock.

The next day, Saturday, my father and I took Spike for a walk around the neighborhood in the morning. We got home in plenty of time to make some pork-chop sandwiches with the leftovers from last night's meal, and we had them on the table when Ma got home from her job a little after noon.

I rested for a while after lunch, preparing myself for the séance ahead. Not that séances in themselves were very tiring, but they did go on for a long time, and then people wanted to talk about them afterwards. I generally didn't get home until quite late. Then, on Sundays, I had to get up early to go to church, where I sang alto in the choir. So a nap was definitely called for. Spike enjoyed our nap, too. I don't think my mother approved of Spike sharing my bed with me, but ever since Billy's passing, she hadn't objected.

When I woke up, I went to the closet and surveyed my choices for the evening. I'd taken out Billy's clothes about six months prior to that day. I couldn't bear to do it for a long time, and I still had them packed away in the basement. I knew I should donate them to the Salvation Army so that some needy person could use them, but . . . well, I just couldn't. Yet. Maybe someday.

Anyhow, I had lots of clothes to choose from since sewing was one of my primary occupations when I wasn't raising the dead. I made clothes for the whole family. One year I even made matching Christmas shirts for all of us, including Spike. The memory of that Christmas now made me sad, so I stopped thinking and perused my wardrobe.

"Oh, bother, Spike. It's probably going to be a warm evening, so why don't I choose something lightweight?"

Spike wagged his tail, as if he thought my idea a splendid one.

I reached in and took out a black silk evening dress I'd made from a bolt end bought for a song at Maxime's Fabrics on Colorado Boulevard. It had short sleeves and a tubular shape to the hips—which was the fashion and the reason women were supposed to be skinny and "boyish" in those days. I had qualified for several months after Billy's death, but had regained some of my curves. To disguise them, I'd made a gray silk overbodice with a slashed V-neckline that reached to my hips. The skirt to the dress had layers. It was a very pretty ensemble, but somber.

The pattern, which I'd copied from a Worth model I'd seen in a fashion magazine, showed the overbodice with a frilly bow where the V ended, but frilly bows were too frivolous for a sober-sided spiritualist. I aimed to pin some black flowers there. Altogether, the outfit would be perfect for a warm June evening.

With pale face powder, black earrings from Nelson's Five and Dime, black shoes with pointy toes bought on sale at Nash's Dry Goods and Grocery, and my dark red hair smoothed into a severe bob, I'd look every inch the pale and interesting spiritualist. I'd also be comfortable. Attempting to be all those things at once could be difficult, but I generally managed.

I laid out everything on the bed and went to the kitchen to see if I could help Vi do anything.

"Set the table, will you, dear?" said she, peeking at something in the oven that smelled really, really good. Whatever it was brought back memories of Turkey.

"What is that in the oven, Vi? It smells divine."

"It's from that cookbook you brought back from Turkey. Eggplant with lamb and tomatoes."

"Oh, my! I'm so glad you're enjoying the book."

"It's fun to try new things every now and then, and the market had nice eggplants and tomatoes. Mr. Larkin ground some lamb for me. If we like it, maybe I'll try it on Mrs. Pinkerton and see how she likes it."

For the record, Mr. Larkin was the butcher Mrs. Pinkerton used. Well, in truth, my aunt used him, but only because Mrs. Pinkerton told her to. That was all right. Mr. Larkin knew the ways of the world, and when Vi was buying for our family, he charged her about a third what he charged when she bought for Mrs. Pinkerton. Was that unfair?

Naw. Mrs. Pinkerton could afford to pay more than we could.

"What's it called?" I asked.

Frowning, Vi shut the oven door and reached for the cookbook, which lay open on the kitchen counter. She puckered her brow and said slowly and carefully, "Patlican musakka. Well, I don't know if that's how they pronounce it in Turkey, but that's what it's called."

"Hmm. However it's pronounced, it sure smells good."

"I'm so glad."

Her smile was a mile wide, so I knew she meant it.

So I set the table feeling almost happy that night. I hadn't been truly happy for what seemed like forever, although I did experience moments of joy. Like when Vi used the cookbook I'd brought her because she felt like it. My feet were happy, too, when they trod upon the gorgeous Turkish rug I'd bought for the dining room. In other words, while the love of my life had taken himself out of it a year earlier, the rest of us slogged on, sometimes whether we wanted to or not. And every now and then life lost its bleak grayness and took on a less maudlin hue. If I liked lavender, I'd say it was lavender, but I don't. Soft peach, maybe.

Evidently my mother and father had been taking naps, too, because they were both rubbing their eyes when they walked into the dining room.

"Something smells really good," said Pa.

"It's from that Turkish cookbook I got Vi last year," I said proudly.

"Quite savory," said my mother. She wore a doubtful expression, however.

"It's eggplant and tomatoes and ground lamb and . . . oh, I can't remember."

"Lamb?" Ma perked up slightly. "I love it when Vi fixes leg of lamb. Maybe I'll like this."

"I tell you, Ma, the food in Turkey was better than anyplace else on that lousy trip. Including France, which is supposed to be the culinary capital of the world."

"Really? What do French folks eat?" asked Pa, looking as if he were really interested.

"Snails," I said, and laughed when both of my parents drew back, appalled.

"Daisy!" said my mother in a shame-on-you voice.

"It's the truth. I read about it in *National Geographic*, and Harold told me so, too. They cook the snails in butter and garlic, and people say they love them."

"I don't think I could eat a snail," said Pa.

"I don't think I could either," I agreed. "But I'm sure they eat other stuff as well. According to Harold, they use a lot of different kinds of sauces."

"Hmm. I can't imagine how a sauce could make a snail taste like anything but a garden pest." Ma went to the linen drawer and got out some napkins, which she laid under the forks on the table. We weren't formal at home, but we still used napkins and a tablecloth during dinnertime. Habit, I guess.

"You have a séance tonight, don't you, Daisy?" asked Ma.

"Yes. At Mrs. Bissel's house, although I think she said Mrs. Pinkerton is going to attend, too. And Mrs. Hanratty."

Pansy Hanratty was the reason Spike was such a well-behaved dog, because it was she who'd taught his obedience class. I liked her a lot, in spite of her mother, who's a snooty southern belle misplaced here in California. Her son is Monty Mountjoy, a current favorite cinematic heartthrob and a very nice man. You could have knocked me over with a feather when I learned that Monty Mountjoy had emerged from the womb of Pansy Hanratty, a horse-faced woman with a deep, booming voice that always sounds rather like a foghorn. You never knew where genes would take a person, did you?

"That should be interesting," said Pa, chuckling. "Is Stacy still behaving herself?"

"As far as I know," said I, not really caring one way or another, except for Mrs. Pinkerton's peace of mind. Stacy could fall off the edge of the world for all I cared.

"Daisy!" called Vi from the kitchen. "Will you come here and take out the salad?"

"You bet!" I couldn't wait to get my teeth around that delicious-smelling dish currently languishing in the oven. Vi had made a nice salad of fresh greens to go with it, along with some of her melt-in-the-mouth bread. We'd have had rolls again, but we'd eaten them all the night before.

Vi's eggplant, tomatoes, and lamb dish was every bit as tasty as it had smelled as it cooked, and we devoured the whole thing.

There wouldn't be any leftovers for tomorrow's lunch, but we could make do with whatever Vi fixed for dinner, which we took at noon on Sundays. I'm not sure why, but lots of people did the same thing. Another tradition, I suppose.

After dinner, Ma and I washed the dishes. Then I fed Spike and retired to the bathroom to do a little washing up of myself and my face, making sure to slather on the cold cream Harold Kincaid had directed me to use.

"You *have* to use the cream, Daisy. You don't want to get wrinkles, do you?"

At the time he said that, wrinkles were about the last thing about which I even thought, much less worried. However, after the first, hideous pangs of my grief over losing Billy had subsided a bit, I began once again to care about my appearance—as a spiritualist. As a regular human being, I still couldn't work up any energy to prettify myself. Still, I used the cream. Harold had actually brought me some from the studio where he works as a costumier.

I suppose it helped. But, shoot, I was only twenty-two. That was too young for wrinkles even if I didn't use the stupid stuff. However, Harold knew better than I how cinema stars kept themselves looking good, so I bowed to his experience.

Then I went to my room, where I got all spiffed up to visit Mrs. Bissel in her lovely home on the corner of Maiden Lane and Foothill Boulevard in Altadena, a darling little community just north of Pasadena. After I powdered my cheeks and nose and used a little mascara on the old eyelashes, I darkened my eyebrows with a stick of eyebrow pencil I'd bought at Nelson's Five and Dime. Eyebrow pencil was fairly new on the market, and I didn't much like spending my hard-earned money on makeup, but my job called for it. Anyhow, eyebrow pencil was ever so much better than what I'd had to use before, which was coal, and *extremely* messy.

Feeling daring for some reason, I drew a line under my lower lashes to see if it would create a dramatic effect and discovered the line to be rather too dramatic, so I rubbed it with my finger, thereby creating exactly the look I'd been seeking. And by accident, by gum!

Then I stood back to examine myself in front of the cheval glass mirror in the bedroom. And I grinned. "Boy, Spike, if I didn't know better, I'd think I was a real spiritualist."

Spike wagged his tail in approval. I picked up my black bag—into which I'd packed the one cranberry lamp and candle I allowed during a séance—departed the bedroom to bid farewell to my family, and drove up the hill in our lovely Chevrolet to Mrs. Bissel's house.

CHAPTER FOUR

Mrs. Bissel lived in a huge three-story mansion with an expansive front porch and a terraced front lawn that spread from the house to the street. The whole place was fenced and gated. She also owned all the property from her house west to Lake Avenue, the main north-south street in both Altadena and Pasadena. She had a couple of horses, although I don't think anyone had ridden them since her children had grown up and left home.

If you wanted to, you could park on Foothill Boulevard and then walk a mile or so from your car to her front door, but mostly everyone parked in the back, where there was a wide circular driveway surrounding a patch of land with a monkey puzzle tree in the middle. That tree was extremely odd looking, and I understood the name because its bark might have been a jigsaw puzzle, the way it would break away from the trunk in little pieces. It wasn't easy to get to the puzzle pieces, however, because of its gigantic, prickly leaves that could spear a person's skin if that person wasn't careful.

By the time I arrived at the Bissel place, several cars were already parked there, so I found a good place for the Chevrolet, got out, sucked in a deep breath—séances weren't difficult to conduct, but they could be emotionally trying, especially in those days, when people tended to ask me if I'd been in recent communication with Billy—headed for the back door, and rang the bell.

Hilda Schwartz, the German girl whom I'd helped gain legal asylum in the United States, used to work for Mrs. Bissel, but she'd married a few months earlier. Now Keiji Saito, the house-boy about whom I'd told my family, answered the door. He smiled when he saw me.

"Good evening, Mrs. Majesty."

"Good evening, Keiji. Have all the ghouls gathered, or are there more to come?"

He chuckled. "I think everyone's waiting for Mrs. Pinkerton to arrive. Otherwise, they're all here. You going to wake the dead again tonight?"

"Sure am. Say, Keiji, could you help me learn how to use chopsticks?"

His eyebrows lifted. "How come you want to learn how to use chopsticks?"

"A friend is taking my family and me out to dinner at Miya-ki's next Saturday, and I want to surprise everyone with my deftness with the old chopsticks."

"Oh, yeah. My uncle owns Miyaki's. Their food's pretty good, although we never eat like that at home. We generally eat rice with fish sauce, which white folks don't like much."

Made sense to me.

"But sure, I can help you with the chopsticks. Not that I'm great at them, either. Heck, I was born in the good old US of A, and I don't take meals at home very often any longer, now that I have this job."

Interested in both of these pieces of news, I asked, "Where were you born?"

"Hawaii. My uncle moved to Pasadena first, and he wrote to us to say we should come here, too."

"I had no idea," I said, trying to remember exactly how Hawaii fitted into the United States.

Keiji must have run into ignorant people before, because he

said with a grin, "Hawaii's a US territory, Mrs. Majesty."

"Of course! You probably think I'm an idiot."

"No. Most white people don't think about Hawaii when they think of the United States."

I gave Keiji the soft black shawl I'd worn over my gown, and he carried it as he conducted me to the living room. "We're an insular society, I reckon."

He shrugged. "Oh, I don't know. I hear Japan's worse. Either you're born there, or you don't belong. Anyway," he said with another short laugh, "how do you think people from New Mexico feel when most American citizens don't even know New Mexico's a state?"

"My goodness, I've never once thought about New Mexico. I'm so used to thinking about California, it never crosses my mind to think about the difficulties people in other states and territories must face."

"It's not so bad," he said, opening the door from the sun room, where I'd entered the Bissel mansion, to the living room. "Anyhow, have a good séance. The breakfast room's all set up for you, and I'm ready to turn off the lights whenever you say." He left me with another smile and a brief wave, and I wafted into the living room, wrapping my spiritualist persona around me like a cloak. I'd practiced wafting, and I did it to perfection.

The guests gathered there had been chatting, but as soon as I entered the room, Mrs. Bissel broke off the conversation she'd been having with Mrs. Hanratty, and both ladies rushed over to me.

"Good evening, Daisy. I'm so glad you could help us with this séance tonight."

"I'm pleased to be here," I told Mrs. Bissel in my low, soothing spiritualist's voice. I tell you, by that time, my voice was so well modulated, I could probably have taught elocution lessons—only that wouldn't have paid as much as spiritualism.

"So good to see you, Daisy," honked Mrs. Hanratty. She eyed me up and down with concern. "How have you been doing? I know what an ordeal you've been through this past year."

"Oh, but Daisy can communicate with her late husband, can't you, dear?" said Mrs. Bissel.

See what I mean?

My heart pinged painfully for a second. Then I bowed my head and murmured, "When a person crosses over to the Other Side, it sometimes takes a while until he or she feels settled enough to communicate with those of us remaining here on this plane." Spewing that sort of garbage was second nature to me by that time.

"Do you mean you *haven't* communicated with your late husband?"

Mrs. Hanratty's head drew back, and I hastened to assure her, "Not at all, Mrs. Hanratty. In fact, I chatted with Billy for quite a while the day before yesterday." And that was the truth. The fact that Billy hadn't answered would remain my secret.

"I'm so glad. Being blessed with the gift you have must be such a comfort," said Mrs. Bissel.

Oh, golly. Sometimes, and this was especially true since Billy's death, I wanted to screech at people who believed my nonsense to grow up and act like sensible adult human beings. That, however, would have been idiotic to do if I wanted to keep pursuing a lucrative career as a spiritualist. So I swallowed my anger—which I admit was irrational. After all, I don't guess it was their fault that Mrs. Bissel and Mrs. Hanratty actually believed my guff—and made a demure noise. We spiritualists are great at producing gentle noises that mean nothing. More and more in recent days, I'd come to think my entire life meant nothing. Not that I aimed to join Billy any time soon.

But honestly. How come was it that all these rich ladies believed the absurdity I fed them? None of my friends believed a body could converse with dead people. They all had too much sense for that.

Hmm. Perhaps I just answered my own question. Folks in my station in life didn't have time to fiddle with spirits and ghosts. We had too much *real* work to do in order to survive from day to day.

But never mind that. These women were my bread and butter, and I honored them for that. At least I tried to.

"Come with me, Daisy. I want you to meet my cousin, Laura," said Mrs. Bissel, her voice lowering as she took me by the arm and led me to the corner of her massive living room. "She suffered a terrible bereavement a couple of months ago when her son died."

"Oh, my goodness. I'm so sorry. What was his name and what happened to the poor fellow?"

"His name was Eddie. Eddie Hastings—my cousin is Laura Hastings, and her husband is Stephen Hastings—and no one quite knows how he died. He was found in his apartment—he was an attorney—when no one could get in touch with him for a few days. So young, too. Only twenty-seven." She lowered her voice even more. "Some of her friends and the police think he was a suicide, but Laura doesn't believe it."

Aha. Now I had something to work with. I wish she'd told me she wanted me to chat with Eddie sooner. I could have gone to the library and read his obituary. I'd heard about the Hastings family, however. Mr. Hastings ran one of Pasadena's most prestigious legal firms.

"What a tragedy," I murmured soulfully. "Did he work with his father?"

"Yes. The current Mr. Hastings' father began the firm late in the last century, and Eddie was carrying on the tradition. Indeed, it was an awful tragedy. It shattered poor Laura. Why, it's been two months, and she's only now getting out and about again."

"Two months isn't a long time when you've lost a beloved son." Or a husband. I spoke gently, because I didn't want Mrs. Bissel to think her comment had annoyed me, even though it had. Shoot, I'd agonized for months over Billy—still was agonizing, in fact—and, while it's dreadful to lose a husband, it must rip a mother's heart out to lose a child.

"Oh, yes, yes," said Mrs. Bissel, sounding chastened. "You'd know all about that. I didn't think."

I certainly did already know about that, and also the part about Mrs. Bissel not thinking—although she was a brilliant light in the universe compared to Mrs. Pinkerton. But I said, "Oh, no. It's quite all right. Losing my husband was awful, but I can't even imagine losing a child."

"Yes. Yes, that's true. Of course, I was crushed when my Francis died. But that was fifteen years ago. I still miss him, but not as much as I once did."

Great. I only had fourteen years left until I didn't miss Billy so much. I didn't say so.

"Why do folks think Mrs. Hastings' son killed himself? Had he been depressed or something?"

"Not that I know of," said Mrs. Bissell. "And Laura is *certain* he didn't kill himself. It must have been something else, although I don't know what."

Something else, eh? Hmm. "Did he have heart problems or anything? I understand that a person who suffers from rheumatic fever as a child might have a weakened heart as an adult. I know my husband suffered terribly after he was gassed in the war. Did the younger Mr. Hastings serve in the war? That might lead anyone to suicide." Dr. Benjamin, our well-beloved physician, who had written on the death certificate that Billy had died a natural death, had told me that.

Mrs. Bissel cocked her head as if this was a new angle for her to think about. "No. Eddie didn't serve in the war. I believe he was still in school during the war. And I don't think he had any medical problems, although I never asked Laura. Here she is."

Mrs. Bissel stopped in front of a gaunt-looking woman who bore traces of grief I'd recognize anywhere. I'd seen them on my very own visage not long ago. She wore a straight black dress with a low waistline and long sleeves. She could have passed as one of Macbeth's witches, with her pallid countenance, tortured brown eyes, and limp gray hair. "Laura, please let me introduce you to Desdemona Majesty, who will be conducting our séance tonight."

Mrs. Hastings gazed dully at me, but she held out her hand for me to shake. I felt so sorry for her that I took her hand in both of mine and said, "I am so very sorry about your loss, Mrs. Hastings. Perhaps we can give you some measure of comfort tonight." I aimed to try, anyway.

"Comfort," said Mrs. Hastings as if comfort was as far from her at that moment as the moon and stars. I understood perfectly. "Yes. Thank you."

"Mrs. Majesty lost her husband only a year ago, Laura," said Mrs. Bissel, again causing my heart to twang. "She understands grief."

"Losing a child must be the most terrible loss a person can suffer," I said in order to make Mrs. Hastings know I understood her pain. Not that I truly did, but I have a great imagination. If I didn't, I'd be in another line of work.

"Thank you," said Mrs. Hastings again, and I saw tears shimmer in her eyes.

I wanted to hug her. Instead, I gave her hands a brief squeeze. "I'll do my best to communicate with your Eddie tonight, Mrs. Hastings."

"Thank you," she said again.

I felt like *such* a fraud.

But, honestly, I did try to give people relief and reassurance. Every now and then, particularly during the past year, I'd felt rage toward my clients. But really, people like Mrs. Hastings truly needed to believe their loved ones were safe and happy on the other side of life. And I always stressed that their loved ones still loved them and wanted them to be safe and to enjoy whatever life remained to them. God forbid anyone go home from one of my séances and decide to commit suicide in order to join her beloved whatever.

So I intended to give Mrs. Hastings as much consolation and solace as I could. Generally my intentions came to fruition, so my confidence was high.

Just then Mrs. Pinkerton burst into the room in her usual flurry. I swear, that woman could stir up a fuss merely by breathing. She was constantly in a flutter about something. I only hoped this dither was normal and not created by something her awful daughter had done.

But no. She was merely dithering because she was late to the party.

"Oh, dear, I'm so sorry to be so late. I couldn't find my— Oh, Daisy! I'm so glad to see you, dear. Why, I don't know what I'd have done without you during—But we mustn't talk about our own problems when your poor husband—My goodness, I can hardly catch my breath!"

That was Mrs. Pinkerton all over. She drove me *crazy* with her hysterical ways. Only once in all the years I'd known her— more than half my life—had I ever given in to my frustration and told her what I truly thought of her daughter, and that had been through my so-called spirit control, Rolly. I felt guilty afterwards, but both Harold and Sam told me I'd done the right thing. And maybe I had, because Stacy Kincaid was still, as far as I knew, living life on the straight and narrow path. One never knew how long Stacy could keep out of trouble, but one could hope. Mrs. Pinkerton was difficult at the best of times, but when Stacy was acting up, she was positively impossible.

"How nice to see you, Mrs. Pinkerton," I lied. But I did it in my best, most professional, soft and calming spiritualist's voice.

"It's so *good* to see you again, my dear." She whirled around, searching for Mrs. Bissel. Mrs. Bissel stood beside me, but I guess Mrs. Pinkerton had been focusing on me and missed her—a difficult thing to do, as Mrs. Bissel was quite a large woman. What's more, that evening she'd decided to wear a startlingly purple gown that made her look not unlike one of Aunt Vi's larger eggplants.

By the way, while Mrs. Pinkerton was doing all her fluttering, Keiji tried to keep up with her, valiantly attempting to wrest her wrap from her so he could hang it in the hall closet. Every time he got close, she veered off in another direction. At last she came to a quivering stop in front of me, and he snatched her shawl before she could run off again. I gave Keiji a speaking glance, which he returned with interest.

"Who is the guest of honor tonight, Griselda?" Griselda was Mrs. Bissel's first name, which wasn't her fault any more than it was my fault my first name was Daisy.

"My cousin, Laura Hastings, lost her son a couple of months ago. Mrs. Majesty is going to get in touch with him tonight."

At the news of Mrs. Hastings' loss, Mrs. Pinkerton slapped a hand to her generous bosom, and sucked in a breath.

"Oh, my dear, what a dreadful thing to happen!" said she.

"Indeed. Here, please let me introduce you, Madeline"—Madeline being Mrs. Pinkerton's first name.

I watched as Mrs. Pinkerton and Mrs. Bissel stopped in front of Mrs. Hastings, feeling terribly sorry for the latter. Mrs. Pinkerton could be a sore trial at the best of times, and poor Mrs. Hastings wouldn't be having a best of times again for the rest of her life, as nearly as I could judge the matter. I lifted a silent prayer to a God I wasn't sure I believed in any longer that I could help the woman that night.

"You're looking quite spiffy this evening, my dear. Somber, though. Incredibly somber."

It took all my considerable acting talent not to whirl around and give Harold Kincaid, who'd whispered those words, a big, fat hug. "Harold! I didn't know you'd be here. I'm so glad you are!" Naturally, I kept my voice well-modulated and soft. No squealing, even if I was overjoyed to see my best friend.

"I drove Mother up here. Thought it would be fun to raise the dead with you tonight."

"Fun?" I shook my head. "I don't know about fun. I'm supposed to get Rolly to talk to Eddie Hastings, Mrs. Hastings' late son."

Harold's jolly expression turned dour. "Yes. I heard about that. Terrible loss for the poor woman, especially since her husband's such a rotten cur."

My eyes opened wide. "Is he really?"

"Yes. Eddie couldn't stand him."

"Oh, you knew Eddie?"

"He used to dine with Del and me on a regular basis." Harold tipped me a wink, and I understood then that Eddie, in life, had been of Harold's ilk. That was okay by me, although I sure wasn't going to tell anyone else, people's prejudices being what they were.

"I had no idea." Taking hold of Harold's sleeve, I dragged him to a corner. "Say, Harold, tell me as much as you can about Eddie before the séance begins. I didn't know I was supposed to communicate with him before I got here."

"Ah. Yes. I suppose a little knowledge of your subject would add verisimilitude to your performance."

"You betcha."

So, in the very few minutes we had together, Harold told me everything he could about the late Edward Montrose Hastings. By the time Mrs. Bissel herded us to the breakfast room—which, by the way, was larger than our dining room at home, although nowhere near as large as her dining room, which contained the biggest table I'd ever seen and could seat a party of thirty without anyone feeling squished—I knew quite a bit about the subject of that night's séance.

God bless Harold Kincaid!

CHAPTER FIVE

As was my custom, I placed the cranberry lamp in the middle of the table and bade everyone sit down. Mrs. Bissel had taken out—or, rather, she'd had Keiji take out—a couple of the table's leaves, so the eight of us who were participating that night could hold hands with ease. I didn't care to have more than eight people at my séances. More than that could become unruly, and I liked to keep strict control over my working environment.

I sat at the head of the table, bowed my head, and was silent for several minutes. Yes, I mean minutes, not moments. This preparation time was very important to the overall scene I created. This was, ostensibly, the time during which I gathered my spiritual resources around me, and everyone who'd ever been to one of my séances knew that complete silence was called for. As an added benefit, the silence made everyone nervous. I used every trick I could think up to perform my job, and a nervous audience was generally a receptive one. Don't ask me why, because I don't know.

After about as much of that as I could stand, I lifted my head and nodded to Keiji, who obligingly turned out the light. The little red glow from the candle lamp in the middle of the table added a good deal to the atmosphere, which was already relatively creepy, thanks to the aforementioned period of silence. I said, "Please, everyone, take hands."

A little rustling told me the sheep were obeying their shepherd.

I'm sorry. I really should stop disparaging my clients. They were my bread and butter, for heaven's sake! The fact that I thought them silly was wrong of me. But to continue . . .

"Remain silent while I summon my spirit control."

You notice—or perhaps you don't—that I refrained from using my spirit control's name, which was Rolly. That's because I'd dreamed him up when I was ten years old and now wished I'd selected a more sober-sounding name. Fortunately for me, most of the people for whom I worked believed his name was spelled R-a-l-e-i-g-h, but the name still caused me some embarrassment.

Another space of silence ensued. When I judged the séance attendees were as receptive as they were going to get, I finally let out a soft sigh and slumped in my chair. This was the signal that Rolly had come to me.

"Och, my darling," came from my mouth in a voice an octave below mine and with a Scottish accent. I had the accent down pat because I used to go to school with a little Scottish girl.

So. Rolly was among us. "You seek my services?" Also, according to my story, he and I had been married some thousand years earlier in Scotland, and he'd remained true to me ever since that incarnation. Heck, if a girl can't have perfect love in her own lifetime, she can dream, can't she?

In my own voice, I said softly, "Thank you, Rolly. Our mission this evening is a sad one. We would like to communicate with one Edward Hastings, son of Laura Hastings. Mrs. Hastings is with us tonight and she misses her son terribly."

A sob came from the other end of the table, and I again felt a pang of regret, this time for Mrs. Hastings. Oh, heck, I felt one for myself, too.

"Aye. Edward Hastings. Let me see . . ."

Rolly went rummaging about in his own personal universe for Eddie Hastings. After only a few seconds, he was back.

"Aye. Eddie's a fine lad. He left your realm too soon, but he's been wanting his mother to know that he's well and happy here. He wants her to enjoy the life that's left to her, and—"

And then something happened that had never happened before in all the years I'd been conducting séances and dealing with tarot cards, Ouija boards, crystal balls, and all things spiritual.

Rolly's voice faded, I felt a sudden rush of energy surge through me, and a voice entirely different from Rolly's came out of my mouth. I couldn't help it. It frightened me almost to death.

It said, "Mother, please don't grieve for me. I know you miss me, but you need to take care of yourself."

A collective gasp went up from my audience. I'd have joined in, but my body was being used by something else at the moment.

Mrs. Hastings almost shrieked. "Eddie! It's Eddie! Oh, Eddie, what *happened* to you?"

"Shhh," said several other people gathered round. I heard Mrs. Bissel whisper, "You need to keep still, Laura. Mrs. Majesty can't be disturbed during her séance, or she may suffer severe consequences."

Those consequences were, as I'd told most of my clients at one time or another, the possibility that I might get stuck between this world and the next if anyone had a fit and disrupted a séance. That night, however, I was as shocked—not to mention aghast, horrified, and rattled—as everyone else present. What was going on? Unfortunately for me, Rolly was as fake as I was, so he couldn't tell me. And I had no control over my body, vocal chords, or anything else of a personal nature. It was the most terrifying thing that had ever happened to me.

I felt the voice emerge again. Against my will and to my utter horror. "I was murdered. And don't know who did it. If you want me to rest easily on this side of life, find out who killed me on that side of it."

And then, although I always fake a swoon at the end of a séance, for the first time in my entire life, I fainted.

I have no idea what happened then. The next thing I remember was when I was jolted into consciousness by the sharp smell of ammonia salts being held under my nose. After I jerked awake, I discovered I'd been deposited on a sofa in Mrs. Bissel's living room. I tried to sit up, confused and still shocked by what had taken place in the lady's breakfast room.

"Be still, Daisy. Don't sit up too suddenly. You might swoon off again."

The voice was that of Harold. I thanked my lucky stars he'd decided to come to my séance that evening. Clutching his hand and staring into his eyes, I whispered, "D-did what I think happened actually happen, Harold?"

"Yes, it did." He sounded severe. "I must say, Daisy, while you generally provide a good deal of entertainment and drama during an average evening, you might have gone too far this time. Mrs. Hastings is in hysterics. So is Mother, although that's nothing unusual."

"But, Harold, I didn't plan it!" I said, wanting to wail but remembering myself in time to whisper. "I had no idea that was going to happen!"

His eyes crinkled to narrow slits. "You didn't?"

"No! It was the strangest sensation I've ever felt. I swear, I—I think Eddie Hastings took over my body for a minute. Or something. That sounds crazy. Oh, Lord, Harold, what have I done?" I envisioned my cozy career slipping downhill faster than Spike snatching food from the air when I threw it for him. "I swear, I don't know what went on in there. It was like I was . . . was . . . possessed by . . . Oh, I don't *know*!"

"It sounded to me as though you were possessed by Eddie Hastings, which doesn't make any sense at all." After another moment or two, Harold, still frowning, said, "I believe you. But what a hell of a turn of events. Good God, do you think you actually *were* visited by the soul of a murdered man, and that the man was Eddie?"

Other people began gathering around me, and I couldn't speak frankly anymore. God forbid anyone besides Harold realize I was a counterfeit spiritualist medium. At least I had been one. At that moment, I wasn't sure what I was. I feared the word "lunatic" might hit the mark. I moaned, genuinely groggy and distressed, and Harold helped me sit up on the sofa.

"Daisy! Are you all right? My sweet heaven, do you think it's true?"

I gazed up at Mrs. Bissel, who'd asked the question, and shook my head slowly, trying to clear away the fuzz. "I—I don't know." Giving myself a hard mental wallop, and knowing I had to reestablish my spiritualist act soon or lose it forever, I said, "I've never received a message like that before. I—I guess Rolly thought we should hear the truth from Mr. Hastings himself. Or . . . or . . ." I ran out of words.

Mrs. Bissel clapped a hand over her mouth, and her eyes went wide with dismay. "Oh, my goodness. Poor Laura."

Poor Laura, indeed. I felt like a louse for putting a grieving mother through additional pain. But I had. It was my fault those words had come from my mouth, even though they'd come without my permission—or my volition, for that matter. "May I see her? Perhaps I can . . . soothe her. Or something." Lame, Daisy Majesty. Very lame. But I didn't know what else to say.

"Yes. I know she'd like that. Perhaps you can speak with her and . . . well, I don't know. But she does want to speak with you."

She did? Uh-oh. I didn't like the sound of that. Nevertheless, Mrs. Hastings' present state of misery was my fault, and the least I could do was talk to the poor woman.

"Can you stand, Daisy?" asked Harold, sounding honestly concerned, which I appreciated.

"Yes." I put a foot on the carpeted floor and re-thought my answer. "Or . . . maybe you can help me, Harold? Just hold on to me so I won't fall. I feel quite woozy still."

"Small wonder," he muttered under his breath.

I wanted to scream at him that I hadn't planned Eddie Hastings' interruption of my usually flawless performance, but I managed to control myself. As he tenderly helped me to my feet, I managed to mumble, "I truly, *truly* don't know how it happened, Harold. I hope you believe that, because I feel crummy enough without thinking my best friend believes me to be a spiteful wretch."

"I'd never think that, Daisy. You sure gave us all a turn, though."

"I think I gave myself a worse one."

"Wait until you see Mrs. Hastings."

"Oh, Lord." I felt tears building in my eyes and had to blink fast a few times to keep them contained. I was pretty sure Mrs. Hastings wouldn't appreciate me crying all over her right after I'd flung her dead son's murder at her feet. Murder. *Murder.* What in the world—or out of it—had prompted me to say that?

Only I hadn't said it. Something else had. As incredible as it sounds, I was truly beginning to believe Edward Hastings had thrust himself into my séance that night. Lord, Lord, Lord. If anything like that ever happened again, I'd be too scared to continue with my profession. But it was too soon to think about my future. Right now, I needed to help Mrs. Hastings. If I could.

Harold led me to another sofa in the living room—I did mention that the living room was gigantic, didn't I? Well, if I didn't, it was. Several of the séance ladies had gathered around the sofa upon which Mrs. Hastings lay, but when they saw me coming, they all backed away, staring at me as if I were either an angel or a devil. Probably the latter.

Mrs. Bissel, who had lowered her bulk to her cousin's sofa and now held her hand, spoke to her gently. "Here's Mrs. Majesty, Laura. She wants to talk to you."

"Oh, yes!" said Mrs. Hastings, surprising me a bit, since I wouldn't want to talk to anyone who'd told me *my* son had been murdered. "Thank you so much, Mrs. Majesty!"

Now she was thanking me? Good heavens. But I had my nerves under control by that time, and I knelt beside her, putting on the soberest expression in my repertoire. I'd even thought of something to say, believe it or not.

"Mrs. Hastings, I can't tell you how sorry I am for what happened during the séance. Sometimes the spirits—"

"No, no!" she cried, and fairly forcefully, too, for a woman who had seemed to be prostrate. "It was Eddie. I recognized his voice. And I *knew* there was something wrong about his death. I *knew* it! You've only confirmed the truth for me."

I had? Sweet Lord have mercy, as my aunt was wont to say.

Suddenly Mrs. Hastings sat up, almost upending Mrs. Bissel. She grabbed my right hand and held it tightly. "But you must discover the villain who killed my Eddie!" she said, sending the faint glimmer of relief that had barely begun to bloom in my heart flying out of it again. "Mrs. Pinkerton told me you have a friend who's a police detective. You must tell him about Eddie. The police weren't interested at the time. They—well, everyone, really—chalked his death up to suicide."

I suffered yet another jolt. She wanted me to find her son's killer and/or enlist Sam? Sam Rotondo, who might or might not love me, but who never believed anything I said? Oh, Lord.

"But I *know* Eddie wouldn't have killed himself," Mrs. Hastings continued. "Please. *Please,* Mrs. Majesty! Please help me. If you could only enlist the help of your friend on the police force."

Blast Mrs. Pinkerton to heck and back! She would go and blab to this woman about Sam Rotondo, wouldn't she? As if Sam would ever take anything I learned at a séance seriously. Was the woman mad?

"Um . . . I . . . Well . . ." Fumbling for words doesn't half describe the state I was in by that time. First a real, honest-to-God spirit had burst into one of my séances like those dratted coppers when they'd raided the speakeasy, and now this woman actually wanted me to tell Sam about what the spirit had said to me.

"Please, Mrs. Majesty."

"Um . . . Actually, Mrs. Hastings, I don't know that Detective Rotondo would believe me if I told him your son had visited our séance."

She looked stricken, and I could have kicked myself. Thank God for Harold.

"She's right, Mrs. Hastings. I know Detective Rotondo, too, and he's a true skeptic if ever there was one."

"But . . . but we must do *something!*" cried the poor woman. "I can't leave Eddie just . . . just *floating* there on the Other Side with no rest. My God, he'd be like one of those wandering spirits in *A Christmas Carol!* You simply have to figure out a way to tell him about Eddie, Mrs. Majesty. Or perhaps *you* could, Mr. Kincaid! You knew my Eddie, and you know that detective. Surely he'd listen to you!"

Harold and I exchanged a couple of wary glances. Sam? Listen to Harold? That was only slightly more fantastic than thinking Sam would listen to me about Edward Hastings having told me of his murder during a séance.

"Um . . ." said Harold.

"Er . . ." said I.

"I know you can do it, Daisy!" came a voice from my back. Naturally, it was the voice of Mrs. Pinkerton, my biggest fan and most troublesome client. "You can do *anything*! Why, you've done wonders for me. And I know others have benefited so much from your work. Surely you can help bring poor Eddie's killer to justice!"

How like her to have stopped suffering from hysterics at that particular moment, blast the woman!

"Well, but it's the police, you see. They don't often give spiritualist mediums much credit for anything, you know," I said, hedging for all I was worth.

"But I thought they called in psychics all the time for police work," said Mrs. Pinkerton.

Psychics? Heaven help us. Not in good old Pasadena. "Um, perhaps some police forces use psychics, but I doubt that Sam Rotondo would ever use one." Even if whatever it was I'd said during the séance had come to me through some otherworldly being that had taken over my body. I shivered, remembering.

"Well, don't tell him you heard it at a séance, then!" said Mrs. Pinkerton.

"Um . . . I . . ." I mulled her words over in my fuzzy brain for a second or two before I came to a startling conclusion.

By God, it was, perhaps, the first time in her entire life Mrs. Pinkerton had ever made any sense.

CHAPTER SIX

I considered how to approach Sam Rotondo with the startling news that Edward Hastings had been murdered, mulling it over for the rest of that evening and through the night. Because I couldn't sleep, I tossed and turned for what seemed like forever—upsetting Spike so much, he finally jumped off the bed and sought a calmer place to sleep—and continued to think about it all the following morning.

But I was left to reflect on my problem all by my lonesome the next day, which was Sunday. My family, naturally knowing nothing of what had taken place at the previous evening's séance, got up, dressed, and ate Sunday breakfast as usual, and then walked to the Methodist-Episcopal Church, North, on the corner of Marengo and Colorado Boulevard. I brooded alone, since I couldn't tell a soul what had happened.

During the choir's anthem, I sang the alto part of "Come Thou Fount of Every Blessing," attempting with every word and note to erase Edward Hastings' voice from my brain. That didn't work, so I tried harder as we all gathered in Fellowship Hall to have cookies and coffee. Still no luck.

My family and I walked home, where we partook of one of Aunt Vi's delicious dinners. Then I went to my room, ostensibly to rest. My family was happy to let me, since they knew the séance had gone on until long past midnight. Fortunately for me, Sam Rotondo didn't pay a call on the family that day, because I still had no idea how to approach him with the news that Edward Hastings was a murder victim. He'd laugh his head off. Or get mad at me. Probably both.

Anyhow, we had a light supper of sandwiches and then went to bed, where I commenced tossing and turning some more. Exhaustion must have claimed me at some point during that night because Spike didn't desert me.

Then came Monday.

Aunt Vi had left us one of her delectable breakfast casseroles before she'd gone to work at the Pinkerton mansion to create more delicious meals for them. Ma had already eaten and gone to her job at the Hotel Marengo, so it was only Pa and me—and Spike, who lived in hope of a dropped morsel—at the table. Pa had the *Pasadena Star News* open in front of him, and I ate what little I could in silence as I considered the Edward Hastings affair.

Staring blankly out the kitchen window as I thought, I heard the paper crinkle. Pa said, "What's the matter, Daisy? You seem a little down in the dumps this morning."

A *little*. That was putting it mildly. I glanced at my father, not quite knowing what to say. "Um . . ."

His brow furrowed with concern. Pa, an unusually perceptive man, laid his newspaper aside. "All right, Daisy. Give. What's troubling you? You were well when you left for that séance. Did something happen there? Would it help you to talk about it? I don't want to butt in, but—"

"No! No, you're not butting in." I'd never, ever accuse my father of being meddlesome. But . . . Oh, Lord.

"Well, if you ever want to talk about it—"

He reached again for the paper, and I cried, "No! No, please. I *do* want to talk about it." Didn't I? Oh, heck, I didn't know. Then, reading the love in his blue eyes—eyes I'd inherited—I decided to take the plunge and tell him the truth.

Sucking in about a gallon of air to sustain me through the

coming ordeal, I said, "I swear, Pa, a spirit actually spoke through me Saturday night at the séance."

"Eh?"

"It's true, Pa. A spirit spoke through *me* and told everyone at the séance that he'd been murdered. It was awful."

Pa's mouth opened and closed a couple of times. "Um, Daisy, do you mean . . . ?"

His skepticism was too much for me, and I kind of folded up, pushed my plate aside, and laid my head in my arms. Spike whimpered, and I threw him a bite of potato from my portion of the casserole.

"I swear, Pa, it's the truth. It was the most ghastly experience of my life—well, except for when Billy died. I've always, until last night, thought all spiritualists and their mumbo-jumbo were hogwash. Piffle. Nonsense. I put on a show for people and try to make them feel better if they've lost a loved one. But on Saturday night . . ."

"Yes?" He sounded genuinely interested and, better, no longer scornful or doubtful.

I lifted my head and almost shouted, "Edward Hastings, the late son of Mrs. Bissel's cousin, showed up while I was doing my Rolly routine and told everyone there that he'd been *murdered*!" Lowering my voice to a whisper, I added, "Pa, I don't know what to *do.*"

"Are you kidding me, Daisy? Because if you are—"

"No! No! Good Lord, Pa, do you think I'd joke about something like that? It was ghastly, I tell you." The tears I'd held in check the night of the séance and all day Sunday started leaking from my eyes. "It was horrible! All of a sudden, it was as if someone or something took possession of me. I felt this . . . oh, I don't know. It was like an electrical shock. And then this voice I'd never heard before in my entire life came out of my mouth!" I pointed at the orifice as if to verify my words. "Harold heard it. Everyone heard it! Mrs. Hastings said it was the voice of her dead son, and Harold said it sounded exactly like Edward Hastings. They knew each other, you see."

"Good God."

Grabbing a handkerchief from the old blue day dress I'd donned that morning, I wiped my eyes. "Yes. Good God, indeed. And now I don't know what to do."

Pa sat there, staring at me, and didn't say a word.

Feeling compelled, I went on, "Mrs. Pinkerton had to open her yap and say that I knew a police detective. And then Mrs. Hastings begged me to tell the coppers her son had been murdered or, failing that, to find out who killed her son myself." I gazed at my father and went on in a pleading—I hate to say it, but perhaps it was even a little whiny—voice, "Sam would never believe me if I told him what happened."

"No, I don't suppose he would."

"But you do, don't you, Pa? Please tell me I'm not going crazy!"

He gave a sharp shake of his head. "You're not going crazy, sweetheart."

"There were witnesses, Pa. Lots of them. They all heard that voice come out of me. I didn't have any control over it. And I've never even *met* Edward Hastings, so I sure as heck wasn't imitating his voice or anything. I couldn't, since I didn't know what he sounded like."

"I see. When did this young man die? And what did he die of? That is—"

"I know what you mean. The police and everyone thought he committed suicide." The last word wobbled on my tongue, because it had such a terrible significance for me. "But then he—or something—spoke through me and told the world he'd been murdered. I don't know the official cause of death. Something that could look like suicide, I suppose."

"Mercy sakes."

"And not only that, but he said he needs someone to find the culprit or he'll never rest in peace!"

"You mean he doesn't know who killed him?"

"Evidently not. Oh, Pa! I don't know what to *do*!" Burying my head in my arms once more, I commenced whimpering.

Pa patted my shoulder in a consoling manner. "That must have been a terrible experience, sweetheart."

"It was," I sobbed.

"Yes." His voice took on a musing quality. "You say you'd never met this Hastings boy before?"

"No. Never. Didn't know he existed. Well, I guess he doesn't anymore, but . . . oh, never mind."

"I see."

Silence prevailed for what seemed like an hour or three, but was probably only maybe a minute. Then Pa said, "Please don't think I doubt what you told me, Daisy, because I don't. But I know this last year has been especially rough on you. You don't think that perhaps . . ." His words trailed off, as if he didn't quite know how to phrase the last part of his sentence.

I knew, though. He thought I'd imagined the whole thing and had somehow managed to project Edward Hastings' voice at the stupid séance out of my own personal misery. My heart sank like a lead weight. My own father, the man who had been the bedrock and strength of my life since its beginning, thought I'd succumbed to the stress of my husband's illness and death and had somehow or other created, not by choice, the scene at the séance. Oh, he believed I didn't know I'd done it or even know how I'd done it, but he didn't believe for a minute that a murdered Edward Hastings had crashed the party and begged someone to avenge his death.

Feeling increasingly desperate, I sat up straight and said, "Harold believes me! So does his mother! Not Mrs. Pinkerton.

I mean Mrs. Hastings, Edward's mother. She said she'd always known her son didn't kill himself."

"I see."

Oh, boy. Another "I see." Almost as hysterical as Mrs. Pinkerton by this time, I said, "Mrs. Hastings said the voice was that of her son! So did Harold! I didn't do it, Pa! Something—or someone, and I suspect the honest-to goodness ghost of Edward Hastings—spoke through me!"

"Oh, dear." My father appeared almost as distressed as I felt.

"And Sam will never, ever believe me if I tell him a real ghost spoke through me. You know he won't. He'll only get mad."

"Well, I don't know if he'll get mad, Daisy."

"I do," I averred with some heat. "Believe me, I know Sam well enough to know that."

"Hmm. We'll have to think of some way to approach him, then. You can't tell him the ghost story—not that I don't believe you," he hastened to assure me.

I sighed. "Right. I wouldn't believe me either."

"Now Daisy, it's entirely possible that . . . something did speak through you at the séance. I know none of us believes in spirits and suchlike, but you never know about these things. Even Shakespeare wrote something about ghosts, didn't he?"

"Yes. *Hamlet.* 'There are more things in heaven and earth, Horatio, than are dreamt of in your philosophy.' "

"You have a good memory." Pa said it proudly.

"Well, we had to memorize entire passages of *Hamlet* when I was in eighth grade. Too bad we didn't read *Othello* before I chose my spiritualist name." I shook my head to rid it of trivialities. "But that doesn't make any difference. Can you think of a way to approach Sam?" I stared beseechingly at my father.

Who gazed back at me. Blankly. Drat.

Then I got mad at myself, pulled my cold casserole back in front of me, and dug in. Darned if I'd let Eddie Hastings' murder go unrecognized or allow myself to go into another decline. Between bites, I said, "One thing I can do is visit the library and look up his obituary and read anything else I can find out about him. And I can talk to Harold and Mrs. Hastings some more. Heck, I can even question Sam about how and where Eddie Hastings was found and who decided he'd killed himself."

"Oh?" Pa seemed nearly stunned by my tone, which was rather forceful.

"Yes. Darn it, I'm at least going to find out how the poor guy died. If there were any marks on his body. Stuff like that. Heck, maybe somebody injected him with . . . something." I liked to read detective stories, and I shuffled through memories of various books, trying to come up with injectable poisons. Then I bethought me that if someone had injected him with something, he or she must have been mighty close to the victim. Close enough to be seen by same. "Or maybe somebody fed him cyanide. I understand that works almost instantly. Heck, maybe you can even sniff some and croak."

"Daisy. Do you really think you should—"

I dropped my fork, raised my hands to my shingled red hair, and tugged. Hard. "*Yes!* Yes, blast it, Pa! I *have* to! I promised Mrs. Hastings I'd look into her son's death, and I won't go back on my word. Especially since . . . well, especially since I'm the one who propounded the murder scenario in the first place, even though I didn't do it on purpose. Or by my own will, for that matter. Criminy, do you think I *wanted* this to happen?"

"I know you didn't, sweetheart, but don't go nutty on us. All right? Calm down, and take your investigation step by step if you honestly intend to investigate."

Trying to take my father's advice, I released my poor hair, rubbed the sore spot I'd created on my scalp, and took several deep breaths. "Yes. Yes, you're right. I'll have to be methodical.

First, I'll go to the library. Then . . . well, I guess I should make an appointment with Mrs. Hastings. She'll have information about her poor son's friends and enemies and so forth." A brilliant thought occurred to me. Or maybe it wasn't brilliant; sometimes it takes a while to discover an idea's worthiness. But it seemed like a good one. "Doc Benjamin! Maybe he treated the Hastings family."

"Lordy, Daisy, you're not going to tell him about—"

"Good heavens, no! He'd think I was crazy. But I could go to his office for a checkup or something and ask him. Heck, I could even tell him I'd met Mrs. Hastings at a séance and ask about her son."

Pa gave a judicious nod. "Yes. Yes, I suppose you could do that. Actually, Vi's been talking about asking the Benjamins to dinner one of these days. Maybe you could convey an invitation and wrangle some information out of him at the same time."

"What a good idea!" I gave my Pa a smile at least as brilliant as my idea had been.

I finished up my breakfast casserole and carried the dirty dishes to the sink. As I began the washing-up, Pa said in a thoughtful voice from the table, "You know, Daisy, maybe this is a good thing that happened. It's at least got you taking action about something. We've all been worried about you, you know. Well, of course, you know."

I heaved another sigh and picked up a dish towel. As I carefully wiped a plate, I said, "Yes. I know. The past year has been rough on all of us, and I . . . well, it's kind of funny. I mean, I knew Billy was destined to die young. After he was shot and gassed in the war, we all knew it. But when it happened, I . . . well, I wasn't prepared."

"You can't prepare for something like that," said Pa.

"No. I guess not. But then Harold hauled me to Egypt, and I got so sick, and I lost so much weight, and . . . I don't know.

It's almost as if I've spent the rest of the year recuperating."

The first three months after Billy died, I was basically stunned. Grieving and lost and miserable. I'd felt marginally better after Harold and I got home from Egypt, but I'd gone into a vast melancholy at Thanksgiving that hadn't eased until well past the new year started. My family had even gone up to watch the New Year's Day Rose Parade on Colorado Boulevard on the first of January, 1923, and the jollity hadn't helped my mood one little bit.

It was now the middle of June, and I'd gradually begun crawling out of the hole of unhappiness into which I'd sunk. Yet until Eddie Hastings showed up at last Saturday's séance, I hadn't seen much point to existence.

It suddenly occurred to me that maybe Billy had been the driving force behind Eddie's appearance, but I scoffed at the idea almost as soon as it popped into my head. Heck, Billy had been dead set—so to speak—against my line of work. If he knew now, after his own demise, that people's spirits survived beyond the grave, he'd never tell me. He was stubborn like that.

As I put the last glass into the cupboard and wiped down the sink and counter, I said, "First I'm going to change clothes. Then I'm going to the library to look up what I can find out about the young Mr. Hastings' death. Maybe I'll pop around to see Flossie and the baby. Dr. Benjamin's office hours don't start until one, so I'll probably have a sandwich at the Tea Cup Inn or something and then visit him."

"Sounds like a good plan to me," said Pa.

I'm sure he was only humoring me, but that was all right. *I* knew what had happened on Saturday night, even if Pa remained doubtful.

I resented it like fire, too.

CHAPTER SEVEN

So I gathered up all the library books my family members had stacked on the little table beside the front door—every time anyone in the family finished a book, he or she would put it there in anticipation of my next library visit—told Spike to sit and stay, and went out to our wonderful self-starting Chevrolet motorcar. My mood was lighter than it had been in many months when I drove north on Marengo, headed for the Pasadena Public Library.

My favorite librarian, Miss Petrie, greeted me when I walked into the library shortly after nine that morning. She reached under the desk she sat behind, which instantly told me she'd been saving books for me. Goody. Miss Petrie was seldom wrong in her selections. She knew my father enjoyed Edgar Rice Burroughs' books, both the outer-space ones and the *Tarzan* ones, and she knew my mother and aunt and I all liked detective fiction and action yarns.

"I've got several brand-new books for you today, Mrs. Majesty. This one just got catalogued." She handed me a book with a yellow cover. Which, when I read the title, seemed appropriate: *Crome Yellow*, by someone named Aldous Huxley. I'd never heard of him. I guess I tilted my head in bewilderment or something, because Miss Petrie said in something of a hurry, "I'm not sure you'll like it. It's set in England. I thought it was most amusing. It's about a poor lad named Denis who visits a grand house called Crome."

"Thanks. I'll give it a try. Um, do you have any new mystery books?"

She gave me a beaming smile. "Oh, my, yes. We have two Doctor Thorndyke books for you: *Helen Vardon's Confession* and *The Cat's Eye*. The latter is brand new, too. It sometimes takes a while for British fiction to cross the Atlantic, but this one was published in America at the same time it was published in Britain."

"Hmm. I think I've read *Helen Vardon*, but unless you have a list of people waiting for it, I'll take it, just to make sure. Anyhow, my mother and aunt might not have read it yet." I didn't mean to sound greedy, but this was turning out to be a most profitable visit, and I couldn't help myself. "Anything else?"

She grinned. "I don't suppose you're interested in a new collection of stories by Mr. Fitzgerald?"

I very nearly shuddered. "No, thanks. His people are too depressed and wealthy for me. I prefer stories about people who don't hate life."

Never mind that my husband had killed himself because he couldn't stand his life. The way I looked at it, then and now, is that if I wanted to be despondent, all I had to do was wake up in the morning. When I read for entertainment, I wanted to be taken away from the real world for a while. Nuts to F. Scott Fitzgerald and all his beautiful and damned young people who didn't have anything better to do than fritter their lives away drinking and brooding.

"Very well. I know you enjoyed the *Father Brown* stories by Mr. G. K. Chesterton. I have a new collection of short stories by him. It's *The Man Who Knew Too Much, and Other Stories.*"

"Oh, that sounds good!"

"It seems like all these wonderful writers are English, which makes them more difficult for us to get them here, as I said before."

"Wish more Americans would start writing detective books," I said, meaning it.

"There's a young fellow named Dashiell Hammett who just came out with a pretty good mystery. It's called *The Gatewood Caper,* and it's not only written by an American—"

"With a really strange name," I plumped in for no reason except than it was the truth.

"Yes, he does have a rather odd name, doesn't he? But the book is quite good. It's set in San Francisco and Los Angeles."

"Oh, my! Los Angeles is right next door. Practically." Los Angeles was actually about twenty-two miles away from Pasadena, but lots of people who worked there had weekend homes in Pasadena, where they got away from it all. These were the folks who worked in the moving pictures and who had the money to have lots of houses in lots of different places. Like Harold Kincaid, for instance. Every now and then it would come as a shock to me that I actually *knew* quite a few wealthy people. But Harold was nothing like the characters in Mr. Fitzgerald's books. He was a nice guy who actually worked for a living.

"And I have a book here by a woman named Patricia Wentworth, another Englishwoman. It's called *The Astonishing Case of Jane Smith.* We only have that one because Miss Hill, our reference librarian, took a trip to London earlier this year and brought back several books."

"Bless her heart. I wish I'd thought to bring books back to the library when I was in England last year." The sad truth was that I hadn't been thinking about books on that voyage with Harold; I'd been too brokenhearted to read or even think about books.

Miss Petrie patted my hand. "Oh, my dear, you had so many

other things on your mind back then."

"Yes. I suppose I did." Besides mourning my deceased husband, I'd been sick as the proverbial dog and beset by a gang of criminals.

"But I have two more wonderful books for you. One's called *Captain Blood,* and the other's called *Scaramouch,* and they're both by Rafael Sabatini."

"Oh, my. He doesn't sound American, either."

"He isn't. He's Italian, but his books are being translated. These are both quite new, and we just got them in. They're . . ." Her voice trailed off, and she put a hand over her heart, which, I presume, was palpitating.

"Adventure stories?" I hazarded.

"Yes, indeed. I loved them. In fact, I bought copies for myself, so I can reread them for years to come."

Poor Miss Petrie. She wasn't awfully attractive, being on the drab, skinny side and with a skin tone that resembled library paste, but she was a sweetheart. As with Lucy Spinks, however, the fact of life for young, unmarried women after the Great War was that there were very few young men left from which to choose—or who might be fit to choose a young, unmarried woman. In some ways, I'd been lucky. At least I'd had my Billy for a while. It made me sad to know a tender, romantic heart beat under Miss Petrie's meager bosom, and that she might never find true love. Ah, well.

"I don't suppose you'd be interested in another book by Mrs. Rinehart."

"I love Mary Roberts Rinehart's books. For the most part." I sure didn't want to read any more of her books dealing with the late war. Miss Petrie had lent me *The Amazing Interlude* last year, and all it did was make me cry. "Has she written any new mystery stories?"

"Alas, I fear the new one we have is another war story."

I shook my head so emphatically, my hat nearly fell off. "Then I don't want to read it. I wish she'd get back to writing mysteries."

With a sad sigh, Miss Petrie agreed with me. "Have you read all of her other books? She wrote several before the war that are funny and have good mysteries in them."

"I'll check the stacks. Thank you very much for these." I indicated the pile of books in my arms.

"You're more than welcome, Mrs. Majesty. I enjoy selecting books for you because we share the same tastes."

"Thank you again. I have to look in the Periodical Room for back issues of the newspapers, and then I'll look in the R section of the stacks."

"Aha. Looking up a person who showed up at one of your séances?"

The question startled me, as did the gleam of avid curiosity in Miss Petrie's pale brown eyes, which were magnified beneath the thick lenses of her eyeglasses. "Why . . . yes. How did you guess?"

"Oh, no reason, really. But I've often wondered what happens in your séances. You're the best spiritualist medium in town, according to many of the ladies who visit the library."

"How nice of them," I said, feeling heat flush my cheeks. One of the problems of having red hair, even if it's more auburn than red, as was mine, is that we redheads blush easily.

Miss Petrie leaned over her desk and asked intently, "So who is it you're looking up?"

"A young man named Edward Hastings. I conducted a séance for his poor mother last Saturday. The dear woman is shattered about his death. I don't blame her, of course. I never knew Mr. Hastings, so I thought I'd try to find out more about him."

Lucky for me she didn't ask why, but only shook her head sadly. "The poor woman."

"Indeed."

"As if that accursed war didn't leave enough grieving parents behind. I hate to hear about a young person's passing."

"Yes," I said. "Me, too."

And I took my pile of books and headed off to the Periodical Room, wishing I'd asked someone the precise date of Edward Hastings' death. I'd been too rattled at the time to do so. But Mrs. Bissel had mentioned "a couple of months," so I decided to begin my search in March to give me some leeway.

It turned out to be a good thing I started my search earlier than "a couple of months," because I discovered an obituary for Hastings in the March 20, 1923, *Pasadena Star News*. It didn't say much; only that Edward had been employed in the Hastings law firm and had died in his apartment on El Molino Avenue on March 18th. Didn't mention the cause of death.

Therefore, I plowed through the archives of the *Pasadena Herald* to see if they'd say more. They didn't.

Nuts. That left me to ferret information from Dr. Benjamin, Harold Kincaid, poor Mrs. Hastings herself, and anyone else she might mention. I was also going to have to tackle Sam Rotondo, too, but I aimed to put that off until I couldn't avoid it any longer. I didn't fancy being roared at any sooner than I had to be.

So I checked out my books, along with *Mind over Motor* and *The After House,* by Mary Roberts Rinehart. Just because I'd loved it so much, I also snatched *The Circular Staircase* by Mrs. Rinehart. Rereading good books is kind of like visiting with old friends.

And then I headed to the Salvation Army Headquarters, not because I needed spiritual guidance, but because I wanted to see Billy's namesake, William Buckingham, Flossie and Johnny's son, who was now eight months old and cute as a button. Flossie welcomed me with open arms and a big hug.

"And you must stay to lunch, too, Daisy."

Flossie had lost almost all of the twangy New York accent she'd had when I'd first met her. She'd done so deliberately, and with great strength of purpose. Johnny loved her unreservedly, but Flossie, having been born on the wrong side of the tracks in a terrible section of New York City, and having grown up poor and then drifted into the arms of bootlegging gangsters as a very young woman, still didn't believe she deserved Johnny or his love. She did, of course. Flossie was one of the kindest, sweetest people I'd ever met. But try telling *her* that.

She'd certainly settled into marriage and motherhood with glee and vigor. She adored Johnny and little Billy. What's more, she loved to cook! That anyone besides Aunt Vi not only liked to cook but could actually do so always astonished me. I was the world's worst cook—and that's even after I'd tried so very hard to learn at my aunt's capable shoulder. My lack of cooking skills ranked as one of my most significant flaws, at least in my mind.

Lunch was simple but delicious, featuring vegetable soup and cheese sandwiches. Johnny joined us, and so did little Billy, who sat in a high chair at the table with us and periodically banged on his wooden tray with a spoon.

After praying over the food and us, Johnny and Flossie took turns spooning mashed muck into little Billy's mouth. I watched with interest and some slight uneasiness. Billy and I had wanted children, but from where I sat, they looked like a whole lot of work. And mess. After Billy got tired of the squished banana he'd been eating, he spat it all over his high chair and his mother. Flossie only laughed, cementing her in my mind as a wonderful mother.

"Too bad you and Billy never had a child, Daisy," murmured Johnny, watching his son and his wife with adoration.

My heart gave a tug, as it always did when I thought about

my lost Billy, but I said, "I guess so, Johnny, but I wouldn't want to rear a child all by myself."

"You wouldn't be alone, Daisy," Flossie told me, running a damp washcloth over her son's messy mouth and hands after wiping banana muck off her own apron. "Your family will always be there for you, and so will Johnny and me. Always. You never have to feel alone."

"Amen," Johnny intoned.

I darned near cried, but restrained myself, thank God, because I didn't want to distress my friends. "Thank you." Then I bethought me of Sam Rotondo, who had claimed to love me almost a year ago, and wondered what kind of father he might have been. Or would be. Or . . . oh, never mind. Anyhow, Johnny spoke again and interrupted my profitless thoughts.

"But in a way," Johnny continued, "it's probably just as well that you and Billy didn't have any children. I doubt that, even with the love and distraction of a child, Billy would have been around much longer than he was." He peered at me with meaning. "He was on the downhill slide when he opted out of life. You know that, Daisy. I hope you don't feel guilty any longer about his passing."

When Billy first died, my guilt had been almost overwhelming. During the year since, I'd developed a better understanding of the reality that had been Billy's life. Oh, heck, even before he finally did the deed, I'd noticed a change in his attitude and worried what it foretold. His death came as a wrenching loss, but it wasn't unexpected.

"Daisy?" Johnny said when I didn't answer immediately.

"Yes. I mean, no, I don't feel as guilty as I used to. I wish I'd been able to help him more. I can't stop feeling guilty about that."

"Oh, Daisy!" cried Flossie, throwing her dishcloth at the sink and turning to give me a huge hug. "You know good and well that it was the war that killed your Billy. There wasn't anything more you could have done for him."

Very well, I sniffled—but I felt silly for it. "I could have been more understanding. More forbearing, if you know what I mean. I allowed his moods to affect mine, and I should have known better. Well, I *did* know better. But we used to have awful quarrels, and I know we wouldn't have if I'd only been more understanding."

Johnny shook his head. "Daisy, as far as I know, only one perfect person has ever existed on this earth, and He was divine. As much as Flossie and I love you, we know you as a flawed human being, as we all are."

I heaved a largish sigh. "You're right. But I can regret not being kinder to my husband, can't I? Because I do."

"Billy loved you. You loved him. You both survived a God-awful ordeal, which neither of you deserved. I suspect you'll beat yourself up forever that you weren't perfect, but that's totally illogical." As I opened my mouth to retort, Johnny held up a hand. "Yes, I know. We're all illogical. Just try to remember, when you're flogging yourself like one of those old monks used to do in the Middle Ages, that you were the wife Billy chose, and he loved you."

After a second, I said, "I guess you're right." Then, remembering our childhood, I added, "Although sometimes it seemed to me that I corralled him and wouldn't let him go." I sobered again instantly. "But he'd still have joined up when he did whether we'd married or not. We both thought it was the patriotic thing to do. Stupid. We were both stupid."

"I was stupid, too, Daisy. I joined up, and you know what happened to me after that cursed conflict."

Yes. I did know. After the war, reeling from memories of blood and mud and lost comrades, Johnny had become a terrible drunkard. As shell-shocked and scarred as my darling

Billy, only less grievously injured in body, he credited the Salvation Army for finally saving him from his degradation. That was why he joined the organization and led his flock every day onto the streets of Pasadena in an effort to save others who yet suffered from various calamities.

Like, for instance, Flossie, whom I'd intentionally placed in his way when she'd come to me for help. I guess I'd helped her. In a way. Only I hadn't been trying to change her life at the time; I'd been trying to get her out of mine. I'd never say that to either of these good people. And I felt guilty about *that,* too.

"Oh, boy," I said upon another sigh. "This old world just keeps turning, no matter what we idiots who live on it do, doesn't it?"

"Yes, it does."

And, after chatting for another few minutes on happier topics, I left the Buckinghams' cozy home, located behind the Salvation Army church, and drove the Chevrolet up Lake Avenue to Beverly Way in Altadena and to Dr. Benjamin's office.

Chapter Eight

Dr. Benjamin's office hours were from one to five in the afternoons. His wife was his nurse and receptionist, and, like most doctors back then, he didn't take appointments. If you or one of your loved ones was sick, he'd come to your home during the morning hours if called to do so. If you had another kind of problem that wasn't urgent, you'd show up at his office in the afternoon and see him when the person in front of you was through with him.

He was a man universally loved in Pasadena and Altadena, and he and his lovely wife had spent many a Christmas or Thanksgiving with us at our bungalow on Marengo. I'd gone to him many a time with my worries about Billy, and he'd come to our house probably hundreds of times to nurse him through bouts of illness, his lungs being prone to infection. As I've already mentioned, he'd even written the cause of Billy's death on his death certificate as "natural." He knew better, of course. We all did.

As luck would have it, I was the first to enter his office's portals that day. His wife greeted me with a warm smile.

"Good afternoon, Daisy. Hope you're not feeling ill."

"Actually, I'm not. I hope Doc won't mind if I ask him a few questions, though."

"You know he never minds chatting with you, dear. Why don't you come right this way?"

So I followed Mrs. Benjamin into the doctor's office. He'd

opened the window facing Lake Avenue, so his constant smoking wouldn't bother his patients too much. It was still kind of foggy in there, but tolerable.

"Daisy!" he cried, giving every indication of being glad to see me. "To what do I owe this visit? Hope you're not sick."

"Thanks, Doctor. No, I'm not sick."

"Good. You're looking well." He squinted hard at me. "I'm glad to see you no longer look like one of the ghosts you chat with for your clients. For a while there, I feared you were going to starve yourself to death or end up in a nursing home."

I felt myself blush. "No, I've gained weight again. Although," I added honestly, "I almost wish I hadn't."

He shook his head. "You looked depleted and totally unwell for a long time after Billy's passing, child. You needed more pounds on you. During Victorian times, it was fashionable for ladies to go into a decline when anything bad happened to them, but I believed you were too sensible for that. Glad to see I was right."

"Well . . . truth to tell, food made me sick for several months after Billy died. I guess . . . I suppose I lost a little too much weight. But women are supposed to be skinny nowadays."

Dr. Benjamin snorted. "Stuff!" He lifted the lid of the cigarette box on his desk, claimed another fag, and lit it. "But please tell me why you've come today. I can see your health is blooming."

Blooming? If he said so. "I . . . just wanted to ask you a couple of questions." Now that I was there, I felt silly about my mission and wasn't sure how to begin my interrogation. Didn't doctors have to abide by some kind of moral code decreeing they couldn't talk about their patients with other people?

Oh, bother. After taking as deep a breath as I dared, given the smoke-filled office, I plunged ahead anyway.

"This is kind of an odd question, but it's asked in aid of

another person. You see, I performed a séance for Mrs. Stephen Hastings, last Saturday at Mrs. Bissel's house."

"Ah. Trying to conjure her dead son, no doubt."

Dr. Benjamin never scolded me about my idiotic profession, but he didn't believe in ghosts or spirits any more than I did. Or than I used to.

"Yes." I hesitated for a moment or two and decided not to tell him about the sudden eruption of young Hastings into the séance. He wouldn't believe me any more than Pa did. Instead, I said, "Poor Mrs. Hastings is sure her son's death was neither natural nor suicide. She's convinced he was murdered. Do you know anything about his death—that you can tell me, I mean?" I held my breath, hoping he wouldn't lecture me about medical ethics or something.

After he tutted once, he said, "Not really. I've treated the Hastings family for many years, but I don't recall anything being especially wrong with young Hastings. He followed his father into the same legal firm, I believe. I didn't handle the autopsy or anything like that—if there even was an autopsy, which I doubt. The police and medical professionals seemed to be happy with the verdict of suicide, if I recall. I can certainly understand why a loving mother wouldn't accept that verdict, but I don't know any different."

Nuts. "Oh. Well, do you have any suggestions about where I might go to learn more about what he died of? Or is that question improper. I don't want to . . . break any rules or anything like that."

"I don't know of any rule forbidding people to learn the cause of a person's demise. If you'd like me to, I'll be happy to telephone the coroner and see what he says."

"Thank you! I didn't expect so much cooperation." That didn't sound right, so I hastened to correct myself. "I mean, I didn't want to step on any medical toes or anything." That sounded even worse.

Fortunately, Dr. Benjamin only laughed at my fumbling attempts to extricate myself from verbal mire. "Don't fret about it, Daisy. I don't mind at all."

"Thank you. Oh, and my parents and Aunt Vi would like to invite you and Mrs. Benjamin to dinner one of these days."

"I'm always happy to partake of your aunt's delicious meals, my dear. Did you have any particular day in mind?"

"That's really up to you. You're more likely to have timing problems than we are. We all live dull, predictable lives." Except, of course, when ghosts interrupted the séances I was conducting.

"Set a date, and we'll be there," he said, smiling happily. Everyone who knew us knew Aunt Vi to be the best cook in the entire city of Pasadena, if not the world.

"How about Friday, then? Vi always comes home early on Fridays, so maybe she can fix something really special. I brought her a cooking book from Turkey, and she's made some delicious dishes from it." Only then did I recall that Sam aimed to take my family out for a Japanese meal on Saturday. Oh, well. We'd just eat huge dinners two nights in a row. I hoped nobody would mind.

Naw. We all loved our food.

"Turkey! My, my. I've never eaten Turkish cuisine."

"I hadn't either until last year. It's really good."

So, after he'd called his wife into the office for a consultation, we fixed Friday as the day of our dinner party.

What's more, he was going to call the coroner! That was more cooperation than I'd anticipated. I wanted to help Mrs. Hastings as soon as possible. If I could. I still had doubts about my ability to do so.

But, darn it, her son had invaded my entire physical and psychical being and spoken from my very mouth! He wouldn't have done that for no reason, would he? I felt as though I *needed* to find the answer to the death of Edward Hastings if there were any way in the world to do so.

Lord. Sometimes I set myself the most difficult tasks.

However, there was something else I could accomplish, and I aimed to do it before next Saturday. From Dr. Benjamin's office, I drove directly to Mrs. Bissel's home on Foothill Boulevard and Maiden Lane in Altadena.

I didn't generally go to a client's house without an appointment, but this time I didn't even want to see Mrs. Bissel. In fact, it would suit my purpose better if she were away from home. I needed a lesson from Keiji on how to use chopsticks.

Fortunately, Mrs. Bissel was away from home when I drove onto the huge circular driveway in her back yard. Also fortunately, it was Keiji himself who answered my ring at the doorbell.

"Mrs. Majesty!" Keiji was clearly startled to see me. "I'm afraid Mrs. Bissel isn't home at the moment."

"That's fine with me. I wanted to see you. If you have a couple of minutes, I want you to teach me how to use chopsticks."

He broke into a huge grin and opened the door for me. "Step right this way," he said in the manner of a carnival barker. "One lesson in how to use chopsticks coming right up."

"Oh, goody! Do you have some here? Chopsticks, I mean?"

"Sure. I always keep some handy. I'll give you a pair so you can practice at home."

"Oh, my, you don't need to do that, Keiji. That's too much."

He stopped walking and turned to face me. "Mrs. Majesty, they're a couple of pieces of bamboo. Trust me, they aren't expensive. My uncle buys 'em by the score for the restaurant, and he's given me about a dozen pairs."

"My goodness. Well, if you're sure . . ."

"I'm sure. Besides, you'll need the practice." He chuckled in a way that told me he meant what he said.

Shoot. I hoped I hadn't mouthed off at Sam and my family about learning to use chopsticks too soon. But no. Surely, since everyone in China and Japan used them, the skill couldn't be all *that* difficult to conquer.

Silly me.

After I'd struggled for almost an hour, attempting to pick up everything from celery sticks to pieces of string, I was so frustrated, I wanted to stab Keiji with one of the blasted things. I told him so.

He only laughed. "Just keep practicing. It's easier to do if you learned as a child, but I have great faith in you."

"That makes one of us," I grumbled.

He laughed again and said, "But I really do have some work to do around here. Do you want to practice some more on your own?"

I glanced around the huge kitchen in which he'd given me my first lesson. I'd been there before. In fact, I'd spent the better part of an entire night there when I cast the ghost from Mrs. Bissel's basement. I'm joking. It wasn't a ghost, although from that day on Mrs. Bissel believed it was. I tell you, my reputation was *great*.

"No, thanks. I'll just take these home, if you're sure you don't mind—"

"Not in the least."

"Thank you, Keiji. I'll practice more at home. Hope I don't drop one of them. Spike would probably grab it and eat it."

"Better not drop it then. I don't think bamboo is good for dogs."

"I'm sure you're right." I rose and put the chopsticks Keiji gave me into my handbag. "I really appreciate this, Keiji."

"Not a problem, Mrs. Majesty."

Only then did I sense the inequality of our stations, and it bothered me. "Please call me Daisy, Keiji."

He squinted at me. "I thought your name was Desdemona."

Borrowing a page from Sam Rotondo's book, I rolled my eyes. "That's my professional name. Everyone who knows me knows I'm really Daisy. But Desdemona sounds so much more . . . spiritual. Or something."

We started walking toward the sunroom and the back door to Mrs. Bissel's house.

"I'd vote for *something*," Keiji said wryly. "Why'd you pick that name, anyhow? You might as well have called yourself Ophelia, except then you'd carry the weight of being named after a suicide instead of a murdered woman."

My nose wrinkled of its own accord. The word *suicide* had that effect on me. "I chose it when I was ten years old. What can you expect from a kid?"

"Golly, you were a precocious kid, weren't you? Knowing Shakespeare at that age."

"Not really. If I'd been forced to read *Othello* before I chose the name, I'd have selected something different. Esmeralda, maybe."

"Ha! Then you'd have had a hunchback fall in love with you and been murdered."

"Gee whiz, Keiji, you really know your books, don't you?"

"I like to read."

We'd reached the back door, which he politely opened for me. "Well, it doesn't matter anymore, because everyone thinks my name is Desdemona."

"Desdemona Majesty." He thought about it for a second while I grabbed my hat from the rack beside the door. "Well, it sounds good for your line of work, although I think your last name really makes it perfect."

"Majesty?"

"Yeah."

"That was my husband's name." I sighed, unable to help myself.

"Oh, jeez, I'm sorry. I didn't mean to make you feel bad."

Impulsively, I took his hand and squeezed it. "Nonsense. You didn't make me feel bad. In fact, I think you've rescued me from a dire predicament." I patted my handbag, where the chopsticks lay, waiting for me.

He grinned. "If you say so. Daisy."

We parted on the best of terms.

CHAPTER NINE

I practiced with those darned chopsticks until I could pick up the tiniest of objects with them. I practiced until my fingers ached. I practiced all week long. By the time the Benjamins came for dinner on Friday, I almost wished I could use them on a real meal, but I didn't want to lessen the impact of my proficiency during Saturday's dinner at Miyaki's. Besides, Sam came to dinner on Friday night, too.

Practicing with chopsticks was far from the only thing I did that week, however. On Monday afternoon, after I returned home from my long day, I greeted Spike, put the family's books on the table near the door, and went to the kitchen. There I picked up the telephone receiver from where it hung on the kitchen wall and asked Medora Cox, an old high-school friend and an operator at the local telephone exchange, to connect me with the home of Mr. Stephen Hastings. She did so.

Naturally, the Hastings being wealthy, a servant picked up the instrument on the other end. "Hastings residence." Whoever it was sounded snooty.

But that didn't put me off. My occupation had accustomed me to snootiness in other people's servants. "May I please speak with Mrs. Hastings? This is Mrs. Majesty."

After a short hesitation, the snob on the other end of the wire said, "One moment, please. I'll see if she's available."

What she meant was that she'd see if Mrs. Hastings wanted

to speak to so puny a specimen of humankind as I. Well, nuts to her.

Anyhow, I heard the flurry of footsteps approaching the instrument, and Mrs. Hastings' breathy voice came through loudish and clear. So there, Miss Snoot. "Mrs. Majesty? Oh, I'm *so* glad you telephoned. I've been wanting to speak with you since Saturday."

"I've wanted to speak with you, too, Mrs. Hastings. I feel terrible about how upset you were after the séance, and I wanted to apologize and—"

"No!" She didn't squeal quite as loudly as Mrs. Pinkerton was wont to do, but she gave a fair imitation of Mrs. Pinkerton in a tizzy. "No. What I want is to hire you to get in touch with Edward again and find out if he can tell us any more about his death and who killed him. I *knew* he didn't kill himself!"

Not on her life. No way was I going to go through that experience again. Drat! Now I wished I hadn't telephoned her until I'd thought of a way to avoid this very thing, which I should have anticipated.

"Um . . . I'll be happy to visit with you. I'll bring the Ouija board or perhaps the tarot cards—"

"I'd prefer you do another séance."

Stupid, stupid Daisy. Of *course* she wanted me to do another séance. Bother! "Well . . ."

She paused before speaking again. When she did, she sounded concerned, and I felt like a big bully. "It was quite hard on you, wasn't it?"

Lifting my eyes to the ceiling in a gesture people generally use as a plea to the Almighty, although I only saw the kitchen ceiling, I hedged. "Yes. Having a spirit speak through me is always trying. Last Saturday's séance was particularly difficult because of the circumstances of your son's death. I can honestly tell you that nothing like that has ever happened in one of my séances before. No one has ever had me call up a murdered relative"—I bethought me of the séance I'd conducted in a speakeasy for a murderous bootlegger and honesty compelled me to add—"unless, of course, they knew he was murdered ahead of time. Your son's plea was a terrible shock for all of us. I'm sure it was harder on you than anyone else there."

"Oh, dear. I'm so sorry."

"It certainly wasn't your fault, Mrs. Hastings. I only hoped I could help you in some way. I . . . well, I've begun a little investigation into your son's death on my own and would appreciate some information from you about him, his associates, his friends, his work, and that kind of thing." I sucked in a breath and held it for about five seconds before saying what I said next. "I'm hoping to interest our family friend, a Pasadena Police detective, in investigating your son's death more fully."

"Oh, *thank* you! The police didn't seem to care one bit that Eddie would never have killed himself."

"No, it was probably easier for them to accept the obvious answer." I mentally apologized to Sam Rotondo, who was a smart, dedicated, and hard-working fellow.

"Exactly!" Mrs. Hastings said with satisfaction. "But when can you visit me, Mrs. Majesty? I'd ask you to come this evening, but . . ."

"I'm awfully sorry," I said at once. I already had one client who expected me to drop everything and come to her aid anytime she had a fit. Not that I equated Mrs. Hastings with Mrs. Pinkerton. The former seemed much more sensible and level-headed than the latter, although I didn't aim to take any chances. "However, I am free tomorrow morning if you have some time."

"Oh, thank you! Yes. Please come tomorrow. I'll be free all morning, so you pick the time."

So I said, "How about ten o'clock?" I probably could have

been there earlier, but then I'd have had to hurry and skip Spike's walk.

"Ten o'clock is perfect. Thank you *so* much! I'm sure you'll be able to straighten out the police."

Hmm. We'd see about that. I had grave doubts—so to speak—that Sam Rotondo would pay any attention to me about Eddie Hastings' possible murder, no matter how much information I amassed on my own.

A shiver overtook me as I recalled the ghastly moment in the séance when *something* took over my will and my body and spoke through my mouth. As little as I believed in those of us alive on the earth being able to communicate with those who'd died before us, I still couldn't help but remember that particular incident and its accompanying sensations. And if discovering the truth—providing the truth was that Eddie Hastings was murdered—would ensure nothing like that ever happened to me again, I was willing to do it. Even if, in doing so, I rattled Sam Rotondo's uneven temper.

"Very well. I'll be at your home at ten o'clock tomorrow. Oh! I just remembered I don't have your address."

She gave me an address in the San Rafael area, an extremely isolated and posh district of Pasadena. Good. My visit might prove painful, but at least I'd carry it out in beautiful surroundings. I aimed to take my Ouija board, too, and see if we couldn't communicate with Eddie via that. Provided, of course, we could communicate with him at all.

The very idea of an actual dead person communicating with me hit a raw nerve. Darn it, I didn't *believe* in communication with the dead! And if such things were possible, why hadn't Billy bothered to ring me up? I almost wouldn't mind talking to him. At least he wasn't in constant pain any longer.

Oh, bother.

After I hung the receiver on its cradle, I took Spike to my

bedroom off the kitchen, removed my day dress and shoes, put my hat away, and lay on the bed. Spike and I were out like a couple of lights until we both heard Aunt Vi bustling in the kitchen, preparing our dinner. Then I rose, smoothed down my hair, put my day dress and shoes back on, and went to the kitchen to help.

Not that Vi ever let me near the foodstuffs. She knew better. But she did allow me to set the table and so forth. As I did my task, I listed the books I'd got at the library. Vi was pleased.

That night we dined on succulent roasted chicken, mashed potatoes and gravy, carrots and peas, and more of Vi's awe-inspiring dinner rolls. She'd even fixed an apple crisp for dessert. My aunt was wonderful.

After dinner, Ma and I washed up, and then I headed for the bedroom with *Crome Yellow* in hand and proceeded to read it. What an odd book. But entertaining. Funny in spots.

The following morning, after I'd washed the breakfast dishes and put them away and reached for Spike's leash—which sent him into a frenzy of joy—the telephone rang.

I looked at Pa, who looked back at me. We both knew the call was for me. We both knew whom the call was from. Nobody except Mrs. Pinkerton in a fuss ever called that early in the morning. I heaved a sigh.

"You're going to have to wait a minute, Spike. I need to answer the telephone."

Spike wasn't happy about it but, being the well-behaved dog he was, he sat and stayed as I answered the 'phone, his tail doing a remarkably good job at sweeping the floor around him.

"Gumm-Majesty residence, Mrs. Majesty—"

"Daisy!" came a wail from the other end of the wire.

Aw, nuts. I'd been right. I grimaced at Pa, who winked at me. "Good morning, Mrs. Pinkerton." It was difficult, but I spoke in my soothing spiritualist's voice. I knew better than to think anyone's low voice or common sense would ever penetrate the woman's self-absorption, but I did it anyway.

"*Daisy!*" she repeated in the same wail. "I need to *see* you! I *must* see you! As soon as possible."

"Please calm down, Mrs. Pinkerton." I don't think I'd ever suggested she calm down before, primarily because I didn't want to ruffle her feathers. However, since they were clearly already ruffled that morning, I figured a gentle command wouldn't hurt.

She ceased wailing and commenced sobbing over the telephone wire.

"Please tell me what's the matter, and we can set up an appointment. I won't be able to see you until eleven-thirty this morning, I fear, because I have another imperative appointment earlier." She wasn't going to spoil my walk with Spike, by gad, or my appointment with poor, bereaved Mrs. Hastings.

"It's Mr. Kincaid!" She'd commenced shrieking, but I was so shocked by her words that I didn't tell her to shut up.

"*Harold?* Good heavens, what—"

"No, no, no! *Mister* Kincaid! Harold's father."

I pressed a hand to my heart, which had taken to thundering like a herd of rampaging hippopotami when I'd thought Harold had suffered some sort of accident. Blast this woman, anyhow!

I modulated my voice to its spiritualistic tone. "What about Mr. Kincaid?" As far as I knew, the villainous Mr. Kincaid, her first husband, was rotting away in a prison somewhere for fraud and theft.

"He's *escaped*!"

Now there was a shock. "Oh, my goodness! I'm so sorry to hear it." If the man had a brain in his head, he wouldn't set foot in Pasadena, but one never knew about these things. "How did he do that?"

"Nobody knows!" More sobbing and a wail or two. "He

wasn't in his cell yesterday morning. The prison administration has only just been in touch with the Pasadena Police Department, and that awful Detective Rotondo telephoned me to let me know."

And why, wondered I, was she calling Sam awful? I felt proprietary about Sam. Darn it, *I* was the only one who could call him names! "Detective Rotondo was the man responsible for arresting Mr. Kincaid, if you'll recall, Mrs. Pinkerton. And he was also instrumental in getting Stacy to rejoin the Salvation Army."

Subdued whimpering. "I suppose you're right. But—oh, Daisy! Whatever will I *do*?"

Beat me. "I'll bring my board and cards to your house at eleven-thirty today, Mrs. Pinkerton. Are the police giving you any kind of protection?" Not that she'd need it. Probably.

"Protection? Oh, Daisy, do you think he'll try to *get* me?"

"I don't think so." I sure wouldn't if I were he. "But you never know. You might want to telephone the department and ask to have a policeman drive by your house every so often. Just to make sure."

"Call them? Me?" Her voice had gone tiny. "Um . . . would you be willing to do that for me, dear? I'm just *so* upset!"

Lord, the woman was impossible. Not to mention incompetent. But needs must, so I capitulated. "Certainly. I'll be happy to call them for you." Liar, liar.

"Oh, *thank* you, Daisy!" And she rang off.

Looking down at my dog and then up at my father, I held up a finger. "One more little call, and we can go for our walk."

I already knew the number of the police department, so I just dialed it up and asked to speak with Detective Rotondo when the officer at the desk answered.

"Rotondo," a growly voice hit my ears a few seconds later.

"Sam, it's Daisy."

Silence. Then: "What do you want?"

"Darn you! I don't want anything for myself. But Mrs. Pinkerton just called me in a dither."

I heard Sam's heavy sigh carry over the wire to my ear. "Yeah. Her ex just escaped from San Quentin. I called her a few minutes ago to tell her."

The name of the prison shocked me. "He was in San Quentin?"

"Well, yeah. He was a thief, Daisy, not a mass murderer. They weren't going to send him to Folsom. He worked in the library in San Quentin."

"I didn't know that."

"Now you do." He sounded bored and not a little snide. "So what does she want?"

Deciding not to waste any more of his precious time, I said, "She asked me to call the police and request that an officer drive by her home every now and then. Sort of patrol the area. She's afraid her ex-husband is going to get her."

"Why'd he want her?"

Reasonable question. "I have no idea, but you know her."

Another sigh. "Yeah, I know her. And I know she's rich, and the chief tries to appease the big taxpayers." This fact of life disgruntled Sam, although I'm sure the same held true the world over. The rich are different from the rest of us peons, and those in high places paid attention to them. "Very well, I'll tell the duty sergeant to dispatch officers to patrol her neighborhood every hour or so."

"Thanks, Sam. I appreciate it. I have to go to see her today and work the Ouija board. I'm not sure why. I sure can't do anything about her problem."

"Lucky you."

"Right."

"We still set for Saturday night at Miyaki's?"

"You betcha. Say, why don't you come to supper tomorrow? Pa needs to play rummy, and Spike misses you."

Daisy Gumm Majesty! I couldn't believe those words had come from my mouth!

"Spike misses me, eh?"

"Well . . . yes. And the rest of the family, too."

"I see." He sounded both disappointed and slightly exasperated. "All right. I'll come over. Six, as usual?"

"Yes, that will be fine."

"See you then." He hung up.

I hoped Vi wouldn't mind that I'd invited Sam to dinner without consulting her first. But no. She loved it when Sam came over. The whole family did. Except me. Well . . . maybe that wasn't true any longer, but I didn't want to think about it.

So Pa and I took a delighted Spike for a walk around the neighborhood until I had to get ready to pay a visit to Mrs. Hastings. Pa was fascinated to learn about the escape of the dastardly Mr. Kincaid from San Quentin, and we propounded so many possibilities to account for his success in the endeavor that we were both breathless with laughter by the time we got home again.

CHAPTER TEN

I chose my wardrobe carefully. As I contemplated my closet, which was stuffed full of clothes I'd made, I tried to decide how to present myself to a bereaved mother in a respectful yet encouraging way. I wanted my appearance, as well as my posture and voice, to be such that I could best wring personal details of her family's life from her. Some folks were chary about revealing family secrets, although I sensed Mrs. Hastings would provide almost any information if it would help determine who had killed her son.

If, of course, her son had been murdered. For all I knew, he really had killed himself. Or died of natural causes. Or ptomaine. One young man I'd known had died of ptomaine poisoning a couple of years back. Made me sad at the time.

In the end, I selected a costume that went well with my mission and the weather, which was warm. A pale coral-colored cotton-voile dress with an unfitted bodice decorated with darker peach embroidery on the loose sleeves would suit the purpose admirably. A belt buckled below the waist, and I topped it off with my all-purpose summer straw hat with a peach rose set thereon. I had a number of fabric flowers in various colors, all of which enhanced that same straw hat from time to time. With the outfit, I wore bone-colored shoes with a Louis heel and carried my bone-colored handbag. Of course, I also aimed to carry my Ouija board in its lovely velvet carrying bag (made by me, naturally), but I don't think it marred the perfection of my outfit much. I also stuffed my tarot cards into my handbag.

When I exited the bedroom after powdering my nose and making sure my visage was pale, interesting, and spiritualistic, Pa said, "You look grand, Daisy. Doing a reading for someone?"

"Mrs. Hastings," said I with some trepidation. After all, Pa didn't believe Eddie Hastings had invaded my last séance.

"Ah. To talk about her dead boy?"

That didn't sound quite right, but I supposed it was. "Yes," I said upon a sigh. "But don't worry. I haven't gone totally 'round the bend. I only want to find out about him and his friends and so forth."

"And then you aim to do some snooping around, right?"

"I . . . Well, yes."

Shaking his head, Pa said, "Be careful, Daisy. If the boy was murdered, you don't want his murderer to claim a second victim, do you?"

It took a second for Pa's words to sink in. When they did, my shock was unfeigned. Pointing to my chest, I asked in a squeaky voice, "You mean me?"

"No one else is looking at the death as anything but natural or suicide, right?"

"Oh, Lord. No. I mean, yes, you're right. Pa, I promise you that if I discover anything at all that seems fishy, I'll tell Sam about it. He's coming to dinner tomorrow night." Which reminded me that I'd best tell Aunt Vi about having invited Sam so she could be prepared. Shoot. Sometimes I didn't know why I did the things I did.

"If you don't, I will," he said with a wry bite to his voice. "I don't want to lose my daughter after just losing my son-in-law."

I gave him a quick hug. "I know you loved Billy like a son, Pa. That's one of the reasons I love you so much."

"Then be careful on this investigation of yours."

"I don't know yet if there will be an investigation."

"Maybe not, but I know you, Daisy."

Upon that not especially happy note, I patted Spike, gave him the command to sit and stay, and went out the side door to the Chevrolet parked conveniently next to the porch. Pa's words thrummed in my head as I drove toward the San Rafael district of Pasadena. In order to do so, I drove across the Colorado Street Bridge and past Busch Gardens into the exclusive district where stood very few homes. The homes that did exist in the area were exquisite, though. The Hastings' mansion sat behind a jungle of shrubbery on South Arroyo Boulevard. Naturally, it also had a gate around it, and a guard at the gatehouse.

I was great pals with Jackson, Mrs. Pinkerton's gate guard, but I didn't know the little Chinese guy who stuck his head out of the gatehouse at Mrs. Hastings' place.

"Name?" he asked crisply.

"Desdemona Majesty," I said. Sometimes I bantered with the household staff in the great homes I visited, but this fellow didn't appear very friendly. Anyhow, I didn't want any hint of frivolity to mar my spiritualistic bearing.

Friendly or not, he must have pushed a button, because the enormous black iron gate parted before my humble Chevrolet, and I drove onto the grounds, although I wasn't sure what to do once I was there. For only a second I considered asking the guard, but then I decided to continue on the paved roadway before me.

I swear to heaven, I must have driven *miles* before I caught sight of the gigantic palace wherein resided the Hastings family. Until that moment, I hadn't realized how profitable a profession lawyering could be.

As Mrs. Hastings had given me no instructions on how to approach her residence, I stopped the machine near the first door I spotted and got out. Then, after looking left and right and up and down, I decided the door must be one of the home's major entrances, since it had big double doors and could only be reached by climbing several concrete steps, which were guarded on both sides by Chinese dragons. Hmm. The Hastings had a Chinese guard at the gate and Chinese dragons on pedestals at the door. Did this indicate a business link with China? No use speculating at that point.

Therefore, I lifted the door knocker—which was attached to a formidable-looking brass Chinese dragon—and clunked it twice.

My heart fox-trotted madly for a minute. Don't know why it did that. I visited wealthy clients who lived in grand houses all the time. I guess the isolation of the Hastings' place, the strange occurrence at the séance, and Pa's dire warning had affected me badly.

Fortunately, I didn't have to wait long. A uniformed maid—Chinese, by the looks of her—answered the door shortly after my knock had thudded. A pretty little thing, she eyed me out of inscrutable black eyes—I possessed inscrutable blue eyes—and said, "Mrs. Majesty?"

"Yes."

"Please come this way."

And she turned abruptly and walked across a vast marble entryway and into a hall leading directly from it. Still nervous, I glanced around and discovered lots more Chinese art every-where. A pair of benches carved out of some very dark wood, which I should probably know the name of, sat beneath a simply smashing Chinese silk painting.

Here I probably should make a confession. Although I know nothing about art, I had learned by that point in my life that I preferred Chinese art to Japanese art. I had a hunch this prefer-ence came from my own natural muddledness of mind. The Japanese art I'd seen was pristine, tranquil, serene, and rather stark. Chinese art, on the other hand, while still definitely Asian, was jolly and fussy and busy. Clearly, tranquillity wasn't one of my better friends at the time.

At any rate, I was terribly impressed and not a little pleased as I followed the maid down the hallway. Chinese artwork decorated the walls and the floors, and everywhere I looked my eyes were treated to more than Oriental splendor, as Rudyard Kipling might have said.

And yes, I've read three *Fu Manchu* books by Mr. Sax Rohmer. Nuts. I still loved Chinese art.

"Please enter here, Mrs. Majesty. Mrs. Hastings is waiting for you."

"Thank you." I smiled at the girl, not expecting a response, but she smiled shyly back at me, and I felt good for having been polite.

"Oh, Mrs. Majesty!" came Mrs. Hastings' voice from a corner of the room. When I glanced over at it, I saw the lady herself, rising from a padded Chinese-style window seat. She placed a bookmark in her book, put it on the window seat, and hurried toward me. I wafted over to meet her, smiling my serene spiritualist's smile. I might not have felt serene, but I could fake it as well as anyone. And my waft was perfection itself.

"Good morning, Mrs. Hastings. I hope I'll be able to help you." As long as her son didn't butt into any more of my séances.

"I do so hope you can, Mrs. Majesty." She took my hand in both of hers.

I always wore gloves when I did any gardening and slathered my hands with cream, so said hands remained soft and smooth. Nobody would believe in a spiritualist with callused hands or a ruddy complexion. My splatter of freckles, which I assiduously covered with pale face powder, was difficult enough to deal with.

"You have a lovely home, Mrs. Hastings. The art alone is awe-inspiring."

She glanced around vaguely. More Chinese art was displayed on these walls, and the furniture had a Chinese air about it. So to speak. "Mr. Hastings has collected Chinese art for decades now. He and Mr. Millette worked in Hong Kong for quite a few years. They were in partnership there."

"Oh, my. I didn't know that. It must have been fascinating."

"It was profitable, at any rate. I'm not sure I completely trusted some of the people with whom he worked, but . . . well, you needn't hear about that."

Aha! Perhaps there was a Chinese connection to her son's death. A couple of scary scenes from a *Fu Manchu* book toddled into my brain and danced there for a second or two.

"Actually," I said as she herded me toward a sofa with a low, carved scrollwork table in front of it—was that teak wood? I couldn't remember—"perhaps we might look into a Chinese connection to your son's death, if you think that's feasible."

She stopped walking and said, "Chinese connection? Oh, my dear, I don't think so. Stephen—my husband, I mean—has no connections with the Orient these days. He's stuck fast in his Pasadena office, and Eddie never had anything to do with China at all."

Hmm. Well, it was worth a question. "I see. That will probably make things easier, if he was murdered. I mean, we wouldn't want to have to go to China or anything, would we?" Good Lord, I was babbling. Mind you, I was babbling in my low, silky spiritualist's voice, but I was still babbling. I told myself to cease instantly.

"Yes, I can see how that might be difficult," Mrs. Hastings said. She didn't sound sarcastic or anything, either, so I guess she didn't think I'd just made a fool of myself. Thank God for small favors.

We arrived at the luxurious sofa where she sat, and as I took a seat on the chair opposite the sofa, I commented on the table.

"That's a beautiful table. Do you know what kind of wood the Chinese use to make such wonderful furniture?"

"Not really," said she, dashing any hope of enhancing my knowledge of the world. "I do know that some of the furniture Stephen bought is cherry wood and some of it is teak wood." She rubbed a hand on the table, which was so perfectly dusted, it gleamed in polished perfection and her hand made a print. "This piece is lacquered. I believe a lot of Chinese furniture is lacquered."

Aha. So I wasn't to be totally bereft of new knowledge. "I see. Yes, I can see that the lacquer makes it shine. I love the scrolled shape of it."

"I believe that's a Ming Dynasty piece. We probably shouldn't use it for every day, but what's the point of having pretty furniture if you can't use it?"

Good question, and one I didn't even attempt to answer. Rather, I said, "Would you like to proceed with the Ouija board, or would you be willing to answer a few questions first? In order to get the police interested in your son's death, we'll have to give them a good reason to investigate it. They won't pay attention to any news collected from séances or Ouija boards." I gazed at her with the most sorrowful expression I could summon, which was pretty darned sorrowful. I'd had tons of practice.

"Yes," she said upon a heartfelt sigh. "I know you're right." She stared at me earnestly. "But that *was* Eddie on Saturday night! It was, Mrs. Majesty!"

"I know it was," I said, suppressing my shudder with some difficulty. "But the police won't believe us. Would you mind if I took some notes of people and places your son might have dealt with?" I'd pondered long and hard whether to take notes, something I deemed far from spiritualistic behavior. But, blast it, I wanted to learn the truth.

"Notes?"

"I know that sounds quite pedestrian, but it might help me in securing the attention of the police."

"Oh, yes. I see. That makes sense." She gazed with longing at the fabric carrying bag in which my Ouija board lay, and I knew she wanted to get to the good stuff. "I don't see why not. Ask any questions you like, although I think we'd get more information from Eddie." Her sentence ended on a high note, as if it were really a question.

"We'll definitely do some work with the Ouija board and see if Rolly can communicate with your son, but I need to know the names of his friends and so forth, too. To give to the police." I stressed the police connection, because even if, God forbid, Eddie Hastings had really and truly launched himself into a Ouija-board session, nobody would believe us if we told them so.

"Of course."

"Perhaps we should start with his place of business. Did he work in his father's legal firm?"

"Yes. After he graduated from Stanford, he got his law degree and began in Stephen's firm. He started at the bottom of the ladder," she said, as if to let me know Eddie was no laggard. "But he progressed rapidly because of his talent, not because he was Stephen's son."

Hmm. Maybe. But I said nothing to cast doubt on her son's abilities. Poising my pencil over the pad I'd taken from my handbag, I asked, "And the name of the firm?"

"Its full name is Hastings, Millette, and Hastings. Eddie had just been made a partner." She sniffled, and I noticed she had a wadded-up hankie in her hand. She used it to wipe her eyes. Poor woman.

I wrote down the name and murmured, "I see. And how long had he worked there?"

"Oh, ever since he graduated from law school." Before I could ask her how long that was, she said, "Since he was twenty-two, so it was five years."

"Thank you. And you say he got along well there?"

"Oh, yes! Everyone loved Eddie."

Trust a mother. I said, "Did he have a secretary? Were there other secretaries in the firm? Perhaps you remember some names?"

"Oh, dear." She hesitated and got a faraway look in her eyes before she blinked and said, "Eddie shared a secretary with Mr. Grover, another youngish man. Her name is . . . oh, let me see . . . Belinda! Yes, her name is Belinda. I'm not sure of her last name. Something simple."

I thought about an old classmate of mine, Belinda Young, and decided to offer that as a last name. "Young?"

Her eyes going wide as dinner plates, Mrs. Hastings cried, "How did you *know*? Oh, but Griselda and Madeline both told me you're the best spiritualist in California."

That was nice. I didn't let on that I already knew Belinda Young had taken a secretarial course at Pasadena City College. Let her think the spirits had told me Belinda's last name.

"Mrs. Bissel and Mrs. Pinkerton are both very kind. Do you know the names of other people in the firm? Other secretaries? And does the Hastings firm employ runners?" I'd heard of runners, who literally ran or bicycled all over town, carrying legal papers from one law firm to another, or from a law firm to the courthouse.

"Oh, dear. I wish I'd paid more attention. I don't find legal work terribly interesting, to tell you the truth, and I fear my mind was on other matters when the men talked about the office. I know Stephen's secretary is Elizabeth Mattingly. She's been with the firm for years, and I think . . . no. I can't recall the name of Mr. Millette's secretary. I'm sorry, dear. Is it important?"

"At this point, I don't know what might be important, Mrs. Hastings."

"Of course. Now I wish I hadn't daydreamed through all those boring dinner-table conversations."

"I'm sure we'll be able to fill in the blanks. Perhaps I can visit the firm and chat with Miss Young. What type of legal work does Mr. Hastings' firm do? Are they criminal attorneys or do they practice civil law?"

"Oh, they never touch criminal cases! Criminal law is so tawdry."

Hmm. Tawdry, criminal law might be, but I'd wager it was more interesting than civil law. I doubt that I'd have paid any attention either if, say, Pa and Billy had chatted about a broken contract or a disputed boundary at the dinner table.

"I see. And do you know the names of your son's friends, or the people he saw most often in or out of the office?"

"Let me see . . . of course, he saw the people at the law firm most often. He had a lot of friends, too, though. Harold Kincaid was one. And a nice fellow named Lester Knowles—his last name is spelled K-N-O-W-L-E-S. Mr. Knowles used to come to dinner here sometimes. I don't know why, but Mr. Hastings didn't care for Mr. Knowles much."

Bet I knew why Eddie Hastings' father didn't care for Lester Knowles, if Mr. Knowles was of Eddie's and Harold's stamp. But I didn't want to crush Eddie's mother, so I didn't say anything. Let the woman live with her illusions. She'd loved her son, and that was the important thing.

"I see. Anyone else? The more names you can give me, the better my chances of discovering the truth. What about clubs and so forth. Did your son belong to any clubs?"

"Oh. The Pasadena Athletic Club. Eddie loved to play tennis and swim. And he'd go to the theater quite often. He and Mr. Knowles would often see a play of an evening. Mr. Hastings and I were quite anxious that Eddie marry and have children, but the only woman he saw on a regular basis was Mr. Knowles' sister, Adele. They often made a threesome. I think Eddie was shy about courting her, and that's why they included Mr. Knowles in their party."

"I'm sure that's it," said I, trying not to grind my teeth. "So he belonged to the Pasadena Athletic Club. Anything else you can think of?"

"Oh, dear. Let me see. We've attended All Saints Episcopal Church ever since it opened in 'fourteen."

"All Saints? The one on North Euclid Avenue?"

"Yes, exactly, although the congregation is growing so large, we're probably going to build a new church building soon."

"I see. Perhaps I might have a chat with the rector there."

"That might be worthwhile," she said doubtfully. "His name is Reverend Leslie Learned."

Mr. Learned. The name alone almost intimidated a person.

After I'd pumped Mrs. Hastings for all I was worth, I tucked my pencil and tablet into my handbag and withdrew the Ouija board. My heart started pounding like crazy. For the first time in my career as a spiritualist medium, which had taken up more than half my life, I was scared witless by the tools of my trade.

CHAPTER ELEVEN

Thank God nobody but Rolly appeared as Mrs. Hastings and I plied the planchette, and Rolly only did so because I made him. He couldn't tell us much about Eddie Hastings' demise, however.

"The poor lad didn't see his killer," Rolly spelled out.

"May I speak to him? Eddie, I mean?" Mrs. Hastings asked breathlessly.

I wanted to smack her. But I only had a sad—one might even say dispirited, if one were in a punning mood—Rolly write, "The poor lad can't speak to you today, ma'am. But he sends his love and wants you to be as happy as you can be."

Wrong thing to write. Instantly Mrs. Hastings began sobbing. "How can I ever be happy again without my Eddie?"

Neither Rolly nor I knew the answer to that one, but Rolly made a stab at it. "It's terrible, terrible to lose a child. My darling one and I lost a boy. Our sixth son." This was quick thinking on my part, because before that day, the story was that Rolly and I had only had five sons together way back when in Scotland. Perhaps "only" isn't the right word, but never mind about that.

By the way, spelling things out on the Ouija board can take a whole lot of time. This was especially true when I first started plying my craft at the tender age of ten. I'd improved a lot over the years, however, and although I still told people that Rolly had no education and couldn't spell well, I now had that planchette zipping over the board like a mad thing.

Anyhow, the lie about my sixth son put a stop to the tears. Mrs. Hastings' gaze flew to my face. "Oh, I had no idea!"

"It was a long time ago, Mrs. Hastings. Your grief is much more recent. To tell the truth, I don't really remember." A thousand years is a long time, for Pete's sake. And I'd made up the story of our deathless love in the first place. Oh, the tangled web one weaves . . . but I'm sure you know the rest.

"I see." Mrs. Hastings sniffled and blew her nose, but didn't seem inclined to sob anymore, for which I was grateful.

The Ouija-board session didn't last too much longer, and I hied myself out of the Hastings' mansion shortly thereafter, leaving plenty of time to drive to Mrs. Pinkerton's grand home on Orange Grove Boulevard. I attempted to fortify myself for her hysteria the whole way there.

Jackson, Mrs. Pinkerton's gatekeeper, of whom I've spoken before, gave me a friendly greeting at the gate, and I drove on up the drive to the front door. Not for Desdemona Majesty, spiritualist extraordinaire, to use the back door like a common or garden-variety grocer's boy or anything. Not on your life. I walked up the marble staircase and rang the booming doorbell as if I deserved to do it. Which I did, darn it.

I love Mrs. Pinkerton's butler, Featherstone. He's always impeccably dressed in suit and tie, and he even wears white gloves, I presume to check to see if the housemaids have done their job to perfection. He's sober and serious, and I can seldom resist teasing him.

"Mrs. Majesty," said he somberly when he opened the door, looking as much like a funeral director as a butler.

"Good morning, Featherstone. Lead me to the weeping woman, please."

"This way, madam." Without even cracking a smile, Featherstone turned and walked down the hallway to the drawing room.

I followed him, as I always did, even though I could have found my way there blindfolded by that time.

When he opened the door to the drawing room—which is like a living room, only bigger and with grander furnishings—I saw Mrs. Pinkerton quivering on the sofa, blotting tears with a lace-edged hankie and in one of her better tizzies. I gave an inward sigh, but wafted to her as if on fairy feet.

"Mrs. Pinkerton?" I said softly, since her eyes were pinched shut and she couldn't see me. Besides which, the Oriental carpet under my feet was so thick, you couldn't have heard an elephant walk on the thing.

Her eyes popped open, and she leapt from the sofa and ran at me. I braced myself, knowing from prior experience that the hefty Mrs. Pinkerton could quite easily knock me to the floor if I didn't. I managed to survive upright by holding tightly to a medallion-backed chair. It was one of those Louis the Some-thingth chairs and quite lovely. It was also heavy, thank God.

"Oh, Daisy!" she shrieked. "Oh, I'm *so* glad you're here. I've been going mad! I'm so worried!"

Feeling secure on my feet once more, I patted her on the back and said soothingly, "Let's try to calm down, and consult the board, shall we?"

"Oh, yes! And do you have your tarot cards? I need to know if that dreadful man is headed here!"

"Why would he do that?" I asked quietly—and reasonably.

"I don't know!" she screeched. "But he's such a terrible person!"

True, but she'd married him. On the other hand, I know several women who'd married bounders and have read about even more of them. To be fair, I'm sure there are men who've married bad women, too, but people didn't tend to write about them as often as the other way 'round. Besides that, if Mr. Kincaid had acted like a wretched specimen before the ceremony, probably even Mrs. Pinkerton would have noticed and backed down. Maybe.

"Well, let's see if Rolly can set your mind at ease." I guided her to the sofa she'd recently left and pulled up a chair opposite the table in front of the sofa. I took my Ouija board out of its special carrying bag and set it on the table with the two rows of letters facing Mrs. Pinkerton. By that time, I could read upside down almost as well as I could right-side up. "But you'd better dry your tears first, so you can see what Rolly tells us."

Once and only once had Rolly materialized, more or less, during a Ouija board session with Mrs. Pinkerton. It was right after Billy's death, and I'd been in a blue funk and a black temper at the time. I regret to this day how hard I was on the woman during that particular session. I must admit, however, that its ultimate result was worth it, since Rolly got Mrs. P to let her pill of a daughter languish in jail for once. I figured it was past time Stacy Kincaid paid the full price for her misdeeds. So she did. Three months behind bars, and she'd been a good girl ever since. Heh.

Anyhow, Mrs. Pinkerton blotted her tears and focused her red-rimmed, swollen eyes on the Ouija board. "What would you like to ask Rolly first?" I asked demurely.

"I need to know if Eustace is coming here," she said promptly.

"Rolly might not know that, but let's see if he can answer." By rights, the Ouija board isn't supposed to be able to answer any questions other than those posed by and for the persons using the planchette, but what the heck.

I had Rolly fumble around on the board for a few seconds, then spell out, "Don't know."

"Oh, dear," said Mrs. Pinkerton. "Should I worry about him coming here?"

That one was easy. Rolly whipped the planchette right up to the word "No" printed on the top right-hand side of the board.

"But what if he does come here?" asked Mrs. Pinkerton plaintively.

Crumb, you'd think she wanted the rat to bedevil her some more, the way she was carrying on. The planchette spelled out, "Don't borrow trouble."

"Oh, dear. Oh, dear." Mrs. P removed her pudgy fingers from the planchette and gave me a beseeching glance. "Daisy, perhaps you should try the cards, since Rolly doesn't seem to be able to tell what Eustace is going to do."

"Perhaps that's a good idea. Rolly really can't tell you what other people are going to do, you know, especially if they're still living."

"Yes, yes, I see what you mean."

That made one of us. However, I nobly reached into my handbag and withdrew my pack of tarot cards, for which I'd sewn a much smaller, but still lovely, carrying bag. After I removed the deck, I shuffled it and laid it out in a simple five-card horseshoe. I didn't want it to be too complicated for Mrs. Pinkerton to understand.

Oddly enough, the cards made sense in a way. Mrs. P's "present" card was represented by the nine of swords, which represents fear of circumstances either current or to come. The card representing her existing expectations was the five of cups, which basically means the person for whom the reading is being done can only see bleakness and none of the possibilities to help herself out of her mood. Sounded exactly like Mrs. P to me.

The card at the apex of the horseshoe is supposed to represent something unexpected. When I laid the card down, I darned near laughed, because it was the ten of wands, which depicts a fellow carrying an ungodly burden who doesn't perceive that help is all around him if he'd only bother to look. The card is supposed to show that the person for whom the reading is being done needs to change her attitude in order to overcome her difficulties. Mrs. P to a T.

On the right of the ten of wands came the chariot, which foresees struggles to come, either physical or, in Mrs. Pinkerton's case, emotional. Fitted right in. And the very last card in the horseshoe depicted the ultimate future. Darned if I didn't turn over the hierophant. Lord. This card meant that Mrs. Pinkerton was destined to receive aid from someone on a spiritual or emotional plane. I feared that meant me. But that's precisely what I'd been doing lo, those many years, so the hierophant didn't come as a complete surprise, although I'd as soon have dealt a different pattern. Shoot. All I needed was for Mrs. Pinkerton to continue telephoning me in a frenzy every day or so.

When the reading was over, I glanced at Mrs. Pinkerton, and she glanced at me. She blinked several times and then said, "But it's all so *indefinite*. Oh, I wish I could get a clear reading of what I should do!"

I wanted to ask her what she expected from a deck of cards but held my peace. Rather, in my most soothing and gentle voice, I said, "The cards are telling you you're fretting over nothing at the moment, but that if something bad *does* happens, you'll find the means to cope with it."

She blinked a few more times doubtfully. "Do you really think so, Daisy?"

I swept a hand in a theatrical gesture over the cards lying on the table. "That's what the cards say, Mrs. Pinkerton. Do you see any reason to doubt them?"

"Well . . . no. I guess not. But I'm not sure what I should *do.*"

"That's exactly the point. You can do nothing. The probability is that Mr. Kincaid is headed for Mexico. That's where he was going when the police caught him originally. I don't see a reason for him to come back to your house, especially with the police patrolling all the time. Do you?"

"Oh." She sounded disappointed. I'm sure she craved more drama. "I see."

I gently laid my hand on hers. "Mrs. Pinkerton, have Rolly or I ever led you astray?"

"Goodness, no!"

"Then please try to take the advice of both Rolly and the cards. Whatever Mr. Kinkaid is doing now, you can't affect his behavior. If, and I think it's a remote possibility, he tries to get in touch with you, simply call the police. You have servants and Mr. Pinkerton here all the time, so you have nothing to worry about, really."

"Well . . . I suppose you're right, although Algie does go to his club most days."

"But you still have the servants. I'm sure Edie Applewood takes excellent care of you. And don't forget Aunt Vi, who has charge of all those knives in the kitchen."

A martial light appeared in Mrs. Pinkerton's eye. "Yes! I forgot. I'm not completely helpless, am I?"

"Not at all. And you have the faithful Featherstone, too."

"Yes. Featherstone is such a rock of dependability."

"There you go then." I shuffled the cards I'd laid out back into the deck and stuffed the deck into its bag. "Truly, your future looks grand, Mrs. Pinkerton. If you could make yourself worry less about things that probably won't happen, you'll be a happier person for it." As if she would ever take *that* sensible advice.

"Yes, yes. Yes, I see."

I gave her my most reassuring, soothing spiritualist's smile. "You can do it, Mrs. Pinkerton. I know you can."

"Thank you, dear. You're always such a comfort to me."

That's why she paid me so much money, bless her. "If you

don't mind, I believe I'll stop in to see Aunt Vi before I leave. Would you like her to assemble your luncheon?" Mrs. P always called the middle meal of the day *luncheon*.

"No, thank you. I believe I'll go upstairs and take a nap. It's been an exhausting morning."

Whoo, boy, I should have exhausting mornings like hers. But I only smiled sweetly. "Now? You don't even want a cup of tea or anything?"

"My nerves are too shattered for me to eat anything right now. I'm going to take a powder and rest for a while. Would you be kind enough to tell your aunt for me?"

"I'd be happy to." What's more, if I were lucky, Aunt Vi would let me eat some of Mrs. P's lunch. I was starving by that time, which was almost one-thirty in the afternoon. "Would you like me to tell Edie to prepare your bed, too?"

"Would you, dear? Thank you so much. You're so good to me."

"It's my pleasure." I picked up my handbag, left the massive drawing room, and made my way to the stairs. I found Edie in Mrs. Pinkerton's sitting room, folding freshly laundered clothes. "Hey, Edie."

She turned and smiled at me. "Hey, Daisy. Mrs. P in a fit again?"

"Isn't she always?"

With a giggle, Edie said, "She's been worse lately, since she learned that rat she used to be married to escaped from prison. But I don't know why she thinks he's coming here."

"I don't, either. Why would he? Do you know of any reason he might come here? Did he leave a fortune stashed in a safe somewhere?"

Shrugging, Edie said, "Don't ask me. I tried to stay as far away from that man as I could. Disgusting pig."

Mr. Kincaid used to corner Edie with his wheelchair and

pinch her bottom. He truly was a ghastly man. Edie had been a mere housemaid in those days. Now she held the exalted post of Mrs. Pinkerton's personal lady's maid, quite a jump up the social ladder of servants. Edie's husband, Quincy, took care of Mr. Pinkerton's horses. Or maybe they were his two sons' horses. All I know is that Quincy loved horses and Mr. Pinkerton's sons played polo a lot. Guess they didn't have to work for a living, either.

"Anyhow, I came up here to let you know Mrs. Pinkerton is going to take a nap now after her exhausting morning."

"Huh. I'll go turn down her bed and get her robe laid out."

"Thanks, Edie. I'm going to see Vi now."

"Good to see you, Daisy!"

"You too, Edie. Say hey to Quincy for me."

"Will do."

Edie vanished into Mrs. Pinkerton's bedroom, and I went down the back stairs, the ones the servants used, mainly because I didn't want to see Mrs. Pinkerton again. But I did want to see my aunt. Not only did I need to tell her I'd invited Sam for dinner on the morrow, but I hoped she'd be able to feed me something.

CHAPTER TWELVE

As luck would have it, when I entered the kitchen, Aunt Vi was just putting the finishing touches on what looked to be a spectacular luncheon for one. She'd even put a single yellow rose in a cut crystal vase on the tray. I couldn't tell what foodstuffs lay thereon, because they were covered with silver lids, but whatever they were, they sure smelled good.

"Boy, Aunt Vi, you're not only the best cook in the world, but you prepare very artistic trays."

"Go on with you, Daisy." She stopped preparing the meal long enough to give me a hug.

"But I'm afraid all your hard work is for naught. Mrs. Pinkerton claims she's too shattered to eat anything right now."

"Oh, bother the woman!"

Aunt Vi seldom criticized her employer, for whom she'd worked for nigh on twenty-five years. I lifted an eyebrow. "Has she been especially difficult lately?"

"You know she has," said Vi with a frown. "That's why she called you here today, isn't it? She's afraid that stinker of a first husband is going to come after her. Lord knows why. He paid little enough attention to her when they were married."

Hmm. Interesting. "Well, I guess the fear that he might show up has put her off her food." I eyed the tray with longing. "But your niece hasn't had lunch yet, if there's any more of whatever that is left."

"Daisy Majesty. And to think a year ago, we feared you were

112

going to starve yourself to death."

"I remember. Those were bad days."

Vi gave me another hug. "I know they were, sweetheart. But you just sit yourself down and eat whatever you want to eat. If the woman wakes up hungry, I'll fix her another tray. There's plenty." Vi walked over to a bell pull and gave it a tug. Featherstone appeared a moment later. "The mistress won't be taking her luncheon now, Featherstone. Perhaps later."

"Very well, Mrs. Gumm." He vanished again. I swear, his movements were almost as wraithlike as mine. Maybe they taught wafting in butler's school or something.

"Eat up, Daisy. I have to get the Pinkertons' dinner started."

She lifted the silver lids to the plates to reveal a fresh green salad, a plate of what turned out to be a delicious soup, and a lamb chop with fresh asparagus and tiny red potatoes, cut up into slices and served with butter and parsley. Everything was absolutely delicious.

I told Vi so.

"Thank you, sweetie. We're having lamb chops for supper tonight when I get home. Hope you don't mind eating chops twice in one day."

"Are you kidding? This is fabulous, Aunt Vi. What kind of soup is this?"

"It's just a plain old vegetable."

"There's nothing plain about it," I said, sipping delicately. I didn't want to annoy my darling aunt by showing bad manners. "By the way, I hope you don't mind, but I invited Sam for dinner tomorrow night, and the Benjamins are coming to dinner on Friday."

"That's fine about Sam, and I have the perfect meal planned for the Benjamins. We're going to dine on roasted turkey and all the trimmings. I know it's the middle of summer, but I've had a hankering for turkey lately, and leftover turkey makes great sandwiches."

Oh, yum. I loved turkey. And the stuffing, potatoes, gravy, and all the other fixings that went with it. And turkey sandwiches. Because I'd been taught never to speak with my mouth full, I swallowed my sip of soup before I told her I thought her plan a brilliant one. "And don't forget that Sam's taking all of us to Miyaki's on Saturday night."

"I haven't forgotten." Vi eyed me as I cut a piece of lamb chop. "I don't know why he asked the whole family. The one he wants to dine with is you."

Her words surprised me so much, I almost dropped my bite of lamb. Hastily shoving it into my mouth, I chewed as I thought about how to respond to Vi. I still hadn't come up with anything when I swallowed, so I sipped some water. When I finally spoke, my voice was soft and my response idiotic. "Nonsense."

"Daisy, if you don't know by this time that Sam Rotondo thinks you're the cat's meow, you're the only one. The poor man is head over heels in love with you, and you treat him abominably."

"No, I don't!" I cried, stung. "We're friends, Sam and me."

"Pish. You're always picking fights with him, and him such a nice man."

"He hasn't always been nice to me," I said, sounding like a whining child to my own ears.

"Stuff. He was your husband's best friend, and he's been trying to take care of you ever since Billy passed. Why, he hared off to Egypt after you and Harold went to that heathen country, don't forget."

My appetite had fled. "How could I forget? I was so sick and sad."

Vi plunked herself down on a seat at the kitchen table. "I know, Daisy. I've lost a husband and my only son. But life goes on."

"Whether you want it to or not," I said feebly.

"Yes. But you have to pick yourself up by your bootstraps and carry on. You've learned that much, but you haven't learned that it's possible to love again."

I thought about Vi's words, my hands folded in my lap, for some time before I said, "I'm not sure I want to love again. The first time hurt too much."

Vi heaved a sigh. "Yes. I know you had a hard time. But your marriage was so badly marred almost from the beginning, that you shouldn't think all marriages have to be like that. Why, my Ernie and I were happy together for twenty-seven years, until he got that deadly flu. I think he only got it because he was so broken up when we got the news about our Paul." Paul, Aunt Vi's son, had perished in Flanders during the war.

"I think Ma and Pa still love each other," I ventured tentatively. At least I never heard them quarrel.

"Precisely. And don't forget Mrs. Pinkerton. She might be a little . . . daft sometimes"—I regret to say I snorted—"but she and Mr. Pinkerton are very happy together. Why, they're like lovebirds, the two of them."

Trying to envision Mr. and Mrs. Pinkerton acting like lovebirds strained even my vivid imagination. Not that I much wanted to. "That's nice."

"And that young woman from church. Lucy? Isn't she seeing a nice widower?"

"Yes, but that's only because all the younger men are dead." I winced as soon as the words left my lips.

"Daisy Gumm Majesty! That's not the only reason she's stepping out with him, and you know it!"

I didn't, actually, but I'd never tell Vi that. She'd smack my hand. "I guess so. But . . . Oh, I don't know, Vi. Sam and I . . . I just can't quite see us together."

"I can. And so can your mother and father."

"They can?" I gulped and stared at my aunt.

"Yes," she said firmly. "They can. You could, too, if you'd only open your eyes. Or maybe it's your heart you need to open." She laid a hand over both of mine, which were still clasped in my lap. "I know you and Billy had a terrible time of it, Daisy, and I know you were crushed when he died, but I really think it's time you stopped dwelling on the past and give Sam a chance."

Oh, boy. My whole family was against me. I wondered if Ma and Vi had talked to my sister Daphne and my brother Walter about my "problem."

On the other hand, I'd come to appreciate Sam. Too, when I'd believed he might be sweet on Lucy Spinks, I hadn't liked it. And, although he'd annoyed me by considering me unable to take care of myself, I was glad when he'd chased Harold and me to Egypt. Huh. Where *we'd* had to rescue *him*.

"I don't know, Vi. I can't just turn off my feelings for Billy and transfer them, like you'd transfer a dinner plate from one place to another."

"Posh! Who's asking you to do that? You'll always love your Billy. Just like I'll always love my Ernie. But there's no telling what might happen. I doubt another man will come along and sweep me off my feet." She laughed. "If he did, he'd have to be a mighty big man."

This was true. Vi sampled the food she cooked, and it showed. She wasn't enormously fat, but she was definitely chunky. I smiled at her, unable to laugh, but appreciating her sense of humor.

"But if one did, I'd be open to another marriage, Daisy," she said, turning sober again. "Don't think I wouldn't be. Ernie and I were happy together for many long years, and that's more than you and Billy ever were."

"Vi!"

"Oh, I know you loved each other, but life was too hard for you. You never had any good years."

"We had a few good weeks," I said, and felt my throat tighten and my eyes begin to sting. "Before he joined up and went off to fight in that . . . blasted war." I'd been going to blaspheme, but I knew Vi would object.

"Yes," she said. "That damned war ruined too many lives, yours and Billy's among them."

I stared at my beloved aunt. I'd never heard her swear before.

"It was a damned war, Daisy." She smiled again. "But don't you say so or I'll have to give you a swat." Heaving a sigh, she rose from the chair next to me. "But I have to start making dinner. Chicken curry tonight."

"Chicken curry? I don't believe you've ever made that for us. What is it?"

"Some East Indian concoction Mr. Pinkerton used to have in India when he was there on business. It's rather spicy, and it's probably an acquired taste. Very pungent."

"Hmm. Do you think Ma and Pa and I would like it? And Sam?"

"I don't rightly know, Daisy. Why don't I try it on the family tomorrow? Then you can all pass judgment. If you don't like it, I'll never make it again. You can make it with lamb, too, and you always eat rice along with it. That's what Mr. Pinkerton said."

"Interesting how many people in the world eat rice, isn't it? We mainly eat potatoes here."

"Potatoes are more interesting than rice." Vi smiled as she took a plate of plucked chicken parts out of the Frigidaire. "Anyhow, lots of places haven't discovered them yet, I reckon."

"Maybe so. I like buttered rice, but the only time I ever ate it with something else was when I was in England, where Harold made me eat something called kedgeree. It was rice mixed with

smoked fish and some other stuff. They eat it for breakfast over
there. It was . . . interesting."

Vi's nose wrinkled. "It doesn't sound awfully tasty to me."

"It was different, for sure. My goodness. You know, Vi, there
are a whole lot of different cuisines in the world that I don't
know a single thing about."

"You helped broaden your family's horizons when you
brought me that cooking book from Turkey."

"I guess I did at that."

"Finish your lunch, Daisy."

So, at my aunt's insistence and even though I wasn't hardly
hungry any longer, I did.

When I got home again, I was pooped. It had been a long
and emotional morning. So Spike and I took a nap. In many
ways, I was a lucky girl. I got to work from home, I made quite
a bit of money, and my hours were my own. True, there were
many late nights involved, thanks to séances and parties and so
forth, but I didn't mind. It was fun to mingle with the wealthy
and meet new people.

As I drifted off to sleep, I considered what Vi had told me as
I'd eaten Mrs. Pinkerton's lunch. It occurred to me that I could
probably fall in love with a rich man as easily as I could Sam.
I'd have been appalled at the notion if I thought there was any
possibility of me falling for anyone besides my Billy ever again.

Vi was wrong. I knew she was.

CHAPTER THIRTEEN

The next day was Wednesday, and I decided to call upon some of the people whose names I'd retrieved from Mrs. Hastings the day before. First of all, after Pa and I took Spike for his morning walk, I visited the offices of Hastings, Millette, and Hastings, figuring I couldn't do better than talk to Belinda Young. At least I knew her, which was more than I did the Reverend Learned, whom I aimed to tackle after I was through at the law firm.

Hastings, Millette, and Hastings was a posh place in a posh building on Colorado Boulevard near Fair Oaks Avenue. Tall and filigreed, the place looked as if no one of less than exalted status would be allowed beyond its portals. I went in anyway.

Besides, I looked good in my light green suit with its tailored three-quarter-length jacket and calf-length skirt. Nobody would ever suspect I wasn't rich by my appearance. Even though the day would surely be a hot one, I wore smart gloves and shoes and a pretty wide-brimmed hat to keep the sun away from my face.

As luck would have it, the first person I spotted when I entered the building was Belinda Young, the very person I'd gone there to talk to. She was leaning over the reception desk, pointing out something to another, younger, girl whom I assumed to be the receptionist.

When I'm out in public I never do anything so crass as to stride, but I wafted more quickly than was my wont up to the

119

receptionist's desk before Belinda could get away from me. I gave both ladies a lovely spiritualist's smile and held out my hand in a languid gesture that would have done Theda Bara proud. "Belinda!" I exclaimed softly, feigning surprise as well as I feigned talking to spirits. "I don't believe I've seen you since we graduated from school."

She lifted her head and peered at me. The electrical lighting in the building's lobby was bright, but she might not have recognized me. We hadn't been close chums or anything. Then she said tentatively, "Daisy? Is that you? Daisy Gumm?"

"I'm Daisy Gumm Majesty now, Belinda."

Taking my hand, she said, "How nice to see you again." She dropped my hand. "Um . . . may I help you? Do you have an appointment or something? Miss Clyde can help you if that's why you're here."

I don't think she wanted to get rid of me exactly; she just wasn't sure what to say next. Accustomed to dealing with strange situations—you can't be a spiritualist medium if you get rattled easily—I said, "Actually, I came here to see you, Belinda."

"Me?" She appeared quite startled. She looked good, too. I guess the firm paid their employees well, because she wore a dignified suit of gray flannel with a pretty white shirtwaist with a ruffled front.

"Yes. I'm here at the request of Mrs. Stephen Hastings." It wasn't a lie. Mrs. Hastings fully expected me to keep my promise to investigate her son's death.

Belinda lifted a hand to her mouth, and I saw her gulp. "M-Mrs. Hastings?"

"Yes. Do you have a minute or two? I know you're working, but I won't take much of your time."

After looking around the lobby for a couple of seconds, as if for inspiration, Belinda seemed to deflate slightly. "Yes. Why don't you come upstairs with me? I can't take long, but Mr. Grover is in court this morning, so I guess it will be all right."

"Thank you very much." I followed her down the corridor behind the receptionist's desk, giving poor Miss Clyde a gentle smile as I passed her. She only looked confused.

A few feet after the corridor started, Belinda took a flight of stairs leading to her left. I padded right after her. By the way, the place was beautifully appointed. Thick gray carpeting covered the floor, and the staircase banister had been crafted out of some kind of dark wood that looked as if it was waxed and polished every day. Dark portraits, I presume of past partners of the firm, lined the walls. All the people were men, of course, and they to a man looked prosperous and somber. Actually, a couple of them seemed downright fat and smug.

Fancy tables with fresh flowers dotted the hallway once we got to the top of the stairs. I wondered if there was an elevator in the place but didn't ask. Electrical fans hummed from the ceiling, so the place was cool. I'm sure the building had thick walls, too, which helped keep the heat of the day out.

Belinda veered into an office on her left. It was as beautifully furnished as the rest of the building. This time the pictures on the walls were of horses and dogs and stuff like that. I guessed Mr. Grover or the late Mr. Hastings had been sporting men. Or maybe Eddie Hastings' father was. I imagine junior partners don't have much say in the decorating of the offices in which they plied their trade, and evidently Grover wasn't even a partner yet.

"Take a seat there," Belinda said, gesturing to a chair in front of her desk as she shut the door behind the two of us. The desk itself was large, polished wood, with a candlestick telephone and lots of papers scattered here and there. Shelves in her room were stacked full of deed boxes. What a lot of stuff to keep track of! Made me glad I'd forged my own profession.

"Thank you." I sat demurely. Belinda took her own chair behind her desk and seemed more comfortable there than she'd been downstairs.

"You say Mrs. Hastings asked you to come?"

"Yes. You see, she doesn't believe her son killed himself. She thinks he had some help, and she's hoping I can find out who might have disliked him."

"Good Lord!" Belinda stood up abruptly, then sat again with something of a *whump*. "I can't believe it. The police never said anything about . . . about . . . Do you mean she thinks he was murdered?"

"I'm sure the police never said anything at all and decided upon suicide because that was the easiest answer to his death. However, Mrs. Hastings knew her son better than the police did."

"Did she? I mean, I'm sure she did. But I'm not . . . Oh, heavenly days, Daisy. I can't imagine anyone having a reason to hurt Ed—Mr. Hastings."

Aha. She'd been going to call him Eddie. Interesting. "Did you enjoy working for the younger Mr. Hastings? Was he a kind employer?"

"Kind? Well . . . Listen, Daisy. You're not going to tell Mrs. Hastings anything I say here, are you? I don't want to jeopardize my job or anything. It's a good one, and I need it."

I held up a hand in a gesture I'd seen Pudge Wilson, the next-door neighbor's kid, make when vowing something. "I promise you I won't in any way compromise you or your job, Belinda. I'm trying to help a grieving woman, and in order to do that, I need to gather as much information as I can about her late son. I won't tell a soul where I get any information you tell me." Very well, I'd just told a little fib. I might have to tell Sam Rotondo who gave me some information, if I ever got around to telling him anything at all.

122

Belinda looked uncertain and chewed on her lower lip for a minute. A pretty young woman, with dark hair and eyes, she'd always been a little on the frivolous side in school. Not any longer, from what I could see. Well, I guess we'd all been through a lot since we left school. Finally, she said, "Mr. Hastings, the late Mr. Hastings, was a very nice gentleman. Much kinder and nicer than his father, who can be a domineering beast sometimes." She cast a nervous glance around the office as if checking to see if anyone might be lurking there. "Don't tell anyone I told you that. But he's really awful. I don't know how Mrs. Hastings can stand living with him. I know Ed—the young Mr. Hastings hated him."

"Really? He actually hated him?"

"Yes." She said the word firmly. "He told me so."

"Ah. You and he were in confidence with each other?"

"It's not the way you're making it sound. We weren't seeing each other after work or anything, but we were friends. I . . . I don't think Eddie actually had much use for women, if you want to know the truth."

"Yes. I'd already suspected as much."

"But he was a good man!" she said in stout defense of her late friend.

"I'm sure he was. One of my very best friends is . . . of the late Mr. Hastings' bent. Men like that make excellent friends."

She seemed to relax. "Yes. Yes, they do. And I miss him terribly."

"Do you suppose his father might have objected to . . . that aspect of his personality?"

"I doubt he'd ever think of such a thing on his own. He's too involved in being lord and master of his universe." She sniffed meaningfully.

"Ah. I see. What about the other man for whom you work?

123

Mister"—I cast a glance at the notebook I carried—"Grover, is it?"

"Yes. Mr. Michael Grover. He's all right. Not awfully bright and a dead bore, but he's all right. Not nearly as friendly and cheerful as Eddie was. He'll probably be made a partner one of these days out of sheer persistence." She cast me a beseeching glance. "I really do miss Eddie, Daisy. If someone did do him in—and I can't imagine such a thing—I hope you find out who it was. And," she added in a defiant tone of voice, "it wouldn't surprise me to learn it was his father."

I'm sure my eyes widened, because Belinda hurried to said, "You didn't hear him roar at his son the way I did. I swear, the old man is a monster."

"I'm sorry to hear it. What did he, ah, roar about at his son?"

Belinda lifted her hands in a helpless gesture. "Oh, everything. Nothing Eddie ever did was right. He didn't work hard enough. He didn't put in enough hours. He didn't take certain cases his father wanted him to take. Things like that. Oh, they'd have terrible fights." Glancing around her room, she added, "These walls are supposed to be soundproof, but nothing can stop a person from hearing that man when he's hollering."

"Curious. What kinds of cases did Mr. Hastings want his son to take that he refused to take?"

"Oh, things like certain property deals. Eddie—you don't mind if I call him Eddie, do you? We truly were good friends."

"Heavens, no!"

"Well, Eddie said his father was as crooked as a dog's hind leg, and he didn't want anything to do with stealing—that's the word he used—from poor people just so his father's cronies could tear down their houses and put up businesses in their place."

"My goodness. Can you think of any examples of that sort of

thing?" If I could get some names, it might help my investigation.

She shook her head, disappointing me mightily. "No. Eddie didn't give me particulars. He had to be very careful in his practice, you know. Lawyer-client confidentiality and that sort of thing."

Drat confidentiality! But there was nothing I could do about Eddie Hastings having been discreet. "And did Mr. Hastings and Mr. Grover get along?"

"Oh, yes. Mr. Grover doesn't have any personality, so he gets along with everyone."

Interesting observation. I wondered if she were right about Mr. Grover, or if he might hide a seething resentment under his bland façade. Which reminded me that I'd better clear that up. "Would you say Mr. Grover has a bland façade?"

"A bland façade? I guess so. He's kind of like oatmeal. You know, bland. Yes. That's a good word for him."

"Did he take any cases the late Mr. Hastings refused to take?"

"That, I don't know, since I never heard any names when Eddie and his father argued."

"I see. And Mr. Millette? What's he like?"

"I don't have a lot to do with him. You'd have to talk with his secretary, Mrs. Larkin."

"Do you think Mrs. Larkin would mind talking with me?"

"I honestly don't know. We're not close. She's ever so much older than I am, and she's worked here since the last century. She's nearly as old as Mr. Millette, and he's got to be seventy, if he's a day."

"My goodness. How old is Mr. Hastings? The older one, I mean?"

"Heavens, I don't know. He's old enough to have a son as old as Eddie was. I think Eddie was about twenty-seven, so I guess he's in his late forties or early fifties." She sat looking glum for a second or two. "I wonder if they're going to paint out the second Hastings on the firm's name. I hope not. Eddie was a good man, and I have no reason to believe he wasn't a good attorney."

"I should think Mrs. Hastings might have something to say about anyone wanting to paint out her son's name."

"Huh. I doubt Mr. Hastings pays her any more mind than he does anyone else."

She was making the older Mr. Hastings sound like an extremely unpleasant fellow. I wonder if she was right about him, or if the father had a legitimate reason to yell at his son. I should think a prudent man wouldn't holler at a business partner in the office, whether he had a good reason for being annoyed or not, but what did I know about the business world? Not a thing, is what.

"Would you mind introducing me to Mrs. Larkin?"

"Well . . . she's kind of an old bat, but I don't mind. Don't expect her to be pleasant, though, because she's not."

Boy, I sure wouldn't want to work in a place where nobody was nice except a guy who got himself murdered.

Belinda had just risen from her desk chair when the outer door of her room opened. I glanced quickly over my shoulder, and Belinda stiffened like a setter on point. "Mr. Grover! I didn't expect you for another little while."

Mr. Grover, who looked as bland as he evidently was, with mouse-brown hair, a clean-shaven face, and a gray suit that sort of blended in with his skin tone, removed his hat and hung it on the hat rack beside the door. "The judge adjourned court earlier than expected." He eyed me with mild curiosity, and Belinda remembered her manners.

"Oh, this is Mrs. Majesty. Mrs. Majesty, this is Mr. Grover. Daisy just came in to ask a couple of questions, Mr. Grover."

He came over to my chair, bowed formally, and took the

hand I held out for him to shake. "Good afternoon, Mrs. Majesty."

"Good afternoon. I was here to see if your firm might be able to handle a bit of work for me."

"I see. And did you make an appointment with Miss Young?"

"Not yet. We were just getting around to that." All right, so I'd just fibbed again.

"Actually," said Belinda, "Mrs. Majesty's inquiry might better be handled by Mr. Millette. I was just taking her over to see Mrs. Larkin."

"Ah. Very well. It was pleasant to meet you, Mrs. Majesty."

I peered into his eyes, which were a watery blue and just as bland as the rest of him, but I didn't detect any emotions seething therein. On the other hand, I've never yet been able to read emotions in another person's eyes. People in the novels I read do it all the time, but I guess they're more perceptive than I am. "Nice to meet you, too," said I mendaciously.

"When you're through introducing Mrs. Majesty to Mrs. Larkin, will you take a letter, please, Miss Young?"

"Certainly, sir." She smiled at me with a professional secretary's mien. "Please come this way, Mrs. Majesty."

So I went that way, which led across the hallway and into another room, where sat a cranky-looking woman with gray hair drawn back into a tight bun and a gray dress that looked kind of like she'd either bought it or made it in 1890. She actually looked rather as though she'd sprouted right there in the room, like a mushroom. She glanced up from her typewriter, upon which she'd been banging out words, and frowned at the both of us.

"Mrs. Larkin, please let me introduce you to Mrs. Majesty. Mrs. Majesty, Mrs. Larkin."

Shoot, now what was I supposed to do? Pretend to have a case Mr. Millette might handle? I told myself to improvise and held out a hand to the grouchy Mrs. Larkin. "How do you do, Mrs. Larkin?"

She didn't want to do it, but she shook my hand. "I'm quite busy, Mrs. Majesty. As you can see, Miss Young," she added for Belinda's benefit. Brenda turned and headed for the door, but not before she mouthed, "I told you so," at me.

"Yes, well, I shan't take much of your time, Mrs. Larkin. I know how valuable it is."

"Do you," the old bat said nastily.

"Yes, indeed. I, too, am a working woman."

"Hmm. Well, what is it? Do you wish to make an appointment to see Mr. Millette?"

"Not really," I said, determining to just ask my few questions and get out. To make sure she answered them, I added, "I'm here at Mrs. Hastings' request. About her son."

I saw Mrs. Larkin's eyes go round behind her steel-rimmed spectacles. "You're here at Mrs. Hastings' request? Why ever did she ask you to come to the business?"

Even though she hadn't told me I could, I sat in a chair in front of her desk. "Mrs. Hastings believes her son was murdered, and she's asked me to do a little investigating."

"Murder! But the boy committed suicide. The police said so!"

"Nevertheless, Mrs. Hastings doesn't believe he took his own life. So I'm here to gather information."

Turning to face me, Mrs. Larkin grabbed her specs, placed them on her desk, and commenced squinting at me. "And just how, pray, are *you* supposed to determine how the young man died? Are you a special investigator for the police or something?"

"Not at all." I decided not to tell this particular woman I was a spiritualist, having gathered that she wouldn't be impressed. "I'm only attempting to assist Mrs. Hastings."

"Well, I never had anything to do with the young scamp, and

neither did Mr. Millette, so neither of us can help you."

Young scamp, eh? "Nothing at all?"

"Nothing at all."

"Why do you refer to him as a scamp? Did he get up to mischief at the office or something?"

"He was young. All young men these days are frivolous and silly. Not like Mr. Millette. Why, in my day, a young man was serious about his work. He didn't go around smiling at people."

"And the young Mr. Hastings smiled at people?"

"And laughed with them."

"How shocking." I know I shouldn't have said that. Sometimes I can't help myself.

"Don't you be sarcastic with me, young woman! The office is no place for frivolity and larks."

"And the late Mr. Hastings cut larks at the office?"

"Well . . . I don't believe he did so here, but he was a frivolous young man, and that's all there is to it. I had nothing to do with him."

"Nor did Mr. Millette?"

"Nor did Mr. Millette."

Very well. It didn't look as though I'd gather much information from this source. "Thank you for speaking with me, Mrs. Larkin. I'll let you get back to your work."

She said, "Hmph," turned, and commenced typing a mile a minute.

CHAPTER FOURTEEN

Determining it would be foolish to tackle Mr. Hastings in his den—heck, if he used to holler at his son for no good reason, can you imagine what he might do to me?—I left the building housing Hastings, Millette, and Hastings and wondered what to do next. Nothing much occurred to me. Then I recalled my vow to visit the Reverend Learned, so I drove to North Euclid Avenue.

I found Mr. Learned in the church sanctuary, puttering about, although I'm not sure what he was doing. A stooped fellow, he looked rather like a desiccated Christmas candy cane that had gone off. He was very nice to me when I held out my hand and told him who I was.

"Good morning, good morning. So nice to meet you. Are you new to our church?"

"Yes. I haven't been here before, but I understand the Mr. Stephen Hastings family attends your church."

"Eh?" He held up a hand to cup his ear.

"Hastings," I said more loudly. This sanctuary was a much more elaborate affair than that of us lowly Methodists, even though our own sanctuary was pretty and had lovely stained-glass windows. We sure didn't have one of those fabulous pipe organs I saw behind the chancel, though. "I'm a friend of the late Mr. Eddie Hastings." Nuts. I'd just lied in a church. Ah, well.

"Tasting?" he said, clearly puzzled. "I'm not sure I understand what you mean, Mrs. Maj-maj- Please forgive me, my dear. I fear I'm going a trifle hard of hearing in my old age."

Oh, dear. This wasn't going so well. I was kind of tired, and the notion of trying to make myself understood to this kind elderly gentleman daunted me. But I decided to persevere a while longer.

"Hastings," I all but shouted.

"Oh, *Hastings.*"

I nodded, feeling something akin to triumph until he spoke again.

"Mr. and Mrs. Hastings are charming people. Such a shame about their son. He was killed in the war, you know."

He what? I wanted to wiggle a pinkie in my own ear after that one. I got the impression that Mr. Learned was not merely deaf, but perhaps a little forgetful.

"Their son died a few months ago," I hollered.

He shook his head mournfully. "Yes, yes. I performed the ceremony for the dear boy. What a tragedy, that war."

"Wasn't it, though," said I, giving up. "Well, thank you."

"You're more than welcome. Please feel free to come on Sunday. We have two morning services, one at nine o'clock and another at eleven, and of course, there's the seven o'clock evening service, which, if I do say so myself, is quite lovely."

"Thank you," I shouted. Then I decided to go home and clean house. You see? I didn't spend *all* my time being snoopy.

I'd finished the dusting and polishing and was running the carpet sweeper over the pretty Oriental rugs I'd brought back with me from Egypt and Turkey when a knock came at the door, and Spike set up such a frenzy of barking, he nearly deafened me. I set aside the carpet sweeper, wiped my perspiring brow on my sleeve, and picked up the dust rag I'd laid on the dining room table.

Although I wasn't fit to greet company or anyone else, clad

as I was in an old ratty housedress and with a scarf tied around my head to keep my hair and sweat out of my face, I told Spike to sit and stay, walked to the door, and opened it. Darned if Sam Rotondo wasn't standing there, glaring at me.

"Sam!" I said.

He eyed me up and down. "New fashion statement?"

Blast him anyhow! "I've been cleaning house, darn you!"

"Yeah? That's not what I heard. What the devil have you been poking around at Hastings, Millette, and Hastings, asking questions about Eddie Hastings and telling people he was murdered for?"

It took me a second or two to disentangle the gist of that question. When I did, I glared back at him. "Darn you, Sam Rotondo, what do you care what I'm doing at any given time and for what reason?"

He stomped past me and on into the house. Aggravated, I shut the door behind him and gave it a quick swipe with the dust rag in my hand. What the heck, I was supposed to be cleaning house, wasn't I?

"Good boy, Spike," said I, releasing my dog from bondage to obedience training. Naturally, because Spike had no taste in human beings, he gamboled delightedly up to Sam, who curbed his fury long enough to pet the dog. Good thing, or I'd have been *really* mad at him. I mean, it wasn't unusual for Sam to be rude to me, but if he ignored Spike, I'd have had to take him to task. Severely.

Sam rose from greeting Spike. "I care," he said, "because Mr. Hastings cares, and he called the station asking what we were doing sending spies to his place of business."

I felt my eyebrows rise in astonishment. "Mr. Hastings? But I didn't even see Mr. Hastings, much less talk to him. Anyhow, why does he care if I visit his offices to chat with an old friend? I didn't take her away from her job, for Pete's sake. We only chatted a bit about Eddie Hastings. We couldn't have taken more than a minute and a half of Mr. Hastings' precious time."

Sam pointed a beefy finger at my face. "There! I knew it! You were snooping around about that damned Hastings kid who killed himself. His father doesn't appreciate you spreading rumors that his death wasn't suicide. And how in hell did you ever get the idea he'd been murdered? Are you nuts?"

Aw, jeez. Precisely the questions I didn't want to answer, especially to Sam. I heaved an enormous sigh. "Sit down, Sam. I'll get us some orange juice."

"I don't want any damned—"

"Oh, stop swearing and sit! If you don't want orange juice, *I* do. I've been working hard all day."

"Prying and poking," Sam muttered as he pulled out a chair at the dining room table and sat.

"Cleaning house," I snarled back at him as I headed for the kitchen, where a lovely pitcher of orange juice awaited my consumption. And Sam's, blast him.

We had two orange trees in our yard, a Valencia and a navel. They provided oranges for us nearly all year long, which was a jolly state of affairs. I got down two glasses, begrudging Sam his, then opened the door to the Frigidaire, lifted out the heavy pitcher, and filled the glasses. I took a hefty gulp from mine before carrying the both of them into the dining room.

"Here." I plunked Sam's glass down onto a coaster I'd snatched from the sideboard.

"Thanks," he growled.

"You're welcome." I didn't mean that any more than he'd meant his thanks.

He guzzled down about half of his juice and set it back on the coaster. "All right. Tell me why you're going around to the Hastings law firm, telling everybody that Edward Hastings was murdered. That's not listed as the cause of death on his death certificate or anywhere else that I know of."

"I . . ." Aw, shoot. Now what? I knew I couldn't tell Sam the truth. He'd never believe me. Being accustomed to dealing with pressure when speaking to people—you have to be quick when you've got a room full of people wanting to chat with dead relatives—I decided to tell as much of the truth as Sam would tolerate. Actually, he probably wouldn't tolerate even as much as I aimed to tell him, but I had to say *something*.

"I conducted a séance on Saturday night at Mrs. Bissel's house."

Sam snorted, but I forged on.

"Mrs. Hastings, Eddie Hastings' mother, attended."

"Daisy Gumm Majesty, if you're going to tell me that the ghost of Edward Hastings showed up at your damned séance—"

"No! If you'll hush up and let me finish what I was going to say, you'll hear the answer to your question, drat you, Sam Rotondo!"

"Huh."

"Anyway, Mrs. Hastings came to the séance. We chatted afterwards, and she's absolutely *sure* that her son didn't kill himself. She believes he was murdered, but she doesn't know who did it. And she claims nobody else will listen to her, *including* the Pasadena Police Department."

Sam put his elbows on the table and dropped his head into his hands. He then proceeded to shake that same head and said, "Good God, Daisy. I don't know how you do it."

"Do what?" I asked, sounding quite snappish to my own ears. But I'd known this confrontation would happen eventually and that it would be unpleasant. That didn't mean I had to enjoy the inevitable.

"Pry into people's lives and get involved in stuff that's none of your business."

"Mrs. Hastings *asked* me to investigate in this case, Sam Rotondo! She said the police didn't even bother to question her son's cause of death. Much. Anyhow, she knows he didn't kill himself."

He eyed me through a couple of fingers he'd parted for the purpose. "How does she know that?"

I shrugged. "She's his mother. I expect she knew him better than anyone else on earth. And she swears up and down that he'd never have killed himself." Because I was curious and because Sam was already mad at me, so it didn't matter, I asked, "What *does* the death certificate say, anyway? How'd the police come to their conclusion of suicide?"

"How the hell should I know? I'm a homicide detective. I had nothing to do with the Hastings case."

"Why'd you come here, then? You said Mr. Hastings called? Did he complain to you personally? I didn't know you hung out in such exalted social circles, Sam." Low, snide blow. But I wasn't sorry. Well, not very.

"Mr. Hastings called the chief. The chief called me. Thanks to our . . . other involvements, he knows I know you. He sent me here to shut you up."

"Shut me up? But what if Mrs. Hastings is right? Darn it, Sam, I talked to his secretary. She's an old friend of mine from school—"

"It figures," he said.

"And Belinda said Eddie was a happy, charming gentleman who was kind and good, as opposed to his father. She characterized the older Mr. Hastings as a cruel beast who was on his son's back all the time, hollering and yelling at him. I'll bet it was his father who did him in!" Very well, so I'd just leapt to an unreasonable conclusion based on insufficient evidence. Sam could sue me if he wanted to.

Sam's head came up, and his hands fell to the table with a *splat*. "You're accusing the head of the most prestigious law firm in Pasadena of murdering his own son? Daisy, I swear you're going to be the death of me!"

"Someone was the death of Eddie Hastings," I said primly. "I should think you'd be interested in knowing who did it."

"For God's . . . listen to me, Daisy. I don't know a single thing about the Hastings case. I came here because the chief got a call from the older Mr. Hastings, who was annoyed that some busybody—"

"I'm not a busybody!"

Sam raised his volume. "All right. He was annoyed because some *nitwit* came snooping around his law firm telling people his son was a murder victim. The lad's been dead since March, his corpse has been laid to rest, and until *you* started poking around, nobody ever thought anything was the least bit wrong about his death. Do you blame the man for being peeved?"

That wasn't true, about nobody ever thinking anything was wrong about Eddie Hastings' death, but I knew Sam wouldn't believe Eddie himself had crashed the séance to tell a bunch of rich women (and me) that he'd been killed. "I don't care what Mr. Hastings thinks of me, but you can tell the chief on my behalf that I don't aim to visit his stupid law firm again. Maybe that will make him happy."

Oh, Lordy, I hoped the rest of the women who were at that séance didn't start pestering Sam or his chief about finding Eddie's killer.

But no. For the most part they didn't have any use for the police, considering policemen on a par with laundresses and housemaids and other menial creatures placed on this earth to cater to their whims. Besides, most of them were too involved in their own lives to worry about other peoples'.

There I go, being mean again. In truth, I don't suppose most of those women were any more self-involved than any other group of people in the world. Well . . . maybe a *little* more.

I had to talk to Harold again.

"The chief is never happy, but he'll be glad to know you're not going to snoop anymore." He gave me a hard squint. "You're *not* going to snoop anymore, are you?"

"No. I wasn't snooping in the first place, curse it. I was carrying out the wishes of a grieving mother. And I aim to continue doing so, whether you like it or not, Sam. I just won't do it at Mr. Hastings' law firm again." So there. I felt like sticking my tongue out at the irritating man, but didn't.

"What do you expect to find out, anyway? The kid killed himself, damn it."

"How do you know? Did you talk to the coroner? Read the death certificate? Look at the body yourself?"

"I already told you it wasn't a homicide case! Of course I didn't do any of those things! Dammit, there was no need—"

"How do you know that?" I demanded. "If you haven't investigated the death, exactly how do you know the man wasn't murdered?"

"If there had been any signs of foul play, my department would have been called in. Believe me, there was no need."

"A likely story."

"Oh, for God's—what do you mean 'a likely story'?"

"If a rich man's son dies, whom are the police going to believe? A grieving mother who's under the thumb of her overbearing husband or a rich father who tells them his son had been depressed—even though none of his friends thought so—and, therefore, took his own life? Answer me *that*, Sam Rotondo!"

Sam's gaze lifted to the ceiling, as if seeking help from the Almighty. I knew from experience how much good that ever did.

"Well? I'm sure you recall that, at the request of a wealthy film producer, you yourself were seconded to a rich woman's mansion to stand guard over a film set. Why is that so different from this?"

"There was no idle chitchat about murder in that case," Sam muttered, his brow beetling in unhappy remembrance.

Sam had hated being posted to watch over a film being produced. I knew it for a rock-solid fact, because I'd been there, too, acting as "spiritual advisor" to a spoiled-rotten movie star. "This isn't idle chitchat," I said, peeved. "Mrs. Hastings is *certain* her son didn't kill himself."

Puffing out his cheeks and then whooshing out the air, Sam downed the rest of his orange juice and rose to his feet. "I'm sure Mrs. Hastings doesn't want to believe her son killed himself. What mother would? Just stay away from the Hastings firm, all right, Daisy?"

"I promise to do just that, Detective Rotondo. I won't promise not to keep asking questions, however."

"Criminy."

"You can 'criminy' all you want, but Doc Benjamin is going to talk to the coroner for me, and if he thinks there's a possibility of murder in Eddie Hastings' death, I expect the Pasadena Police Department to pay attention. I already know they won't pay attention to me."

"Oh, they pay attention to you, all right," said Sam, heading for the front door. "Especially when a filthy-rich lawyer complains about you."

"Huh. Well, that same man's wife is the person who begged me to investigate."

Shaking his head, Sam got down on his knees to say good-bye to Spike. "Just try to stay out of trouble, all right? For my sake? No, wait. You don't give a rap about my sake. For the sake of the Pasadena Police Department. Please? Just this once?"

"For pity's sake, Sam, you'd think I was a thorn in the PPD's side. They gave me an award of merit a year or so ago, if you'll remember."

Standing to the sound of creaking knees, Sam muttered, "How could I ever forget? Holy crap, I thought for sure you were going to be tommy-gunned to hell and back."

"Nonsense. I was never in danger."

Very well, both Sam and I knew that was a lie. Therefore, I amended my statement.

"Well, I wasn't in much danger, anyway. And it all turned out all right."

"It turned out all right," said Sam in a high-pitched imitation of my voice. "Good God."

And he snatched his hat from the rack beside the door and left.

"See you at six tomorrow," I said as he stomped down the porch steps.

"Huh," he replied.

I looked down at Spike, who looked up at me.

"Bother, Spike."

He wagged his tail.

"I hope Sam hates chicken curry, whatever it is," I told my dog.

Spike only wagged some more, so I decided to finish carpet-sweeping the living room rugs, brush my hair, put on a less decrepit house dress, and take him for a walk.

CHAPTER FIFTEEN

I didn't mind eating lamb chops for two meals in a row. Dinner that evening was every bit as delicious as lunch had been.

The following morning, after breakfast, Pa and I took Spike for a walk, as was usual. Although I was tense all through breakfast and washing up, the telephone didn't ring with Mrs. Pinkerton on the end of the wire, weeping into it. It was a relieved Daisy Majesty who fetched Spike's leash, clipped it to his collar, and set out with my wonderful father for a good tramp.

As we walked Spike around the neighborhood, I made up my mind to give Harold Kincaid a telephone call. If I truly wanted to get to the bottom of how Eddie Hastings died, I needed to ask Harold more questions about Eddie and his behavior right before his death. I'd have to wait until after dinner that night in order to chat with Harold, since he spent his days at the picture studio where he created costumes for various pictures.

Of course *that* meant I'd have to wait for Sam Rotondo to leave the house, since I'd invited him to dinner. Sometimes I wondered about my sanity. I also wondered why I hadn't telephoned Harold on Wednesday, when I wouldn't have had Sam to worry about.

But it couldn't be helped. Sam was coming to dinner, and that was that. So after we got home from walking Spike, I decided to set the table in preparation for foodstuffs to come. I wasn't sure if one ate chicken curry from a plate or from a bowl, but I set out plates. I could always exchange them later if necessary.

I also went into the garden and cut a whole bunch of roses. We had twenty rose bushes of differing varieties, and they bloomed steadily during the summer months and far into autumn. We also had anemones and ranunculus, but they were pretty much spent by mid-June. So I went with the roses and created a spectacular bouquet, which I set in the middle of the dining room table. So what if we couldn't see each other over the flowers? Roses looked better than most of us did anyway. I spent the rest of the late morning and early afternoon with Spike on my lap, rereading *The Circular Staircase*. I love that book.

Vi got home around three-thirty and was impressed by my industry. "Oh, my, Daisy, the house looks beautiful, and you've already set the table! And look at that gorgeous bouquet. Are you trying to impress someone?" she asked slyly.

Ah, crumb. It had never occurred to me that Vi might think I'd cleaned house and picked roses in order to get on Sam's good side. I decided to be honest with her.

"No. Wouldn't work anyway, because he came over yesterday afternoon when I was in full housekeeper mode. Even had a scarf tied around my head. I wasn't a pretty picture, believe me."

"Oh, get along with you, Daisy. I don't know why you won't admit you like the man."

"I admit I like him. But we're forever butting heads. If you honestly believe there will ever be a romance between Sam and me, I think you're deluded."

"Bosh. But there's no use arguing with you, and well I know it." Vi took off her hat and trotted upstairs to change into more comfortable clothes before beginning dinner preparations.

I heaved a largish sigh and told Spike, "I wish Vi would stop trying to make a match between Sam and me. We have enough trouble getting along without crushing other people's expectations along the way."

While I'm sure Spike was sympathetic, he only wagged his tail. It was his usual form of communication. I sat back down in the overstuffed chair where I'd been reading, and Spike jumped into my lap to help me read. I loved that chair and Spike and reading, especially in a nice clean house I'd spiffed up myself.

A few minutes later, Vi surprised the heck out of me by coming into the living room and asking, "Want to help me fix dinner?"

"Me?" I pointed at my chest, astonished. "You want *me* to help you cook dinner? You know I'm a disaster in the kitchen."

"I know cooking isn't one of your more prominent talents."

"That's putting it mildly."

"But I could use some help. There's a lot of chopping involved in preparing the curry dish, and I only have two hands."

"Oh, sure," I said. "I can chop with the best of 'em." That probably wasn't true, but Vi herself had taught me how to chop stuff when I'd been forced to teach that wretched cooking class at the Salvation Army a year or so ago.

"Just tuck your fingers under so you won't accidentally cut one of them off."

Gee whiz. You'd think I was particularly clumsy, and I'm not, darn it. Anyone who can waft as well as I can isn't clumsy. Granted, my cooking skills stink, but still . . .

Vi was right about the chopping required for chicken curry. I had to peel and chop potatoes, carrots, onions, and even a couple of apples into a big mixing bowl. Then Vi dumped a bunch of raisins on top of all that. I eyed the pile of chopped foodstuffs askance. "Apples and raisins and onions? Along with potatoes and carrots and chicken?"

With a shrug, Vi said, "There's no accounting for how people in foreign parts eat. You should know that better than anyone by this time."

I guess she was right, but raisins? And apples? Along with onions and carrots? I wasn't sure about this curry thing.

But Vi, mistress of the cooking arts that she was, went blithely along her way, plopping everything together in a big bowl and adding other stuff to the mix, including various chicken parts and a pungent spice that made me wrinkle my nose. Vi eyed me with amusement.

"This is Mr. Pinkerton's favorite dish. Your mother, father, and I sampled many of your Turkish favorites. Give this Indian concoction a try."

"Oh, I will, all right." Couldn't avoid it unless I aimed to skip dinner than night, and I didn't. Still, it smelled unlike anything I'd ever smelled before.

"That aroma comes from the curry spices. Mrs. Pinkerton orders them premixed from Jorgenson's, and I got myself a tin the last time I ordered from them. Just an experiment to see how the family likes the dish. If everyone hates it, I'll just take the spice tin to the Pinkertons' and use it there."

"Interesting." Jorgenson's was where rich folks' servants shopped. The grocery store carried all sorts of things none of the other stores in town stocked, ordinary folks like us Gumms and Majestys not being accustomed to vary our diets the way rich people were.

Vi continued to mystify me by pouring stock, milk, lemon juice, and some tomato paste into a saucepot into which she then dumped the chicken and vegetables. Then she further amazed me by opening the Frigidaire and removing a jar of a thick, milky substance.

"Is that *yogurt*?"

"It is, indeed."

"I had yogurt in Turkey, but I didn't know you could buy it here."

"Jorgenson's has everything," Vi said.

"Wow. Maybe you could make some of that yogurt soup I had in Turkey. It was about the only thing I could eat for several days when I was so sick. It was delicious."

"I think there's a recipe for yogurt soup in that Turkish cooking book you gave me."

Oh, yum. I hoped she was right.

Vi dusted her hands together in a satisfied gesture after she turned on a burner underneath the curry concoction. "There. We'll just let that cook for a while, and then I'll fix some rice to have with it, along with some of this flat bread I brought from the Pinkertons'." She opened the bread box and lifted out a plate covered with a towel, which she removed to reveal several flat things that I presumed to be some kind of Indian bread. "Mr. Pinkerton calls this stuff *naan*. With two *a*'s in the middle."

"Mercy."

"No. *Naan*." Vi giggled like a schoolgirl. "Mr. Pinkerton gave me the recipe for it."

"The man's amazing," I said, meaning it. How many men do *you* know who carry recipes around with them?

"Not really. He just knows what he likes and can afford to have it made for him."

"I guess."

The front door opened just then, and Ma and Pa walked in together, holding hands. Another surprise. "Hey there. Have you been together all afternoon?" I'd wondered where Pa was when I'd been reading.

"Nope," said Pa, letting go of Ma's hand and hanging his hat on the rack beside the door. "We met in the front yard. I've been at Donald Parker's place most of the day, helping him with his machine."

Pa was an inveterate tinkerer with automobiles and their innards. I think I've already mentioned he used to chauffeur rich people around until he had a bad heart attack a few years ago.

"And I just got off work at the Marengo," said Ma. She sniffed the air. "My goodness, what's that smell?"

Vi and I exchanged a couple of glances. I answered my mother's question. "Chicken curry. Vi says it's an acquired taste."

Ma removed her hat, too, and carried it toward her and Pa's bedroom. "I think it's an acquired smell, too."

Vi, Pa, and I laughed, but I feared she might be right. The curry had a *very* pungent aroma.

Sam arrived promptly at six o'clock. One thing about Sam: he was never late to anything, especially a meal. In one of his large hands he clutched a Whitman's Sampler, which he shoved at me.

"Here. I thought your family might like these for dessert."

I grabbed the box before it hit my stomach. "Thanks, Sam. This is very nice of you."

"Huh."

Typical Sam.

Before I could scold him for his lack of manners, the telephone rang, and my mother called out, "Daisy! It's sure to be for you!"

She was right about that. "Well, come in, Sam. Hang up your hat and come visit with the family. I have to get the 'phone." I handed off the candy to my mother before I dashed into the kitchen to grab the telephone.

I heard her say, "Oh, how thoughtful! Thank you so much, Sam," as I lifted the receiver. Huh. Thoughtful, my foot.

"Gumm-Majesty residence. Mrs. Majesty speaking," I said, as I always did.

"Daisy, this is Dr. Benjamin."

145

"Dr. Benjamin! What a surprise!"

"Don't know why my call's a surprise. You asked me to call the coroner, didn't you?"

"Well, yes, but I didn't think you'd telephone with the results. I figured you'd wait until Friday and tell me then. But I'm happy you called!" I bethought me of our party-line neighbors and added, "But wait until everyone else on the line hangs up, will you?"

We both heard a couple of *clicks* as folks on the party line hung up their receivers. When I didn't hear a third one, I said in my most severe tone, "Mrs. Barrow, please hang up your telephone. This is a private conversation."

At last, and after a perceptible pause, a third and decisive *click* came over the wire. Mrs. Barrow was *such* a nosy Parker.

Dr. Benjamin chuckled. "Forgot about the party line."

"I imagine you have a private line."

"Have to have one in my business."

"I suppose that's so. Anyhow, what did the coroner's report say?"

"It was quite interesting. The coroner's report is conclusive as to the cause of Mr. Hastings' death. He died of an overdose of heroin, injected into his body."

"Heroin? What's heroin? I thought a heroine was a female hero."

After a good guffaw or two, Doc Benjamin said, "Heroin, without the *e* on the end, is an opium derivative that can be quite effective in reducing pain. But it's being used more and more by people who only want the feeling it gives them. Rather like alcohol, but not illegal yet. I expect the government will get around to banning it one of these days."

"You mean it's like morphine?" The drug that killed my husband.

"In a way. They're both opiates. I never offered Billy heroin,

146

because I worried about what he might do with it. Guess it didn't matter in the end."

"No," I said, my heart suddenly squeezing in pain, "it didn't."

"I'm sorry, Daisy. I didn't mean to bring up old sorrows."

"That's all right. They aren't that old. But this heroin stuff, it's injected and not drunk, like the morphine syrup Billy used?"

"That's correct. Well, some people probably eat it, but more often it's injected into a vein."

"Golly. Maybe Eddie Hastings did kill himself."

"That's where things get really fascinating. I took a peek at the police report—"

"How'd you get to do that?" I asked, interrupting him and becoming instantly ashamed of myself. "I'm sorry. I didn't mean to interrupt."

"That's perfectly all right, Daisy. I know you're concerned about this matter. Actually, I am, too, now that I've read the police report. And I got to read it because I have friends in high places." He chuckled. "Actually, you could read it, too, if you wanted to go to the police station and ask to see it."

"You mean anyone can read a police report?"

"Yes. According to the police report, there was neither a syringe, nor any other traces of heroin in the lad's apartment, so it's curious to me why the police determined the cause of his death to be suicide. And they did write 'suicide' on the report."

"Even with no evidence to support the finding?"

"Even with no evidence."

"Hmm. Wouldn't you think that if the poor guy injected the stuff himself, there would at least be a syringe nearby? I mean, maybe he didn't have any more heroin . . . how do people inject heroin, by the way? I've heard about people smoking opium, but I've never heard of heroin at all before your call. I mean, do you just stick a needle in your arm or something?"

"It comes in powder form. People cut it with sugar, melt it in a spoon over a flame, fill the syringe, and plunge it into a vein."

Ew. "Doesn't sound like much fun to me."

"Me neither, but I understand that many young men who were wounded in the war are seeking heroin now to ease the pain from their wounds. As I said before, it's legal, unlike alcohol. God knows what those poor boys will do after somebody passes a law making it illegal."

"The people who started that war should have fought in it themselves," I said bitterly and not for the first time.

"I agree with you about that, but it'll never happen. Folks with money will never have to fight the wars politicians start."

"That's so unfair."

"Yes, it is." Doc Benjamin resumed his crisp tone, "But we can't change anything about the war. However, it might be a good idea to discuss this matter with your detective friend."

His words shocked me. "How did you know about—"

"Detective Rotondo?" Dr. Benjamin asked, interrupting me for a change. "Daisy, I've spoken to him about many topics over the years, not the least of which was your husband. Detective Rotondo considered Billy a good friend, you know."

I swallowed a lump that had suddenly taken residence in my throat. "Yes," I said. "I know. They were very good friends."

"He's consulted me on a couple of other cases, too. So you know a homicide detective. You might ask him about this matter. I believe it bears some looking in to."

Oh, Lord. Dr. Benjamin wanted me to talk to Sam about Eddie Hastings' death being a possible homicide. But wait. That was a good thing. Wasn't it? I wouldn't have to bring up Eddie's appearance at that séance if I used Doc Benjamin as an excuse to talk about it with Sam. Never mind that he'd paid me a visit this very day specifically telling me to butt out of the matter. Now *he'd* have a good reason to investigate the death.

When I hung the receiver up, I turned to find Ma, Pa, Aunt

Vi, and Sam all staring at me. Well, so was Spike, but his tail was wagging, so he didn't matter.

"Dinner's ready, Daisy," said Vi.

"Who was that, dear?" asked Ma.

"Dr. Benjamin," I said.

"Shoot, what's the matter?" said Pa.

"Nothing, really," I said, "but Sam, I need to speak with you after dinner."

I heard Sam mutter, "Aw, criminy," before he turned to head to the dining room.

CHAPTER SIXTEEN

I saw Sam visibly square his shoulders, relax his features, and don a smile after he held out a chair for Ma and took his own seat at the dining table. His acting ability surprised me, because I know he wanted to wring my neck. He was a detective, after all; I'm sure he'd deduced that my conversation with Dr. Benjamin had been about Eddie Hastings.

"This smells just like my friend Kamal's house back in New York. I loved to go to his place for lunch."

"You had Indian friends when you were growing up in New York City?" I asked, also pretending that nothing was amiss.

"There are people from everywhere in New York," Sam said. "Kamal and I used to play stickball together. I don't think my parents liked me playing with a dark-skinned kid, but we did it anyway."

"You have an advantage over me," said my mother, her nose wrinkling slightly. "I've never smelled anything like this in my life."

"Me neither," said Pa. "But it smells good."

"Hmm," Ma said. Not an adventurous diner, my mother.

"If you don't care for the curry, Peggy, I saved out some chicken and vegetables without the sauce."

Ma shot a grateful glance at Vi. "You're so kind to me, Vi."

"Nonsense. I know you and food."

"I feel like such a sissy," Ma muttered, shamefaced.

"Nuts, Ma," I said in my most bracing tone. "This is an

150

experiment for all of us." I shot a look through the roses at Sam. "Except Sam."

"Exactly," said Vi. And she proceeded to fill plates with rice, curried chicken, and spinach. I guess East Indians eat spinach along with their curries, although I hadn't thought to ask Vi if Mr. Pinkerton had told her that.

As we dug into our dinner, I had to admit, if only to myself, that curries must, indeed, be an acquired taste, and that I hadn't acquired it yet. But I ate it anyway. If Sam Rotondo had grown up eating the stuff, it couldn't be *that* bad. It sure hadn't stunted his growth, big lug that he was. Anyhow, I wanted to please my aunt. And darned if I'd let Sam know I didn't like the stuff. Actually . . . it wasn't so much that I didn't like it, as that it was so odd to my untrained taste buds. And here I'd thought I'd learned to be a cosmopolitan diner after visiting England, France, Turkey, and Egypt. Shows how much I knew.

Anyhow, Vi served us a soupy rice pudding for dessert that was very good.

"Another recipe from Mr. Pinkerton," she told us.

I thought rice for dinner and rice for dessert was a trifle too much rice for this particular middle-class American girl, but I didn't say so. Anyhow, the rice pudding was spectacular. Tasted as though it had coconut in it, although I didn't remember seeing any coconut in the kitchen. Vi must have concocted it after I'd finished chopping stuff.

After dinner, as Sam and my father retired to the living room to chat, Ma and I washed up the dinner plates and pots. I was glad to see there wasn't any of the chicken curry left over. I'd never tell Aunt Vi, but I hoped she'd forget all about curry dishes for a year or three.

"You ate all your dinner," I commented to my mother as I wiped down the sink and she hung up her apron.

"Yes. I'm surprised, but I actually enjoyed it."

Well, there you go. Ma was more open-minded than I in the curry department.

Then I had to tackle Sam and tell him what Dr. Benjamin had revealed to me about the coroner's report and the heroin someone had injected into poor Eddie Hastings.

We conducted our chat on the front porch, where we sat on the steps and Spike romped in the yard.

"Heroin?" Sam sounded darned near shocked.

"Yes. Heroin. I'd never heard of it before."

"It's becoming more and more popular. Some of the bootlegging operations are handling drugs like heroin and cocaine as well as booze."

"Bootleggers?"

"Yeah."

"I thought heroin was legal."

Sam held out his right hand and wobbled it back and forth. I'd seen that gesture before and knew thereby that heroin's position in the United States was an equivocal one. "It's not as if you can go into your corner pharmacy and buy it, since the politicians passed the dangerous drugs act. It's still readily available, and you can get it at your local pharmacy if you have a prescription for it."

"Like Billy's morphine syrup."

"Yeah. Like his morphine syrup. For that matter, heroin's an opium derivative like morphine. In fact, lots of doctors prescribe heroin as a cure for morphine addiction."

I stared at Sam's profile. The sun was about to set on that warm June evening, and I noticed his strong chin and jaw in the half-light. I saw no trace of a smile on his mug. "Are you serious?"

"As serious as the influenza."

"That's crazy."

"Yes, it is."

"They should outlaw all of them," I said, sounding kind of savage.

"Right. That would solve the problem. Like Prohibition has made everybody quit drinking liquor."

"You're right," I said upon a dispirited sigh. "But then, how'd Eddie Hastings get his hands on the stuff that killed him, and how come nobody found a syringe or anything else involving heroin near his body?"

"Good questions." I could hear in Sam's voice that he hated saying so.

"So are you going to look in to the matter?"

He gave me a hard stare. "Are you going to stay out of it and mind your own business?"

Oh, bother Sam Rotondo and all his kin! "I can't stay out of it. I promised Mrs. Hastings—"

"Dammit, Daisy, if somebody killed the Hastings kid, you're dealing with some rough customers. Do you want to be next on their list?"

My mouth opened, but the instant retort I'd been going to fling at Sam died unsaid. "Well, no." I said, then pointed to my chest. "But why would anyone want to do anything to me? I don't have anything to do with anything, and I've only been asking a few people some questions, is all."

"Oh, for God's sake!" Sam dropped his face into his cupped hands for a second or two. Then he lifted it and glared at me. "You think the boy was murdered, but you don't think whoever murdered him will mind you prying into his death? Whoever did it will be happy to have you asking questions of all his friends and coworkers and so forth? The murderer will have no problem with you badgering all his acquaintances?"

"I didn't badger anyone!" I cried, indignant as all heck.

"I see. Mr. Hastings called the chief of police because he enjoyed you chatting with his staff. Do I have that right?"

"Nuts to him," I muttered, feeling abused. Then something interesting, if not pertinent, occurred to me. "I wonder why Eddie Hastings wasn't a Junior."

"Huh?"

"Mr. Hastings thinks he's such a big muckety-muck. I should have thought he'd have named his son after himself. But Eddie's name was . . . well, Eddie."

"What the devil difference does that make?" Sam asked in a voice bearing some resemblance to thunder.

I shrugged, accustomed to Sam's temper by that time. "Nothing, probably, but I think it's curious."

"Lord, you drive me crazy."

"Yes," I said. "I already knew that."

"Just try not to annoy Mr. Hastings again, all right?"

"I don't plan ever to meet Mr. Hastings."

"Thank God for small favors. And you won't return to the Hastings law firm?"

"No. I won't return to the Hastings firm."

"Good." Sam stood. "Now I'm going to go inside the house and play some gin rummy with your father, if you can stay out of trouble for the rest of the evening."

"Don't be nasty, Sam. Anyway, you haven't told me if you're going to look into Eddie Hastings' death. Are you?"

Sam had stood up, and he now loomed over me like a monster out of one of the Grimms' grimmer fairy tales. A large man, Sam. He didn't scare me. Much. "Yes," he growled. "I'm going to look into Eddie Hastings' death. In fact, it might tie into something—"

He stopped speaking suddenly, and I jumped to my feet. "You already know something, don't you?"

"I don't know anything."

"Drat you, Sam Rotondo, you do too! I can tell. You almost let it slip, didn't you?"

"Let what slip?"

"You were going to say Eddie Hastings' death is tied into something you're working on, weren't you? *Weren't* you!"

Spike came bounding up to us, glad to see his humans standing, because that meant we were going to enter the house, where he could find laps to sit on. Sam and I glared daggers at each other for several heartbeats.

Then Sam said, "There's an ongoing investigation into a heroin operation in town. It's not something I'm involved in personally, but I know about it."

"Aha. Then perhaps Eddie Hastings discovered something and was killed in order to silence him."

"Maybe."

"That might explain why no syringe was found at the scene, which it would have been if he'd injected himself with the stuff."

"Maybe. But if Eddie Hastings was silenced because he was prying, it sounds like an excellent reason for you to butt out of anything to do with him and his demise."

He had a point. "Well . . . I'm going to talk to Harold about Eddie. Maybe he'll know about some of his friends and so forth. Harold can be a mine of information when it comes to the doings of the upper-crust Pasadena set, which is the one in which Eddie Hastings lived, you know."

"Harold's all right. If—and it's a big if—you find out anything from him, *tell me*. Don't go poking around on your own or telling anyone else. Don't even tell Harold if he says something that triggers an inspiration in your brain." He sounded as though my brain having an inspiration was about as likely as snow in Hades.

Nevertheless, I thought about his demand. Should I endanger my person by yakking with villains I didn't know or tell Sam about them? Not a difficult question to answer. "You bet I'll tell you. I don't want anything to do with criminals."

"Ha! There's a first!"

"Darn you, Sam. I don't consort with criminals on purpose. It's not my fault I find myself in . . . difficult circumstances from time to time."

"Difficult circumstances," Sam grumbled as he climbed the porch steps and headed to the front door.

Spike beat him to it, so Sam opened the door, Spike rushed into the living room, and Sam politely held the door open for me. I regret to say I stuck my tongue out at him as I brushed past him and into the house.

Naturally, I was ashamed of myself as soon as I did it, but it was too late by then, so I let Sam and Pa get out the card table. Then I headed to the kitchen, where I proceeded to place a telephone call to Harold Kincaid at the San Marino home he and Del Farrington shared.

"Daisy! What's up?"

Harold's jolly greeting cheered me up some. "Hey, Harold. I need to talk to you soon. Will you be in town one of these days, and maybe we can go to lunch or something?"

"Matter too delicate for the telephone wire?"

I thought of Mrs. Barrow and said, "Yes," firmly.

"About Eddie?"

"Yes."

"Sure. I'll be in town tomorrow, because we just finished wrapping up a western shoot-'em-up in El Monte. Don't have to go back to the studio until next week. How about I pick you up at half-past noon, and we can dine at the Hotel Castleton?"

He would pick the most expensive place in town. Then again, he was richer than Croesus, whoever he was. "Sure, Harold. That would be fine. But I invited you, so I'll be paying."

"Don't be ridiculous, dear girl." He laughed as if he meant it. "I'm going to treat you as a lady should be treated, even if you aren't one."

"That's not nice!" But I giggled.

"Maybe not. And I must say, you play the lady impeccably most of the time."

"Thank you."

"You're welcome. See you at twelve thirty tomorrow."

"Thanks, Harold. You're a pal."

"Don't I know it?"

I might not have been born a lady, but I sure looked like one when Harold drove his snazzy, low-slung, bright red Stutz Bearcat up in front of our house that Thursday at twelve thirty.

"You look like a million bucks," my father said as I headed to the door.

"Thanks, Pa. Harold's taking me to the Castleton."

"Mercy me, you do travel in exalted company, don't you?"

I laughed. "Sometimes."

"Have fun."

"Thanks, Pa."

After greeting my father as a gentleman should, Harold escorted me to his machine. "You look smashing, as always, Daisy."

"Thanks, Harold. This is a copy of a Chanel design I sewed up this spring."

"Chanel is perfection. Excellent choice, my dear."

As a costumier at a big studio in Los Angeles, Harold, better than most folks, could appreciate my flower-printed pink, mid-calf-length silk afternoon dress with a pin-tucked, boat-shaped neckline. The dress had short, three-tiered sleeves, which matched the detail around the hemline. I wore with it a cloche hat with two pink flowers on it and string of real, honest-to-goodness pearls that had been given to me by a grateful customer three or four years earlier, and little pearl earrings. In a daring gesture, I wore flesh-colored stockings and pointy-toed high-heeled shoes. Naturally, I'd made the dress myself. What's more, I'd done so for a song, with a bolt end of artificial silk I'd bought at Maxime's Fabrics on Colorado Boulevard.

I'd also powdered my freckles into submission, and wore the lightest of eyelash and eyebrow darkeners. Not for the world would Desdemona Majesty, spiritualist extraordinaire, be caught in a swanky place clad in anything less than elegance.

Harold and I chatted about nothing much as he drove up Marengo to Colorado Boulevard, turned right, took another right on Lake Avenue, and headed to the Castleton. I knew Miss Emmaline Castleton, daughter of the robber baron who'd built the place. She was a sweet girl whose fiancé had died in the ghastly war.

But I didn't want to think about the war that day. Harold handed his keys to one liveried boy while another one opened my door and helped me out of the auto. Then Harold escorted me into the hotel and to the Castleton Arms, the fanciest restaurant in the place. There were others. Restaurants, I mean. There was a bar and grill and another little dining room where people who were staying at the hotel could partake of light breakfasts and luncheons.

Harold, who was a trifle plump and who enjoyed his food a whole lot, left those places to others. He went whole hog or not at all. I'd learned that much about him years before, and the knowledge had been cemented a year prior when he'd taken me on the trip to Europe and Egypt. I'd never lived on so exalted a plane—or been less able to enjoy it—as on that trip.

After the waiter led us to our table and held out my chair, I sat and gazed around me. The place was truly grand. Harold ordered mineral water for the both of us—"We should have a nice white wine with our luncheon, but we can't do that in these benighted times"—and then looked at me. "All right,

Daisy, give. What's up?"

So I told him.

CHAPTER SEVENTEEN

"Heroin?" Harold stared at me as if I'd suddenly grown a second head.

"Yes. Dr. Benjamin told me he died of an overdose of heroin. I'd never even heard of the stuff until then."

"Lord. I'd never have thought it of Eddie. He was such a prudish fellow. He and Lester Knowles frowned upon any sort of less-than-healthy behavior."

"Lester Knowles was his best friend, right?"

Harold eyed me aslant for a second. "Yes. Sort of the way Del and I are best friends," he said wryly.

"I see. Mrs. Hastings said that Eddie and Lester and Lester's sister Adele used to go to plays and other functions together."

"Yes, they did. Adele was quite an effective smokescreen."

"By that, I expect you mean that she was there to keep folks from believing Edward and Lester were . . . um . . ."

"Lovers," said Harold bluntly.

"Er, yes." I felt heat creep into my cheeks.

"Precisely. And Adele is a very sweet girl. Both she and Lester were cut up over Eddie's death, and neither one of them believe for a minute that Eddie killed himself."

"No. Neither does Eddie's mother."

"Well, you'd expect that from a mother, I suppose."

"I suppose." Something occurred to me, and I decided to broach it boldly. "But Harold, not everyone is as comfortable in his skin as you are. Do you think Eddie might have felt some kind of pressure from his father for being . . . different? If you know what I mean."

"I know what you mean. And yes, Eddie was embarrassed about his attraction to men. Fought it for years, then finally gave up. But that's not to say he blabbed about it all over town. I doubt his mother and father even knew. In fact, I expect he would have married Adele eventually."

"Really? Wouldn't that have been kind of hard on Adele?"

With a shrug, Harold said, "Oh, I doubt it. Eddie was rich, she's a nice girl, and I'm sure he could have performed his husbandly duties well enough to beget a child or two with her."

What an embarrassing conversation! But it might be important. "So, Lester Knowles is out and so is his sister."

"Out?"

"Neither of them murdered Eddie Hastings."

"Oh. No, I'm sure they didn't."

"Then can you think of anyone who might have hated Eddie? Or might he have killed himself? Perhaps he couldn't stand the pressure of being different from his peers." Then I bethought me of the missing syringe, but I didn't tell Harold about it.

Harold made a face, by which I gathered he didn't care for that scenario.

"You've got a commonsensical temperament, Harold. Not everyone is so fortunate."

"Maybe not, but Eddie showed no inkling that he was so dissatisfied with his life that he'd want to end it. In fact, pretty much everything seemed to be going his way."

"Hmm. You liked him, right?"

"Yes. He was a nice fellow."

"Did you ever talk to him about people who *didn't* like him?"

Carefully buttering a piece of roll, Harold thought for a second, then said, "We didn't talk about stuff like that. When we got together, it was usually at social functions. Charity balls and so forth."

"Charity balls? You go to charity balls?"

Harold borrowed a gesture from Sam and rolled his eyes. "Can't get out of 'em. You know my mother. Besides, attending such functions looks good to the folks who employ me. You read the newspapers, don't you? How many times have you seen picture stars attending a benefit for some cause or other?"

"Well . . . lots of times."

"There you go. That's mainly the type of place I'd see Eddie. Sometimes at a friend's house at a dinner party or something like that."

"And he never mentioned anyone threatening him or anything like that?"

"Lord, no."

We were interrupted by the waiter, who'd kindly left us the basket of flaky rolls and a couple of menus, which we were supposed to have been looking at. I felt guilty for not having selected my menu choice. Clearly, I wasn't born to the purple, as it were.

Harold suffered no such qualms and wasn't intimidated by waiters in snobbish restaurants. "We'll need another minute."

"Certainly, sir."

As the waiter loped off, Harold said, "Decide what you want to eat, Daisy. I recommend the lobster Newburg."

Who was I to reject lobster? Nobody, that's who. "Sounds good to me."

Beaming at me from across the small table, Harold said, "I must say, Daisy, it's nice to be with you in a restaurant, now that you're eating again. Last year, I feared you'd starve yourself to death."

"Yes. I remember you telling me so. But that's over. We're here to talk about Eddie Hastings. It doesn't sound as though you have any idea who might have done him in."

"Don't have a clue," Harold admitted. "But I can tell you he never would have dabbled in drugs. He was sort of a bore when he got to talking about healthy living."

"Really?"

"Yes. For instance, he never drank alcohol even before it was prohibited. And he used to turn up his nose at people when they'd offer him cocaine."

It wasn't the first time my mind had boggled when Harold dropped a juicy tidbit into a conversation. "People offer each other cocaine? Where? When? No one's ever offered *me* cocaine!"

With a chuckle, Harold said, "I'm sure that's true, Daisy. You lead a pure life." His countenance darkened considerably. "That's because you don't know too many people within the moving-picture community. You wouldn't believe the number of actors and actresses who use cocaine and heroin."

"My goodness! I've read that some of them are known for heavy drinking, but . . ." I leaned as far over the table as I could without being considered crude. "Oh, Harold, *who*? And do you think any of them might have had anything to do with Eddie Hastings?"

"I don't think Eddie had much to do with motion-picture folks as a rule. He was more apt to be swimming at the Pasadena Athletic Club than raising hell with the Hollywood set."

He saw my quelling stare and capitulated. "Oh, very well. Mind you, these are all rumors, but they're from reliable sources. Mabel Normand, for one."

I gasped, shocked.

"And surely you read about Wallace Reid."

"He died earlier this year."

"Yes. In a sanitarium, into which he checked himself after finishing *Thirty Days*. But he was too far gone on the drugs. He died of drug use."

"Oh, my goodness. What a tragic loss."

"Yes, it was. Then there's John Barrymore, but his vice is alcohol, which, of course, no law can stop him from consuming."

"I suppose not." The conversation had become downright depressing.

"And, of course, it was alcohol that proved to be Fatty Arbuckle's undoing."

"If he'd stuck to alcohol nobody'd ever know he wasn't a gem of a man. I think it was killing that young woman that did him in."

Harold shook an admonishing finger at me. "Arbuckle didn't kill anyone. That's been proved three times so far. You're surely not going to be one of those 'no smoke without fire' preachers, are you?"

"Well . . . I guess not. Still, that affair seems awfully sordid to me."

"You haven't seen sordid until you've been to some of the Hollywood parties I've had to attend. I don't like them, either. Unfortunately, many of the youngsters who flock to Los Angeles to become *stars* wind up on the wrong side of a needle."

"That's sad, Harold."

The waiter approached us again, and this time Harold ordered lobster Newburg for each of us. As he walked away, I said, "But that doesn't have anything to do with Eddie Hastings. He didn't hang around with movie stars, you say?"

"Not that I know of."

"Well, then, why are we talking about them?"

"You're the one who asked," Harold reminded me.

"You're right. But can you think of anyone who disliked Eddie Hastings enough to murder him?"

"No." Harold shrugged. "Except maybe his father."

I sat up straight. "Well . . . a couple of people have mentioned that possibility before, but I haven't taken them seriously. I know the man's a beast, but do you really think he'd kill his own son?"

Grinning, Harold said, "How do you know the fellow's a beast?"

"Belinda Young told me so. She was Eddie's secretary, and she said his father was always hollering at poor Eddie at the office."

"Figures. There's someone whose background could bear some scrutiny."

"Mr. Hastings, you mean?"

"The very one."

"What do you mean by scrutiny? What would anyone be scrutinizing?"

"Well, you know he made his fortune in the Chinese trade."

"Yes. Mrs. Hastings told me as much when I visited her at her home. It's full of gorgeous Chinese art."

"According to sources, the man's been importing more than Chinese art for years now."

I felt my eyes widen. "You mean, you think he's smuggling *drugs* into the country?"

"That's what I've heard. And from more than one reliable source."

"Good Lord." I considered the matter for several seconds. "To tell you the truth, Harold, I don't know much about the trafficking of drugs."

He snorted. "Don't look at me. I wouldn't be caught dead dealing with opium."

"But I thought Eddie died of a heroin overdose."

Once more rolling his eyes, which I resented, Harold said, "Heroin is derived from opium. I thought you knew that."

"Oh. Right. I forgot."

The waiter came back with our lobster Newburg and crispy salads, and we stopped speaking for several delicious minutes.

Everything was *so* good.

After the first pangs of my hunger had been assuaged, I said, "Maybe Eddie found out about his father's illicit drug dealing and called him to task for it."

With a shrug, Harold said, "Maybe. The Eddie I knew wasn't too keen on stirring up trouble. I can't imagine him confronting his father about anything at all, much less accusing him of smuggling drugs."

"Hmm. According to Belinda, they were at each other's throats in the office all the time."

"Maybe his father didn't think Eddie was doing his job satisfactorily."

"Maybe, although he'd just been made a partner."

"Well . . . he was the grandson of the founder, and his father's head of the firm. A partnership for the kid seems kind of like a foregone conclusion."

"I suppose so."

Nuts. I'd hoped to come to some sort of positive finale about the Eddie Hastings affair after speaking with Harold, but a definite perpetrator seemed as far away as Jupiter at that point. Nevertheless, I said, "Say, Harold, do you suppose you could introduce me to Lester Knowles? I'd like to talk to him about Eddie Hastings."

"Sure. When and where would you like to meet him?"

"Shoot. I don't know."

"Well, maybe I can have the both of you over—and Adele, in order to even out the numbers—this coming Saturday."

I was about to pounce on the offer when I recalled that Sam intended to take my family out to dinner at Miyaki's on Saturday. "Pooh. Saturday we're all dining at Miyaki's."

Harold's eyes brightened. "I love Miyaki's! Why don't Del and I take Lester to dinner there, and we can make introductions then. Maybe you two can agree to meet sometime to discuss Eddie. It's possible that Lester has a better idea than I as to how Eddie met his end. He sure knew him better than I did."

"Sam will love that," I muttered.

"What does Sam have to do with anything?"

"He's the one who's taking my family to Miyaki's on Saturday."

Harold gave me what can only be described as an evil grin. "Better and better. Perhaps we can all dine together around one of their larger tables."

"Lord, Harold, you must be joking."

"Am not. Sam has to be polite to me. I helped save his life a year ago, don't forget."

I shuddered. "How could I ever forget that?"

"I even shot a man for him." It was Harold's turn to shudder.

"I remember." I chewed thoughtfully on my lobster for a moment. Then I decided, "Why not? Sam can't object, and my family will be happy to see you and to meet Lester and Del."

Harold eyed me speculatively. Then he said, "I imagine you're right about that. You have a very nice family, Daisy. Hell, even Billy wasn't all that bad once he got over being peeved about our friendship."

"Billy was a wonderful man. It's not his fault he held certain prejudices. I'd bet anything that if he hadn't been so grievously wounded in the war, he wouldn't have given a rap about you and Del."

"Maybe you're right. I have to tell you, though, that it's rather disconcerting when people hate me for something I can't help. I wouldn't mind if they hated me because I'm an evil person or something."

"But you're not an evil person."

"My point precisely."

"A valid one, too," I said, feeling sad.

Oh, but it galled me that men like my darling Billy and Sam Rotondo disliked Harold merely because of the one quirk in his makeup. Take that one quirk away, and Harold was a practically perfect person: happy, friendly, helpful, personable. Charming, even.

Then it occurred to me that he might be all of those things *because* of that one quirk, and I decided human nature was too complicated for me to figure out over luncheon.

"So," Harold said after taking another bite of his second or third dinner roll, "Saturday night at Miyaki's, right?"

After a barest second of pondering, I said, "Right. We'll probably get there around six thirty. Is that all right with you?"

"Fine with me. My Saturday is free. I don't even have to hold Mother's hand. I hope. She's all cut up over Father's defection from San Quentin, but I can't imagine why the ghastly man should bother coming to Pasadena."

"No. I can't either."

"Not," said Harold, with a somewhat vicious twinkle in his eye, "that my mother and sister aren't perfectly charming specimens, whom my father would probably love to see again."

"Whoo, boy," said I.

We both laughed, and then Harold ordered chocolate soufflés for the both of us for dessert.

CHAPTER EIGHTEEN

Naturally, things didn't work out as serenely as I'd hoped they would between Thursday's luncheon with Harold and Friday's dinner with the Benjamins.

For one thing, as soon as Harold pulled up to the curb in front of our Marengo Avenue bungalow, my father opened the front door, Spike raced out to greet us, and Pa said, "Mrs. Pinkerton is on the wire. I told her to hold on when I heard Harold's nifty car pull up." He waved at Harold, who waved back as he, the perfect gentleman, exited his side of the machine and went to mine to open the door.

"Is she in a tizzy, Mr. Gumm?" Harold asked, grinning.

Pa grinned back. "Daisy will have to decide that for herself, but she wanted to wait rather than have Daisy call her back."

As he walked me to my father, Spike frisking at our heels, Harold said, "Good luck, Daisy. Better you than me."

Pa laughed.

I didn't. I did, however, sigh rather heavily as I stooped to pet my darling doggie. I'd been hoping for a little nap after that spectacular meal at the Castleton. But no. Not for Daisy Gumm Majesty. I had to deal with crazed middle-aged rich women who wanted me to solve all their problems for them. "Thanks, Harold. Hey, Pa."

"Sorry, sweetheart," Pa said, kissing my forehead in welcome. "But you know Mrs. P." He glanced guiltily at Harold. "Sorry, Harold."

Lifting his arms, palms out, Harold said, "Don't apologize to me. I don't know how Daisy stands dealing with Mother the way she does."

"It's not easy." But I walked to the 'phone hanging on the kitchen wall, lifted the dangling receiver, and purred, "Good afternoon, Mrs. Pinkerton."

"Daisy!" she shrieked. "I think the villain was Eustace!"

I stared at the receiver for a moment, then glanced at my father and Harold, who were both grinning at me like a couple of idiots.

"Um . . . which villain? I mean, what do you think Eustace—I mean, Mr. Kincaid—did?"

"Why, he murdered poor Laura's son!"

My mouth fell open in shock for a second. I cast another wild glance Pa-ward, swallowed, and said calmly, "And why do you think Mr. Kincaid killed Mr. Hastings, Mrs. Pinkerton?"

"Well, it stands to reason! He escaped from prison, and poor Laura's son died a horrible death! It had to be Eustace, don't you see?"

I shut my eyes and shook my head. "Ah . . . Mrs. Pinkerton, poor Mr. Hastings died in March. Your husband escaped from prison last week, didn't he? I doubt he had a thing to do with Mr. Hastings' untimely demise."

Silence greeted my practical statement. In the background, I heard Pa and Harold stifling laughter. I glared at the both of them.

After a moment, Mrs. Pinkerton said, "Well, who did it then? Laura told me herself that her son didn't kill himself."

"We don't know the answer to that yet, Mrs. Pinkerton, but we're working on the matter."

"We? We who? I mean, is that awful detective helping you?"

Bridling, I said more sharply than usual, "Detective Rotondo isn't an awful man, Mrs. Pinkerton. He does a hard job very well, he's helped you more than once, and yes, he's looking into Mr. Hastings' death."

"Oh. Well. I . . . well, I don't mean to say he's *awful*, but he's quite gruff."

"Perhaps he seems gruff, but he has a difficult job to do. I expect many policemen become a little tired of fighting crime all the time."

Even I rolled my eyes at that one. Harold and Pa were nearly convulsing with muffled hysterics by then.

"Oh, Daisy, I'm sorry. But I'm so very rattled, you see."

I saw, all right. I didn't say so.

"Could you please come over with your Ouija board? This afternoon? I'd be ever so grateful if you would. Just a short session, dear. Will you please? Please?"

Shutting my eyes, I said, "Of course, I can do that, Mrs. Pinkerton. It will take me a few minutes to change my clothes." Darned if I'd waste my gorgeous fake Chanel outfit on Mrs. Pinkerton.

"Oh, *thank* you *so* much, Daisy! I'm so *very* upset and worried, don't you know."

I knew. "Recall what the cards told you, Mrs. Pinkerton. In essence, they told you not to borrow trouble, remember?"

"That's easy for Rolly to say, Daisy, but I find it difficult to do."

Perhaps a guy who'd been dead for a thousand years and no longer had to deal with the problems of the living might spout platitudes with some facility. However, *I* was Rolly, *I* had only been alive on this green earth for twenty-two years, and *I* didn't find dealing with Mrs. Pinkerton so blasted easy. But I merely said, "I understand. I'll be at your house in about a half hour. Try to calm down in the meantime." As if she'd ever do that.

"Oh, *thank* you!" And she hung up the receiver on her end of the wire.

Out of curiosity, I listened to the empty line and heard a couple of other *clicks* as party-line neighbors hung up their own receivers. I should charge them an entertainment tax or something.

I turned and stared sternly at my father and Harold, who'd stopped trying to be quiet. They both whooped with hilarity.

"It's not funny," I said.

"Is too," Harold gasped.

"He's right, Daisy. I don't know how you do it."

"I don't either," said Mrs. Pinkerton's loyal son. "My mother is the biggest pain in the neck around, barring my idiot sister."

"Touching family feelings," I muttered, peeved.

"Just telling the truth, sweetie. Say, would you like me to drive you to Mother's? I don't have anything else to do today."

"Thanks, Harold, but I think I'll take the Chevrolet. By the time I ply the Ouija board and calm your mother, it'll probably be time for Vi to get off work, and I can drive her home."

"Good idea," said Pa.

"Very well, but I think I'll pop by the old family manse just to see what's going on there. You never know. Mother might actually have heard something pertinent to Eddie's death, although I doubt it."

"She told me your father did it."

Harold and Pa roared with mirth at that one. I hoped they'd both get a cramp.

After the two of them had quieted down some, I said, "You can follow me. Or I can follow you."

Harold had to wipe tears of laughter from his eyes. "Or I can just leave now and you can join me at Mother's house."

"Good idea."

Harold shook hands with my father—the two of them were still smirking like idiots—and I went to the bedroom to change clothes and grab my spiritualist's tools. Spike helped.

By the time I arrived at Mrs. Pinkerton's gigantic home on Orange Grove Boulevard—or "Millionaire's Row" as some wag at a newspaper once called it—Harold's Stutz Bearcat sat in the curving drive, and Harold himself opened the door before I could ring the doorbell. I wondered what Featherstone, Mrs. Pinkerton's butler, thought of this breach of protocol.

"You taking over from Featherstone?" I asked Harold as I stepped into the entryway.

"Poor Featherstone didn't want to let me open the door, but I think he'll recover."

"You really shouldn't upset his schedule, you know, Harold. He takes his job very seriously."

"Don't I know it. Kind of like an automaton."

"Don't be mean. I've always been impressed with Featherstone, and I'm quite fond of him, too. And if you're going to take his place, at least try to do it correctly. Now you're supposed to say, 'Please follow me,' and lead me to the drawing room."

Harold complied with his usual good humor. He bowed formally and said, "Please follow me, madam."

"You can leave off the 'madam' next time."

"Nuts. Better than being a madame."

"What's the difference?"

"A madame is the proprietress of a whorehouse, Daisy, you charming innocent."

"Good Lord! I didn't know that."

But we couldn't continue our fascinating conversation because we'd reached the drawing room, which would have been a living room to us plebeians. I whispered, "Is she in a total fit, or just in a nervous dither today?"

Harold paused before opening the door to the drawing room. "I'd say she's in a partial fit. But I have faith in your ability to calm the wild beast, my dear."

"Thanks."

Harold opened the door and I glided into the room in full spiritualist mode. I'd changed into a lightweight gray day dress, suitable to the weather and my profession.

Mrs. Pinkerton, who had been drooping on the sofa, leaped to her feet. She didn't charge at me today, but only clasped her hands to her largish bosom and said, "Oh, Daisy, I'm so very glad you could help me!"

"I'm happy to help, Mrs. Pinkerton," I lied. Harold elbowed me in the ribs for it, but I pretended not to notice.

"I'm going to the kitchen to see if I can nab a cookie or two," Harold told us.

"After lobster Newburg, salad, and chocolate soufflé?" I blurted out. I didn't mean to. Blurting was totally unspiritualistic behavior, but I couldn't help it. I was still so stuffed, I wasn't sure I'd be able to eat dinner that night.

"Harold told me the two of you had taken luncheon together today," said Mrs. P, beaming at her son and then at me. "I think it's wonderful that you two are such good friends."

"Indeed," I said, grabbing my lost dignity and wrapping it around me like a cloak.

"Oh, Daisy and I are best buddies," said Harold with a farewell wave as he headed out of the room. I expected him to turn right and go directly to the kitchen, where Aunt Vi would certainly pamper him to the nth degree.

After the door closed behind him, Mrs. Pinkerton led me to the sofa. I sat in a medallion-backed chair across from the coffee table and she plopped down where she'd been drooping before, only her droop was gone. In a lowered voice, she said, "Are you sure Eustace didn't have anything to do with that poor boy's death, Daisy? I'd never forgive myself if he were in any way responsible."

"I don't see how he could have been responsible, Mrs.

Pinkerton. He was in prison when the young man died. Anyhow, even if he did it—and he couldn't have—that wouldn't be your fault."

"Yes, yes, I suppose so," she said, her brow furrowing. "But it's *just* like something he might do."

Desperately attempting to keep from curling my lip, I said sweetly, "Kill someone? Your husband never killed anyone before he stole those bonds, did he?"

Eustace Kincaid had been convicted of stealing thousands of dollars' worth of bearer bonds, nearly causing his bank to collapse, which was why he'd been sent to San Quentin. I'd never liked the man, but I'd never considered him a deadly force before. A sneaky, mean-spirited, cruel, thieving force, but not lethal.

"Not that I know of." Mrs. P sniffed meaningfully. "But I wouldn't put anything past that man."

That man. The one she'd married. But never mind. "You need not worry about him having had anything to do with Mr. Hastings' death," I said soothingly. "But let me get out the board, and we can start our session."

"Yes. Thank you, Daisy. I don't know what I'd do without you."

I didn't either.

As much as Mrs. Pinkerton tried, she couldn't get the Ouija board to tell her where her ex-husband was, if he aimed to come to Pasadena, or what his future plans were. Nor could she get it to tell her if her daughter would continue going to the Salvation Army or get into trouble again.

Although I'd told her as much at least ten thousand times before, I once more said, "Remember, Mrs. Pinkerton, the board and Rolly can only answer questions about you, not about others. In order for you to learn about the intentions of others, you'd have to ask them."

"Or have them use the board with you," she said, as if upon an inspiration.

There was absolutely no possibility of an iota of the tiniest hint of a chance that I'd *ever* use the Ouija board with Stacy Kincaid or her ghastly father. I know my nose wrinkled, because I couldn't help myself. Fortunately, Mrs. Pinkerton was staring at the board at the time and didn't see. I did, however, say— and firmly, too—"A person needs to believe in order to garner assistance from the spirits, Mrs. Pinkerton. I doubt Stacy or Mr. Kincaid would qualify."

She heaved a gigantic sigh. "Oh, that's so true, Daisy. And it's so unfortunate. I know Stacy would benefit from your helpful guidance."

In a pig's eye.

I didn't speak.

"But I doubt there's anything anyone can do to redeem Eustace. I don't know why I ever married him."

I didn't, either. Heck, she was the one who'd brought money into the marriage. He'd just spent it. He was supposed to be president of a bank, but he'd done his best to ruin it. Del Farrington, Harold's partner, had been the one to salvage the bank from total wreckage. Again, I said nothing.

Mrs. Pinkerton took her fingers from the planchette, sat back, and gazed mournfully at me. "Oh, dear, Daisy, I just don't know what to do."

"There's nothing you can do, Mrs. Pinkerton. Not about Mr. Kincaid or Stacy. All you can do is pray they both find the light one day." Such folderol tripped off my tongue like a prima ballerina at that point in my career.

"You're so right, my dear. Oh, but I wish Stacy would meet a nice man and settle down. I don't suppose she will at that Salvation Army place. The people there are so . . . so . . . well, common."

And worth sixteen or seventeen of Stacy Kincaid. Each. "I'm sure Captain and Mrs. Buckingham will help Stacy find her pathway." Provided she didn't slide off it and into a bottle of booze.

"I suppose so. I only wish she could meet people in her own station in life."

"The last time Stacy consorted with people in her own station in life, she had to spend three months in jail," I reminded Stacy's fond mother.

"Oh, Daisy! But they aren't *all* like that. Why, just look at poor Eddie Hastings. He was a fine, upright man."

And, therefore, totally anathema to Stacy Kincaid. Not that he'd have been interested in her even if he hadn't died.

"One can always hope and pray," I said sweetly. "But I need to get home now, Mrs. Pinkerton. It's just about time for my aunt to be finished with preparations for your evening meal, so I'll visit her in the kitchen and drive her home."

With another huge sigh, Mrs. Pinkerton allowed me to leave her presence. "Thank you for coming, dear. I only wish I could do as Rolly advises and relax."

"You might practice meditation," I said, thinking of the Chinese décor in the Hastings' home and the curry we'd had for dinner the night before. Didn't East Indians and Hindoos meditate? I think I'd read about the practice in the *National Geographic*.

"Meditate? Whatever do you mean, dear?"

Phooey. I didn't want to get caught up in more conversation with Mrs. P. "It's an Eastern practice, Mrs. Pinkerton. You sit calmly and try to rid your mind of all thought. I believe that in order to do so effectively, you hum something—a single syllable—over and over so that your thoughts can't come back to bother you."

Or maybe I was full of baloney. All I knew was that I wanted to get out of there, fetch Vi, and go home.

"Goodness. I've never heard of such a thing."

"Visit Grenville's Books on Colorado Street. I'm sure Mr. Grenville can point you in the direction of Eastern meditation techniques." Besides, George Grenville was a friend of mine, and I'd done a huge service for his wife once. I liked sending business his way.

"What a good idea. I do believe I'll send Featherstone to the store for me."

Lord, she couldn't even fetch her own books. I lammed it out of the drawing room and almost ran to Aunt Vi's lair, craving normal company.

I found it. Aunt Vi and Harold were having a jolly time in the kitchen, and Vi had plied Harold not merely with cookies, but with a piece of what looked like a heavenly pie. I'd have had hunger pangs if my stomach weren't already so full of lobster and chocolate.

"Aunt Vi, you're not good for Harold's diet," I said as severely as I could.

"What diet?" asked Harold around a piece of pie.

"Piffle," said Aunt Vi.

Both valid comments. Vi packed up her belongings, and we drove home together.

CHAPTER NINETEEN

On Friday morning, just as Pa and I finished eating breakfast, I received a telephone call from Mrs. Stephen Hastings. I was surprised, although not terribly. After all, she probably wanted to find out if I'd learned anything about her son's death. I hadn't, and I didn't relish telling her so.

"If you have nothing else to do this morning, Mrs. Majesty, would you mind dropping by for a few minutes? I found something that might be of interest to your investigation."

My investigation? Huh. "Of interest? To whom? Is it about your son's death?"

"I'm not sure. I just don't know. But I thought you might be able to look at it and decide what to do." Her voice was hoarse, as if she'd been crying.

I felt very sorry for her. "Don't you think it might be better to call the police department? I know Detective Rotondo is now investigating your son's case."

"Is he? I'm glad to know it."

"I'm sorry. I should have told you." Guilt swamped me. Sometimes I thought "guilt" might as well be my middle name.

"Oh, no. I understand that you've been working very diligently to honor my request. My . . . Stephen told me you'd dropped by the law firm on Monday."

Uh-oh. "He . . . um, didn't appreciate my visit."

"Yes, he told me. He was quite angry."

"I'm sorry. I didn't mean to create a muddle and hope he

didn't blame you for my clumsiness. But I knew Belinda Young from school and didn't think it would hurt anything if I paid her a visit."

"You didn't create a muddle, Mrs. Majesty. I don't know why Stephen was so upset. He disagrees with me about Eddie's death and thinks I'm silly to believe it was anything but suicide, but he had no reason to be such a bear about your visit. He was furious when I told him I'd asked you to look into the matter. He hopes to avoid a scandal, you see."

"A scandal?" The word puzzled me; not an uncommon occurrence.

"Yes. He thinks suicide is bad enough, but murder would put a blot on the family name."

A blot? Oh, dear. "Well, I hope he didn't take his ill temper out on you. I was the one who irritated him."

"No, no. Stephen never touches me."

She sounded almost sad about that, which I considered odd. Unless . . . did she mean the man really and truly *never* touched her? At all? Not even for a kiss or anything? If I possessed a brassier nature, I'd have asked, but I didn't. I was sure curious, though.

"Will he be annoyed if I visit your home again?"

"He will if he finds out, but he won't. The servants are all most discreet, and . . . well, they don't care much for Mr. Hastings."

I didn't blame them. I'd never met the man, and I loathed him. "I'll be happy to visit you, Mrs. Hastings. What time would you like me to come over?" What the heck. After Pa and I walked Spike, I'd aimed to spend the rest of the day tidying up the house and reading anyway.

"Will eleven o'clock be all right with you?"

"Perfect. I'll be at your home at eleven."

"Thank you very much."

That settled that. I turned, aiming to clear the table and wash the dishes.

"Who was that?" asked Pa, who'd put down the paper to look at me.

"Mrs. Stephen Hastings. She's the mother of Eddie Hastings. You know. The one who . . ." *Crashed my séance.* I couldn't say that to my father. Not again. He'd think I was nuts. "She's the mother of the young man who died in March."

Pa's eyes narrowed. "The one who . . ."

Aw, fudge. "Yes. The one who spoke through me last Saturday night." I shivered, remembering, and felt tiny icy feet clamber up my spine.

"Daisy . . ."

"I know, I know. It's unbelievable. If it hadn't happened to me, I wouldn't believe it, either. It was the most horrible experience of my life, barring when Billy died."

"Hmm."

"Now Mrs. Hastings claims she's found something that might relate to her son's death and wants me to come over so she can show it to me. She thinks I can advise her what to do with it. I know what I'd like to tell her to do with it," I said darkly—and, to be honest, untruthfully. I was wildly curious about whatever it was she thought she'd found.

With a frown, Pa said, "I don't know, Daisy. Maybe I should come with you. I don't want you to put yourself in any danger."

Shaking my head, I said, "There's no danger from Mrs. Hastings. There might be from her husband, but he won't be there. She told me the servants hate his guts, so they won't blab."

"They what?" Pa stared at me.

"She told me the servants don't like her husband. If he's as awful as Belinda Young told me he was, I can understand why."

"Who's Belinda Young? I'm getting confused here."

"She's a girl I used to go to school with, Pa. She was Eddie

Hastings' secretary. But don't let's think about that now. Let me wash up the dishes and then we can take Spike for a walk."

The two words, "Spike" and "walk," galvanized my dog, who instantly stood up and started madly wagging his tail. Staring at his hopeful doggy eyes, I said, "Or maybe we should walk Spike first. I shouldn't have said the word w-a-l-k aloud."

With a laugh, Pa folded the newspaper and rose from his chair. "Sounds like a good idea to me. Let me get my hat, and you get the leash."

So I rinsed the breakfast dishes, fetched my own hat and Spike's leash, and we took a nice, long ramble around the neighborhood. We got back home in plenty of time for me to wash the dishes, change clothes, grab the accumulated library books on the little table next to the door, and head to the Hastings' estate.

The same Chinese gate guard asked for my name and let me into the grounds, and the same Chinese maid opened the massive front door to the palace in which the Hastings family lived.

It occurred to me that I'd never asked Mrs. Hastings if they had any children besides Eddie. I imagine his death would have been even more devastating if he'd been their only child, although losing any child would be wrenching. I don't think a person, especially a mother, can really recover from that sort of blow. I know Vi still grieved for her lost Paul.

The maid led me to another room in the giant house, this one a sunroom that lived up to its name. It was all windows, and white wicker furniture occupied it along with splashy orchids of different colors. The effect was stunning. In fact, I must have stood at the door, blinking at the room and looking like a fool, for long enough that Mrs. Hastings noticed me.

"Mrs. Majesty. How kind of you to come." She rose from where she'd been kneeling, a pair of secateurs in her hand. She wore gardening gloves, and I had a sudden panicky feeling, as if the woman were a monster who aimed to stab me in the heart with those pointy shears. Too much imagination can be a scary thing. I mentally shook myself, and Mrs. Hastings went from ogre to grieving mother in half a second.

"Happy to help," I said lamely.

Laying down the secateurs and stripping off her gloves, Mrs. Hastings said to the maid, "Will you please bring us tea, Lee?"

"Yes, ma'am," said the maid, and hightailed it out of the room.

I gazed around some more. "What a beautiful room, Mrs. Hastings. I've never seen anything like it."

She smiled, as if my comment had pleased her. "I'm quite fond of gardening, and orchids are my particular favorites. Would you like me to cut a stem or two for you to take home?"

"Oh, but . . ." I didn't know what to say.

"It's no bother, and I love to share my orchids. But please, let's sit at the table and wait for Lee. I have what I want to show you in my apron pocket."

She patted a pocket in the apron she wore, which I'd heard my aunt call a "shopkeeper's apron." Mrs. Hastings bore no resemblance whatever to any shopkeeper I'd ever seen. And her apron was a beautifully scalloped affair in a pretty blue-checked calico. Then she waved at a little table and two chairs in front of the largest window in the room.

"What a magnificent view," I said as I gazed out over rolling green lawns before taking my seat. When Mrs. Hastings sat with a sigh, I did likewise, only without the sigh.

"Yes. Mr. Hastings likes to have his grounds as perfect as everything else in his life. They are pretty, though, aren't they?"

I saw what looked like miles of green grass with splashes of color here and there. I suspected the color came from azaleas and hydrangeas, although I also spotted what looked like a big rose garden with an arbor off to the right. "Magnificent," I said again, wishing I could think of more words to describe the fabulous view.

"We have a staff of gardeners to take care of the grounds, of course."

Don't ask me why, but I asked, "Are they Chinese?"

"Why, yes, they are. Why do you ask?"

"Just curious, I guess. I noticed all the rest of your staff whom I've seen are Chinese."

"Yes. I believe I told you that Stephen—Mr. Hastings—used to work in Hong Kong. He still has many connections in the Chinese community."

Jeepers, I didn't even know Pasadena had a Chinese community. I should have. After all, just north of Colorado on Marengo sat the Chinese Methodist Church. Evidently, according to Keiji Saito, Pasadena also boasted a Japanese community. One can become so isolated in one's own tiny little society of souls, couldn't one? I decided then and there to branch out more. I knew there was a Chinatown in Los Angeles. For all I knew there was a Japantown, too. Keiji could probably tell me.

"Interesting," I said.

Lee entered with a tray bearing a gorgeous Chinese tea service and some delicate little cookies at that point, so both Mrs. Hastings and I merely smiled at the girl as she laid out the tea things.

As soon as Lee left the room, Mrs. Hastings poured us both a cup of tea. Then she reached into her apron's middle pocket. "Take a look at this. I don't know what it means, if anything, but it might mean something."

I took the piece of paper she handed me and read. I'm sure my eyes grew two sizes as I did so.

You have to get me out of this place. You know how much you have to lose if I tell the authorities what I know, and those fellows you work with aren't a pack of pansies. They deal hard and rough and don't care whom they step on. I'm sick of rotting here in this prison. I know I said I'd keep my mouth shut. Lord knows, it won't do me any good if our business dealings became public, but San Quentin isn't a picnic, and I want out.

Eustace Kincaid

"My goodness!" I cried, looking up from the paper and staring at Mrs. Hastings, who appeared rather paler than she had a moment before. "Was this sent to your husband by Mr. Kincaid?"

"I honestly don't know to whom it was sent. I found it in a nook in a hall cabinet. It might have been sent to Mr. Hastings or . . ." She waved at the note in my hand. "I just don't know. I'm sure Eddie wasn't involved with Mr. Kincaid in any way, and I don't believe Stephen had anything to do with him. Wasn't Mr. Kincaid the one who robbed his own bank? I remember feeling terrible for poor Madeline at the time."

"Yes, he was." I glanced down at the note and then back at Mrs. Hastings. Bewildered doesn't begin to describe how I felt. However, I did think this was something Sam should probably know about. "Would you mind if I took this to Detective Rotondo at the Pasadena Police Department? I know the police are investigating something that might possibly involve your son's death."

Mrs. Hastings goggled at me. "What could possibly involve Eddie's death?"

Nuts. "Well . . . you do know that your son died from an overdose of heroin injected into his body, don't you?"

After blinking at me in incomprehension for a second or two, Mrs. Hastings said, "Heroine? How can a person inject a human female into the body of another person? I'm sorry, Mrs. Majesty. I don't understand."

"I didn't know what it was either, until I began investigating your son's case. Heroin—without the *e* on the end—is a drug derived from opium. According to Sam—Detective Rotondo—traffic in both heroin and cocaine is growing, and bootleggers have begun dealing the drugs as well as illegal liquor."

"Eddie was injected with a drug?" Tears started rolling down Mrs. Hastings' cheeks. I wished I could hug her, but I didn't dare. "Why did no one tell me? Stephen must have known. Why didn't *he* tell me? I'm Eddie's mother. I deserve to know how he died! Oh, I *hate* men! They always think they need to protect women from things. As if the cause of Eddie's death wouldn't have been of vital interest to me."

I didn't know what to say, but it didn't matter, because Mrs. Hastings wasn't through yet.

"My God, do you suppose *Stephen* was in league with Mr. Kincaid in the illegal drug business? I'll *kill* him!" She rose and grabbed her secateurs as if she aimed to rip right down to the law office and stab her husband in the heart.

I rose and put a hand on her arm. Tentatively. I didn't want any secateur stab wounds on my own personal body. "Please, Mrs. Hastings. Don't jump to any conclusions. This note might or might not mean anything at all. And it might or might not pertain to your son's death. I'm going to take it to Detective Rotondo and see what he thinks about it." Not, of course, that he'd tell me what he thought. Drat Sam anyhow!

Mrs. Hastings sat with a plunk, her secateurs dropping to the floor of the greenhouse, put her face in her hands, and sobbed. Poor, poor woman.

"Mrs. Hastings, I'm sorry this has come as a . . . shock to you. I don't believe the cause of your son's death should have been kept from you. If it's any comfort, everyone I've spoken with so far has told me your son had nothing to do with drugs."

"Of course he didn't!" she cried through her tears.

"So that increases the probability that someone killed him. But you're right. Men are always thinking of women as the weaker sex and try to protect us from things we don't need to be protected from. In fact, if you stop to think about it, women are ever so much stronger than men. Why, you even bore . . . well, at least one child." I was making a botch of this, drat it.

She sniffled several times and wiped her eyes on her apron, which made me wince a little. I mean, she'd just been digging in dirt. On the other hand, it was orchid dirt and, therefore, probably too refined to contain germs.

"We have two daughters. Eloise and Erica. They were crushed by Eddie's death, too."

Hmm. A bunch of *E*s in the family. "Do they live with you?"

"No. They're both married. Eloise and her family live in San Marino. Erica and her husband—they were only married last summer—live in Santa Barbara. It's a lovely beach community."

I wouldn't know. "I'm glad you have other children, although I know they don't make up for the loss of your son."

She sniffled again. "They are a comfort, I have to admit."

I'm glad she had some kind of comfort. Her dearly beloved Stephen sounded like an ice-cold fish to me, and I doubt he was any solace at all for the poor grieving woman. Speaking of whom . . .

"I think it would be better if you don't mention this note to anyone, Mrs. Hastings, including your husband. I sincerely doubt that a successful attorney like him would have anything to do with the illegal drug business, but clearly someone knew something about whatever it is Mr. Kincaid was involved with. That may or may not be drugs, but it's still probably better if no one knows about the note but you and me. And, of course, the police."

"Yes. Yes, I agree with you. Anyhow, Stephen and I are long past being chatty with each other."

How sad. I wonder if Billy and I would ever have reached that stage of indifference—or downright dislike—if our marriage hadn't suffered such a tremendous blow at the beginning. Ma and Pa still chatted with each other. Heck, they even held hands sometimes.

I heaved a huge sigh. "Well, I suppose I'd better take this to the police. Thank you for calling me this morning. This might help with the investigation."

"I hope it does. But let me give you some orchids first, Mrs. Majesty. They aren't much in the way of compensation, but I want you to have some."

"Thank you. I'd be very happy to take some sprays home with me. I'm sure the whole family will love them."

So, what with an armful of simply gorgeous orchid sprays sitting on the seat next to me in the Chevrolet, I had to drive home and deal with them before I drove to the police station and then the library. That was all right. I didn't have anything else planned for the day.

Mrs. Hastings had been more than generous. There were orchids enough for the dining room table, orchids for the living room, and even a spray of orchids for my bedroom. I chose yellow ones for my room, purple not being my favorite color, and most of the others were purple, pink, or white. Pa was terribly impressed. I presumed the Benjamins would be, too, when they arrived for dinner that evening.

Then I betook myself to the Pasadena Police Department. I wasn't looking forward to it.

CHAPTER TWENTY

Sam snatched the note from me as if I'd been withholding evidence regarding the biggest case in his career.

"When did you get this?" he demanded, although I'd already told him.

With a sigh, I said, "This morning. From Mrs. Hastings. She found it in a drawer—well, she said it was in a nook, whatever that might be—in a hall cabinet. Don't ask me to whom it was sent or why, because I don't know anything other than that she found the note and called me."

"Huh." Sam gave me a hard look. "It beats me why all these people call *you* instead of the police when evidence shows up."

I sniffed. "I'm nicer than you are."

"Huh."

"Anyhow, for what it's worth, there's the note." I waved a hand carelessly in the stuffy air of Sam's office.

Actually, it wasn't merely his office. There were four other desks for four other detectives in the room. The first time I met Sam at the police department and walked into that room, I got some mighty odd stares. I guess the other detectives were used to me by this time, because the two of them in residence in this instance simply glanced up and then went back to their paper-work.

As Sam glared at the note, I figured there was no need for me to hang out at the police department any longer. I rose. "Well, I don't know what you can do with it, but I thought you should have it. I have to go to the library now." Because it was lunchtime and I was hungry, I added, "See you tomorrow. I'm looking forward to it."

Sam cast a fevered glance around the room, but my voice hadn't been loud, and none of his colleagues had heard my comment. *Huh* to him! For a man who was supposed to love me, he sure didn't act like it. Not that I blamed him. I wouldn't want a herd of policemen teasing me, either.

"Yeah," he said, standing and getting ready to see me to the door. Then inspiration must have stricken because he added, "Want to go to the Chop Suey place for lunch? I'm hungry."

Oh, boy. Big fat dinner tonight with the Benjamins. Big fat dinner tomorrow with Sam and my family. Why not a big fat lunch? Then I could go to the library.

With a smile, I said, "Why, thank you. Don't mind if I do."

Sam said, "Huh," again.

The Crown Chop Suey Parlor was within walking distance of the Pasadena Police Department, so Sam and I strolled up the street together. Luckily, I'd worn a coolish dress that day, because it was quite a warm one. Sometimes the months of June and July are foggy and overcast in the fair city of Pasadena—and, I presume, the rest of the Los Angeles area—but not that day.

I tried not to stuff myself, in deference to the turkey Aunt Vi aimed to fix for dinner that night, but I was pretty darned full by the time we left the restaurant. Sam paid, which was nice of him. Oddly enough, I didn't feel any tension between us as we chatted over our lunches. How different this time was from the time we'd taken luncheon together at the same restaurant, when I'd been worried to death about Billy, and Sam had been trying to reassure me. No need for that now. Now we just chatted about stuff in general. I think our conversation ranged from Spike's excellent retention of his year-old dog-obedience training to books. We'd never spoken about books before.

"I'm heading to the library as soon as we finish here," I said after I'd swallowed a bite of sloppy noodles and wondered how the Chinese managed to eat that kind of stuff with chopsticks. I didn't have mine with me or I might have attempted it. But no. I wanted to astonish my family, not to mention Sam, with my ability to handle those two little bamboo sticks the following evening.

"I go there a lot after work. I'm glad they're open until nine on Fridays."

"What do you like to read?"

He shrugged. "Biographies and history mainly." He gave me a squinty-eyed look. "I expect you enjoy detective books."

I sniffed imperiously. "You already know I do. You've seen me reading enough of them."

"True. And they've given you ideas about police work that are stupid, too."

"They have not!"

He held up both hands in a gesture of surrender. "Not stupid. Uh . . . inaccurate, I suppose might be a better word."

With another sniff, I conceded the point. "Especially the ones set in England."

"Right," he said, a sardonic edge to his voice. "Especially those."

Aside from that slight skirmish, lunch was a pleasant affair, and we walked back to the Pasadena Police Station in amiable converse. Sam even opened the driver's-side door of the Chevrolet for me, which was more gentlemanliness than I'd expected of him.

"Have fun at the library," he said before he turned to go back to work.

"Thanks. See you tomorrow."

He lifted his hand, his back to me, and I felt a pang, although

I don't know why.

My visit to the library was pleasant, although Miss Petrie wasn't working that day. The library opened on Saturdays twice a month, so the librarians who worked on Saturday took another day off during the week instead of Saturday. I turned in the books my family had read and came away with several others, which we'd devour in their turn.

By the time I got home it was almost four o'clock, and the house already smelled like Thanksgiving. Good thing I'd had a substantial lunch or I'd have been famished. As it was, I put the library books on the table beside the front door and walked to the kitchen with Spike, who gamboled at my feet. Naturally, I'd given him a hearty pet when I first entered the house.

Aunt Vi was industriously snapping and stringing beans as I entered the kitchen. She'd probably started working on our dinner as soon as she'd come home from working at the Pinkertons' place.

She glanced up and smiled at me. It beat me how anyone could be happy after having cooked all day for one family and now had to cook for another. But Vi claimed to love her work, and I believed her. I was also intensely glad of her enjoyment, from which the entire family benefitted.

"Good afternoon, Daisy. Where have you been all day?"

"Oh, here and there. I had to take something to Sam at the police station—"

"Good Lord, now what?" she demanded, pressing a bean-green hand to her aproned bosom.

"Nothing very exciting, I'm afraid. Mrs. Hastings found a strange note in her home. She gave it to me to give to the police."

"Why didn't the woman give it to them herself?"

I tilted my head and gave my aunt a cynical glance. "You know better than that, Vi."

She heaved a sigh. "Yes, I suppose I do. Not for the high and mighty to consort with the likes of policemen and so forth."

"Precisely. But Mrs. Hastings also gave me all the beautiful orchids you see scattered around the house."

"I wondered where they came from."

"She grows 'em herself."

Vi blinked at me, as if surprised that a wealthy woman chose to do anything more or less useful with her time.

"Then I went to the library, and now I'm home. May I chop anything for you? The house smells wonderful, by the way."

"Thank you, dear. Yes, you can chop the celery and onion for the stuffing if you will, and then peel those potatoes I put on the sink. Just a cup each of the celery and onion will do. I didn't get a huge turkey since we're dining out tomorrow, and we don't want too many leftovers."

"I do," I assured her.

She only laughed, and I grabbed my own apron from the hook on the kitchen wall. I set about industriously chopping onions and celery. Because of the chopping lessons that Vi had given me when I'd had to teach that lousy cooking class at the Salvation Army, my piles of chopped vegetables looked very respectable and evenly diced when I was through with them. None of your oddly shaped pieces of celery or onion for Daisy Gumm Majesty—not anymore, at all odds. Then I peeled the potatoes.

"Thank you, dear. I'll just plop these into a pot of salted water and boil them a little later."

I don't know how she coordinated everything so it came out all right at just the appropriate times, but she always did. Not only was she plugging away at the main course and the side dishes, but I saw an apple pie sitting on the windowsill. Oh, my, what a feast we would have that night! I could hardly wait—and this, after a big lunch at the Chop Suey Parlor. Maybe I'd gain all my lost weight back eventually if I kept eating like this.

The Benjamins arrived promptly at six p.m. I hardly recognized Mrs. Benjamin without her nurse's apron and cap, but Mr. Benjamin looked his same dapper self. A rather short man, and whip thin, he always wore a black suit and vest, but he varied his ties. This evening he wore a nice tie with blue and red stripes running diagonally across it. Spike and I welcomed them at the door, and I took their hats and coats and hung them on the coat tree.

"Your home always smells so delicious when I come over, Daisy," said Mrs. Benjamin, smiling at me and handing me a box that had clearly come from Jorgenson's.

"That's because Aunt Vi does the cooking," I assured her. "Doc can tell you it doesn't always smell like this." A twinge of pain assailed my heart as memories of Dr. Benjamin's many visits to Billy tumbled through my mind.

The good doctor patted me on the shoulder. "I know it's not a comfort, but you're not the only family so grievously wounded by that damn—"

"Richard!" Mrs. Benjamin said in a stern voice.

He swallowed the end of the word and said, "By that miserable war."

"I know it," I said, smiling at the both of them. They were a very kind couple of people, and I liked them enormously.

By that time Ma and Pa had arrived at the front door and were greeting the doctor and his wife. I held the box and wondered what to do with it. I guess Mrs. Benjamin saw my confusion, because she said, "It's just some chocolates I picked up. They aren't for tonight, but for whenever you or your family feels the need for a pick-me-up, dear."

"How very nice of you. I'll just put them—" I glanced down at my dog and amended my first plan, which had been to put the box of chocolates on a short table in the living room. "On the shelf of the dining room hutch." The hutch was built into the wall of the room, making the hutch extremely convenient and very pretty. That's where we kept the few display pieces we owned along with some miscellaneous chinaware that had survived various generations of Gumms and Majestys.

Dinner was a rousing success. Luckily for me, I sat next to Dr. Benjamin, so we managed to chat a little about Eddie Hastings.

"I truly doubt the boy did himself in, Daisy. There were no signs of drug use on his body."

"Really? How can a doctor tell if a person uses heroin on a . . . what would you call it? A regular basis?"

"Injection marks, generally on the inside of the arm, along the vein. If a fellow is in a very bad way and has been using the drug for years, he might have what they call tracks on both arms and even his legs."

I'm sure my nose wrinkled, because he smiled at me. "Not a pleasant habit to think about, is it?"

"No, and I can't imagine why anyone would want to do such a thing to himself."

"Or herself."

I think I stared at him, because my mother said, "Daisy, what on earth is the matter with you?"

Gathering my wits together, I said, "Nothing, Ma. Something that Dr. Benjamin just said . . . surprised me, is all."

She opened her mouth to ask what could have accounted for my astonishment, but Mrs. Benjamin, I think stirred into action by a quick move on her husband's part, asked her a question, and she gave up on me.

Dr. Benjamin said, "Yes, women use drugs, too. Of course, they're more apt to become addicted to laudanum, which comes in a syrup form, than to inject heroin, but I've seen cases."

I gulped. "That's . . . so sad."

"Yes. It is. I fear addiction to opiates has increased greatly since the war. Well, you saw it in your own home, sweetheart, with your Billy. Those poor boys can't help it."

Boy, how depressing *this* conversation had become. "Yes, of course."

"I apologize, Daisy. I didn't mean to make you sad. I only wanted you to know that I now agree with Mrs. Hastings. I don't believe her son killed himself. Especially since no syringe was found in the poor boy's apartment. Unless he was with another person, there should have been a means to administer the drug evident at the scene. And if another person was present . . . well . . ."

"Yes. Whoever was there with him must have injected Mr. Hastings himself." I cast a despairing glance at Dr. Benjamin. "Or herself."

He gave me a faint smile. "I believe we can acquit any ladies of his acquaintance of doing the deed. As far as I've been able to determine, Mr. Hastings was a young man of steady habits. I don't believe he had a lady friend in his life."

"No, I guess he didn't. Harold Kincaid told me he expected Mr. Hastings to marry a young woman named Adele Knowles one day, but not any time soon."

"Ah, yes. They would have made a nice couple. I know the Knowles family."

With a soft chuckle, I said, "You know everyone in Pasadena and Altadena, practically."

"Well, I wouldn't go *that* far."

"Now what are you two laughing about?" asked my mother. I think she didn't approve of me hogging the doctor's attention.

"Daisy was quizzing me on how many families we know in common."

"Oh, my, that's probably a lot of them," said Ma. "Daisy gets around to places the rest of us never see." She didn't sound sorry about it.

"That's the truth," said Pa. "Our Daisy travels in distinguished circles."

They were embarrassing me.

I suspect Dr. Benjamin noticed my discomfiture, because he said, "Believe me, the only thing that separates most of those so-called *distinguished* families from yours is more money than they can use wisely."

"Precisely," I said. "Just think about Stacy Kincaid if you doubt Dr. Benjamin's words."

"I don't doubt them for a minute," said Aunt Vi.

"That's the sad truth," Mrs. Benjamin plopped into the conversation. "Why, I've never seen so many women who don't have enough to do so they invent medical problems for themselves." She shook her head. "You don't find that sort of thing in normal families that have good, honest work to do in order to put food on the table."

"True, true," said her husband. "Speaking of food, this is the best meal we've had in ages, isn't it, Dorothy?" Dorothy being Mrs. Benjamin's first name.

"My goodness, yes," she concurred. "No one else I know can match Viola Gumm when it comes to fixing delicious meals."

"Pshaw," said Vi, although I could tell she was pleased.

After that, dinner passed peacefully enough. Even though we all said we were too full for dessert, we ate apple pie and cheese anyway. What a feast! And it was a real treat to have a Thanksgiving meal in the middle of the year, although the house did get sort of warm. We fixed that by opening the windows, and soon a soft breeze cooled us off.

I knew Ma and I were going to have to do the washing up, but we didn't want to rush the Benjamins, so we all sat on chairs on the front porch and jawed until almost nine o'clock. Spike enjoyed the attention of everyone at different times, and I threw his ball for him until my arm ached.

All in all, the evening had been a great success. What's more, Dr. Benjamin had confirmed what Eddie Hastings himself had told me—along with every living soul present at that awful séance. Someone had murdered him.

Now all I had to do was find out who'd done the evil deed. Well, I suppose Sam might help, too.

CHAPTER TWENTY-ONE

When the Benjamins finally left, I sent Ma off to bed, since she had to work a half day at the Hotel Marengo on Saturday, and I washed and dried all the dishes myself and put them all away. It took forever, even with Aunt Vi having stored the leftover food in the Frigidaire first.

At any rate, I slept late the next morning, but I didn't feel guilty. In truth, I felt rather virtuous for having spared my mother an hour's worth of work and a late night.

Pa and I took Spike for a walk after I had a turkey sandwich for breakfast, Vi not having left any delightful surprises for breakfast that morning. Then, since I sing alto in the church choir, and wanted to be sure of my part, I sat on the piano bench in the living room and, while Pa read a book, I practiced the alto part of "Oh, for a Thousand Tongues to Sing," which is always the first hymn in a Methodist hymnal. I don't know why.

Since we aimed to go out to dinner that night at Miyaki's, after I had my part down pat, I retired to my room with Spike and commenced practicing with the chopsticks Keiji had given me. I was darned good at wielding them by that time, and I made myself grin as I thought about how astonished my family would be that evening when I scooped fried vegetables and whatever else Keiji's uncle planned to serve us with chopsticks, while everyone else had to use their forks and knives.

Keiji had told me that it was not considered impolite to pick up, say, a fried shrimp, hold it between the sticks, and take bites out of it. Using the manners my mother taught me, I'd ordinarily cut a fried shrimp into pieces first. I hoped she wouldn't scold. If she did, I'd just tell her I'd been taught how to use the chopsticks and was therefore using Japanese table manners. She probably wouldn't buy my excuse, but oh, well.

When the telephone rang, I was so involved in picking up pieces of paper with my chopsticks, I dropped one of the darned things on the floor. Spike, ever on the alert, bounced to retrieve it, but I snagged it before it could become decorated with doggie tooth marks.

My father got to the 'phone before I did, but the call was for me. The calls at that house were almost always for me—and generally presaged an hysterical fit by Mrs. Pinkerton. I held my breath and prayed as I took the receiver from Pa. In my sweet, soothing spiritualist's voice, I said, "Yes?"

"Daisy!"

Drat. It was Mrs. Pinkerton, all right, and she was as close to hysterical as made no never mind, as my father sometimes said.

Suppressing my annoyance, I said gently, "Yes, Mrs. Pinkerton?"

"It was Mr. Kincaid! I know it was! I saw him!"

I blinked a time or two, trying to sort out this ranting declaration in the chopstick-induced fuzz in my brain. "Ah . . ." She wasn't going to tell me he'd killed someone else, was she?

"I did, Daisy! I saw him! He was with another man, and they were arguing!"

"Ah." Not another murder, but a sighting. After shaking my head, trying to rid it of irrelevancies, I said, "Where did you see this? And you're sure it was your husband—"

"No! It was my *ex*-husband."

Criminy. "Yes, of course. Your ex-husband. You're sure it was he? Where was this?"

"I'd just come from a committee meeting for the Women's

Hospital. We were driving west on Green Street"—Jackson not only served as Mrs. Pinkerton's gatekeeper, but also as her chauffeur when she deigned to leave her home to go anywhere—"when I *saw* him. He and the other man were arguing."

"They were arguing on Green Street?"

"Well, they were sort of tucked away in an alley off Green. Near Marengo. I'm not sure of the address."

"Why didn't you telephone the police?" I asked, still straining to be polite. "Or you could have driven to the police station in less time than it took Jackson to drive you home. You could have told the police, and they could have scooted down to Green and Marengo and caught him right there and then."

"*I?*" she asked, clearly astonished. "You think *I* should go into that tawdry police station and speak to a *policeman?*"

Lord, give me patience. "You could have had Jackson run inside and tell the police, Mrs. Pinkerton. That makes more sense than having him drive you home so you can call me. Do you expect me to drive to Green and Marengo and arrest Mr. Kincaid and his crony?" All right, so I'd slipped from pleasantry to sarcasm. I couldn't help it.

"Oh, no, of course you can't do that," said she, sounding shocked.

"But you want me to call the police for you? You realize both men will be long gone by this time, don't you?"

"Oh, Daisy! You don't think Eustace will come here, do you?"

Not if he had a brain in his head. "I have no idea. All I know is that you lost a brilliant opportunity to get him re-arrested."

"Oh. Do you really think so?"

"Yes, I really do."

"Oh, dear."

"And it's Saturday, so Detective Rotondo won't be at work today." Actually, I didn't know that. For all I knew Sam worked every day of the week. "But I'll call and tell whoever's on duty what you believe you saw."

"I *did*!" she cried. "I *did* see him!"

"Do you have any idea who the other man was?"

"No . . . I don't believe so."

I shut my eyes and counted to ten. "Mrs. Pinkerton, you either recognized the other fellow or you didn't. Which was it?"

"I didn't recognize him."

"Was he young? Old? Middle-aged?"

"Um . . . oh, *I* don't know!" Now she was whining. Pretty soon she'd start weeping piteously, and I didn't want to stick around for that.

"Surely," I said, trying to pacify her with my gentlest tones, "you can tell me if he was old or young."

"Middle-aged, I think."

"Thank you. I'll telephone the police right now."

"Oh, *thank* you, Daisy! Do you think you can come over this afternoon? I'm *so* upset!"

My eye! "I'm very sorry, Mrs. Pinkerton, but my day is filled with appointments already."

"Oh." She'd begun crying. I wanted to scream. "What about tomorrow?"

"I sing in the church choir on Sundays, and then my family and I spend the day together." Because I didn't want to lose her patronage completely, I said, "I can visit you Monday morning. Will that be all right?"

She sniffled as she thought about it. "Oh . . . yes, I suppose it will have to be. Please bring the Ouija board. I truly need Rolly's advice."

Rolly would have advised her to call the police as soon as she got home if she didn't have brains enough to drive to the station—which was practically right up the street from where the purported Mr. Kincaid had been—and have Jackson tell them what she'd just seen. The whole calling-the-police thing seemed pointless to me now. Whoever those two men were, they were assuredly long gone by this time.

"Very well. I'll come over on Monday at ten thirty." Darned if I'd skip walking my dog for her sake.

"Thank you, Daisy." She hesitated for several seconds, and for a moment I thought she'd hung up on me, but she hadn't. She said, "It was foolish of me not to telephone the police immediately, wasn't it?" in a very small voice.

Darned if I was going to agree that she'd been foolish, although she had been. "You were rattled by what you'd seen," I said, graciously letting her off the hook, but hoping the process of its removal stung at least a little bit.

"Thank you, Daisy." She hung up.

I waited for three other clicks on the line, but only heard two. "Mrs. Barrow, please hang up your telephone."

Another click sounded, louder than the rest. Stupid woman. Mrs. Barrow, not Mrs. Pinkerton, although Mrs. P was plenty stupid on her own.

So I called the Pasadena Police Department. When I asked for Sam, the policeman at the front desk told me he wasn't working that day. So I told him Mrs. Pinkerton's story, and he said he'd give the information to another detective who was, in his words, "working the case."

Huh. Wish I could have all the information the police had on "the case." At that point, I didn't even know what "the case" entailed. Were they looking for Eddie Hastings' killer or merely the operators of a drug ring? Or did they think both crimes pertained to each other? Nuts. If I thought Sam would give me an answer, I'd ask him over dinner, but I knew better.

The rest of that day passed peacefully enough. I had another turkey sandwich for lunch and made one for Pa. When Ma came home shortly after noon, I made one for her, too. After that I took a nap with Spike and then read for a while.

Then it was time to dress for dinner at Miyaki's. Deciding I wanted to look my best—after all, Harold, Del, and Mr. Knowles would be there—I selected an ankle-length striped brown dress with a high round neckline and what the magazine from which I'd copied the pattern had called "bishop" sleeves, which were gathered into brown velvet cuffs that matched the draped buckled hip belt. I wore my brown felt cloche hat trimmed with two black pompoms I'd made out of yarn. I got my pointy-toed, low-heeled shoes with wide buttoned straps. They hurt my toes, but that couldn't be helped. I could always slip them off under the table and nobody'd notice. It wasn't as if I had to be on my toes—so to speak—as I had to be while conducting a séance or anything. Black jet beads and a black handbag completed my outfit, and I was pleased with the result after I'd bathed and put it all on.

The whole family looked great that evening. It was difficult to get my father into an evening suit, but he still fit into the ones he wore when he was a chauffeur, and he looked grand. Ma wore a lovely blue creation I'd made her for Christmas. It, too, was ankle-length, and she borrowed my pearls to go with it. Vi looked very nice in her sober black velvet gown, another Christmas present made by my very own hands—well, and my swell, side-pedal White sewing machine. She wore with it a brooch given to me by a grateful client some years ago. I'd always thought it looked too old for me, but it looked great on my aunt's dinner gown.

As he'd promised, Sam picked us up in his big Hudson motorcar about 5:45 that evening. Even he looked as if he'd gone to some trouble with his toilette that evening. He was for once unrumpled, his black suit, vest, and tie were quite formal, and his hat, a black bowler, looked as if it had been cleaned and brushed. He'd even tamed his somewhat unruly curly black hair into submission.

After Spike had been subdued—since we were all in our fancy duds, none of us much wanted to cuddle him, but we did pet him—we trooped out to Sam's motor.

"You all look swell this evening," said Sam, holding the back door of his Hudson open.

Ma, Aunt Vi, Pa, and I all looked at each other, and then Ma got into the back seat, followed by Pa and then Aunt Vi. I sensed a conspiracy, but I didn't say anything. I did give Sam a little mouth quirk when I sat in the front seat of his car. He only smiled benignly at me and walked around to the driver's door, opened it, got in, and started the motor.

Miyaki's was on South Los Robles Avenue, not really very far from where we lived, so we got there in plenty of time for our six-o'clock reservation. A black-robed—actually, I think they call those robes kimonos—woman led us to a table for five in the left side of the restaurant sort of in the middle. The place was already getting full. I glanced around, hoping to see Harold and Del, but evidently they hadn't arrived yet.

The décor was amazing. There were silk hangings everywhere in beautiful blues and greens, reminding me of a peacock's tail. I noticed that there were very short tables and regular-sized tables and wondered about that until I saw some folks sitting at a short table. Actually, they were sitting cross-legged on the floor. I still wasn't sure what that was all about, but presumed it to be some sort of Japanese custom, although all the people were white. I told myself to remember to ask Harold about the differently sized tables next time I saw him—well, the next time after tonight, if he ever showed up. He'd better, darn it. I wanted to meet Lester Knowles, if only to assess what I could of his character. I know that sounds silly. After all, I couldn't very well interrogate the man. But I could at least take his measure in some way. I hoped.

Naturally, my family maneuvered themselves so that Sam and

I sat beside each other. I really didn't mind, since I aimed to tell him about Mrs. Pinkerton's telephone call to me that day.

When we were handed menus, we all stared at them with blank expressions on our faces. I know that for a fact, because I peeked. I didn't know about Sam, but I knew none of us Gumms or Majestys knew what any of the foods mentioned on the menu were. Then I noticed something called "teriyaki" listed. Leaning a little closer to Sam, I pointed to the word. "Is that what your copper friends pick up with their fingers and dip into sauce?"

His brow furrowed, and with a frown on his face, he said, "Blamed if I know. I wish somebody'd come by and translate this menu for us."

And then, as if by magic, Harold appeared! He, Del, a man I assumed to be Mr. Knowles, and a woman I assumed to be Adele Knowles were being seated at the table next to ours. I'd been happy to see Harold lots of times, but that night seemed particularly propitious. He spotted us and didn't sit when his chair was pulled out for him, but strode a foot or two over to us.

Beaming at the whole family, and Sam, too, he said, "Good evening, all. How lucky to meet here, of all places." He didn't wink or anything that might have given away the fact that he and I had planned to meet at the restaurant.

"Harold. How nice to see you," I said, beaming right back at him.

The rest of my family greeted him politely. Even Sam nodded and said, "Evening." I think it was meant to be a shortened version of "good evening."

"Say, Harold, we don't know what any of this stuff is," I told him, whispering so as not to let the rest of the folks in the restaurant know we were middle-class people unused to restaurant dining—especially in Japanese restaurants.

"I'll be more than happy to help. Let me bring the rest of my party over and make introductions."

So he did. My family already knew Del, from him having come to Billy's funeral, so Harold introduced the Knowles siblings. Lester was a nice-looking fellow who wore the hollow-eyed look of grief I'd seen on my own face after Billy's death. I recognized it at once, and my heart hurt for the man. After all, no one gave a second thought to my grief, which was to be expected. But Lester had been in love with another man and, therefore, his anguish couldn't be accounted for by the general population. I wanted to console him, but that was neither the time nor place.

Adele Knowles was a pretty girl, perhaps my age or a little older. She was clad in a smashing dinner gown with no hat, which made me wonder if hats for women in evening wear were going out of style. Time to check the *Vogue* magazine out of the library. I had to keep up with these things, after all. Anyhow, she had brown hair that was cut short and waved, either naturally or via a curling iron. If she were as rich as Harold, she probably had a maid to dress her and do her hair.

She possessed a sweet smile, and was a little pink when she said, "It's so good to meet you at last, Mrs. Majesty. Harold is always talking about you. You certainly had a harrowing trip last summer together, didn't you?"

"Yes, we did. And Detective Rotondo here was with us at the time, too," I said, nodding at Sam, who still frowned. He managed a civil greeting after I kicked his calf with one of my pointy-toed shoes.

"I don't even like to think about that time," Harold said with a theatrical shudder. He turned to his companions. "But you three go sit down. I want to chat with Daisy for only a minute or two."

"Good to see you again," said Del with one of his wonderful

smiles. He reminded me of Billy. In fact, when I'd first seen him at one of Mrs. Pinkerton's séances a few years back, my heart had almost stopped. He'd had his back to me, and he'd had on the uniform he'd worn during the war.

Mr. Knowles smiled politely, and guided his sister back to their table.

Harold leaned between Sam and me and pointed to the items on the menu. "I'd suggest a bowl of the miso soup, the teriyaki beef—or chicken, if you'd prefer—which comes with a delicious sauce. And I'd recommend you try the tempura."

"Ah," said Sam as if a light had just gone on in his brain. "It's tempura that's the fried vegetables you dip in the sauce, isn't it?"

"Precisely," said Harold. "I love the stuff. I'm sure it's fattening." He sighed and patted his rounded tummy. "They'll serve you green tea, which I guess is a Japanese thing, and then they have different desserts, but you'll know what those are."

"Thanks, Harold. I appreciate the lesson."

"Do they give you knives and forks if you ask for them?" my mother asked, rather shyly, peering down at the pair of chopsticks resting on a little bowl before her. I know she was intimidated. As a family, we didn't dine in fancy restaurants, but the ones we did go to came complete with American-style silverware. I was more comfortable than the rest of my kin because I'd hung out with Harold for so long.

"Yes, they do. I always ask for a fork and knife because I can't handle those little sticks."

"Well, *I'm* going to use the chopsticks."

"Oh, boy, I can't wait to see that," Sam muttered.

"You just wait," said I. Smugly.

Chapter Twenty-Two

Harold went back to his table, and we chatted together while we waited for someone to come and take our orders.

"I think Sam ought to order for us all," I said. "Since we don't know what anything is, we might as well follow Harold's advice."

"Sounds like a good plan to me," said Pa.

"And me," said Aunt Vi and Ma in chorus.

Sam said, "What did he say to order? I can't remember it all."

"Miso soup," I recited, having a better memory than Sam, "Teriyaki and tempura. I guess everything comes with rice."

"Yeah. The guys at the station mentioned getting rice with whatever they ordered," said Sam.

Therefore, when another kimono-clad person, this one male, came to our table to take our orders, Sam did a good job ordering for all of us. I suppose I could have reminded him that we could select chicken or beef teriyaki, but I didn't want to confuse the poor man.

"This is great," I said, smiling at him and then at my family. "It's like an adventure to another land, only we don't have to leave Pasadena."

"I suppose it is rather like that," said my mother doubtfully.

"If you don't care for the food, Peggy, we still have leftovers from yesterday's dinner at home," said Vi in an effort to sooth her.

"I'm looking forward to the grub," said my father, who, like me, was happy to experience new cuisines.

"The people at the station who've eaten here have liked it," said Sam.

"I can't wait," I said, hoping he wasn't feeling defensive. Then I remembered Mrs. Pinkerton's telephone call. "Oh, Sam, I have to tell you something."

His gaze paid a visit to the ceiling and he sighed. "What now?" he asked, growling slightly.

"I got a call from Mrs. Pinkerton today. She claims she saw Mr. Kincaid and another man having an argument in an alleyway somewhere around Green Street and Marengo."

He turned in his chair and gave me a hard stare. "And she called *you*?"

"She did. After she had Jackson drive her home."

"With the police station within a couple of blocks from where she says she saw the man she claims to be frightened of?"

I shrugged. "You know Mrs. Pinkerton."

"Yes," he said. "I know Mrs. Pinkerton. I hope you had the good sense to call the station."

"I did. And I asked for you, but you weren't there. So I told the man who answered the 'phone to relate the information to whomever might be interested, and he said he'd tell someone who was, in his words, 'working the case.' "

"Good God."

"My sentiments exactly."

We didn't get to talk much after that, because our waiter came with a pot of green tea and a bunch of tiny little cups with no handles. We all looked at the teapot for some moments, and then Ma said, "Um, Daisy, would you please pour the tea for us?"

"Sure."

So I did. Shortly thereafter, our soup was served. There were no utensils handy, so Sam asked for forks, knives, and spoons. I, having been taught by Keiji Saito the proper way to drink Japanese soup, picked up my chopsticks, which were quite elegantly lacquered, settled them in my hand the way Keiji had taught me, and dipped a chunk of something from my soup bowl. I think Keiji said it was tofu, whatever that is.

When I glanced up, everyone at the table was staring at me as if I'd grown a second head. I smiled serenely back at them.

"You know how to *use* those things?" Sam asked.

"Daisy, you amaze me sometimes," said Ma. She didn't sound as if my amazing qualities were always to her liking.

"You're so talented," said Aunt Vi.

"Mrs. Bissel's houseboy is Japanese," I told my audience. "He taught me how to use chopsticks." I'd sort of planned on keeping my struggle with the utensils a secret and surprise everyone, who would then think I'd just managed to conquer the skill at that very dinner table, but I couldn't stop myself from blurting out the truth. "I've been practicing all week long."

"Good work," said Pa.

"Good God," said Sam.

"My goodness," said Ma.

Vi only smiled at me. It was nice to be appreciated by someone.

Our dinner was scrumptious. Ma's eyebrows dipped when she saw me pick up my soup bowl and drink the remains of my soup, but I told her that's how Keiji'd taught me.

"Hmph," she said.

"It's all right, Peggy," said my father. "I'm sure dinner table manners differ the world round."

"They do indeed," I said, putting my soup bowl back on the table. "Why in Egypt, the Egyptians sit on the floor around a huge platter and only eat with their right hands. Or is it their left hands?" I glanced at Sam, hoping he'd remember which hand was used.

He only shook his head, dipped his spoon into his soup bowl, and said, "Beats me. I don't remember seeing any Egyptians eat. I met you in Turkey, remember?"

"Sure, but they're Moslems in Turkey, too."

"Maybe the *National Geographic* will have an article about Arabic eating habits one of these days," said Pa.

That seemed a good suggestion to me, and I considered writing to the magazine to suggest an article about the different ways people around the world take their food. Sounded interesting to me, but I suspect if I did write a letter, it would go into the nearest trash basket of whoever read it.

The waiter arrived with huge platters of food and set one in front of each of us. He noted I was holding the chopsticks and nodded his approval. I felt as though I'd conquered an Alp or something.

Anyhow, the food was delicious. Even Ma liked it. Pa raved. Aunt Vi instantly wondered if she could find a Japanese cooking book anywhere, and I told her I'd look at Grenville's Books the next time I went downtown.

For dessert, we were each served a slice of pineapple that had been cleverly carved into wedges and then separated so we could spear little pieces of pineapple. Those Japanese were intelligent folks.

After we'd stuffed ourselves, Sam drove us all home and we marched into the house, greeted Spike, who was delighted to see us, and I went to my bedroom to take off my fancy duds and get into a comfortable housedress and shoes. Those toe-pinchers were all right to wear out to the occasional fancy dinner, but I was glad to see the last of them that evening.

Pa and Sam set up the card table, and I played the piano for a while. Ma and Aunt Vi sat on the sofa and rested. I'd played "April Showers" and "Carolina in the Morning" when the telephone rang. Everything sort of halted in the house, and we all looked at each other. It was past nine o'clock by that time, and nobody, not even Mrs. Pinkerton, ever called us at that late hour.

Figuring that, whoever was on the end of the wire, the call would be for me, I trotted to the kitchen and picked up the receiver. "Gumm-Majesty residence, Mrs. Majesty speaking," I said. It was my usual telephonic greeting.

"Daisy?" a woman whispered.

"Yes?"

"It's Belinda Young. Do you have a minute?"

Why was she whispering? I didn't like this. I said, "Sure, but just a minute. We have a party line, and I want to be sure no one else is listening to our conversation. Mrs. Barrow?"

I heard a *click* that sounded downright angry and a couple of other clicks that just sounded normal. Then I said, "What is it, Belinda? Why are you whispering?"

"To tell you the truth," she said in a more normal voice, "I'm not sure. But something very strange happened at the office today, and I wasn't sure, but I thought I should tell you about it." She hesitated for a second or two and I was about to say something, but she suddenly started speaking again. "I may be way off base about this, but it was all so . . . strange. It may have absolutely nothing to do with Eddie's death, but . . . well, you were interested, so I thought I'd telephone you and see what you think."

Merciful heavens! "I'm glad you did, Belinda. Are you at home now?" I sure didn't want her telephoning from the office if odd and possibly dangerous things were going on there.

"Yes. I live at home with my mother and aunt."

Would it be nosy to ask where her father was? I didn't have to think about it because Belinda enlightened me the next time she spoke.

"My father died last Christmas, and Mother is still quite cut up about his passing. Well, we all are, but I'm closest to home and unmarried, so . . ." Her explanation petered out.

"So you're the one who brings home the bacon? And comforts your mother?"

"Well, Dad left her enough money to get by on, but she likes me to be here. I don't mind. I have a gentleman friend who takes me out occasionally, and Mother likes him, so it all works out. My mother and aunt do all of the cooking." She paused to sigh. "I really should learn to cook, since I expect Jerry and I will marry one of these days."

Good luck to her. I'd never yet learned to cook, in spite of Aunt Vi's tutelage.

"It's good of you to take care of your mother," I said, thinking my own mother would be inconsolable if Pa died. So would I, for that matter. But back to business. "Do you work half days on Saturday?"

"Not always, but I had to type a brief for Mr. Grover, so I went in today. But then Mr. Millette and a stranger showed up, and they had a terrible row. They walked right past my room, and since the door was shut and I'd just taken a sheet of paper out of the typewriter, I don't think they knew I was there. They went to Mr. Millette's office, but I could hear them. I didn't dare begin typing again because the machine is so loud, and I didn't want them to find me there."

"That was very wise of you." My heart palpitated at the notion of Mr. Millette and—could it be Mr. Kincaid?—discovering Belinda when they thought they were alone in that huge, empty building.

"I was scared. I didn't dare make any noise."

"Makes sense to me. What were they rowing about?"

"I couldn't make out all the words, but I distinctly heard the name 'Kincaid.' Isn't that the name of that fellow who robbed his own bank and went to jail a couple of years ago?"

I was right! "That's the one, all right."

"Anyhow, after a good deal of yelling, they quieted down. Mr. Millette must have used the telephone—I didn't even know he knew how to dial a telephone for himself," she added with something of a sniff. "That old bag of a secretary, Mrs. Larkin, does everything for him. He probably can't even brush his own teeth."

I entertained—if that's the right word—a vision of Mrs. Larkin brushing Mr. Millette's teeth for him, and my nose wrinkled.

"How do you know he telephoned anyone?" I asked, believing it to be a reasonable question.

"Because Mr. Grover showed up about twenty minutes later. He must have forgotten I was working today, because he almost jumped out of his skin when he opened the door and saw me sitting at the desk in my room. He said, 'What are you doing here?' And I told him I was typing the Cushing brief. He tried to pretend my presence hadn't startled him, but he was rattled. I could tell. Then Mr. Millette yelled at him to go to his office—Mr. Millette's office, I mean—and Mr. Grover left and did as Mr. Millette ordered. First, though, he said, "Well, go on home now. You can finish that brief on Monday morning." He looked frightened, Daisy. I don't know what's going on, but I don't like it one little bit."

"No. I don't blame you."

"What do you think I should do?"

Good question, and one I had to think about. "Well, I don't think you should do anything to tip the men off that you thought anything strange was going on. Go to work as usual on Monday. I have a policeman friend who's looking into the case—"

"You mean they changed their minds and think it was murder and not suicide? I *knew* Eddie wouldn't kill himself!"

Oh, dear. "Please don't tell anyone else about this, Belinda.

There's a lot more involved than murder, and my friend, who's a Pasadena Police detective, would kill me if he thought I'd told anyone there's an investigation going on."

"Very well. I'll keep mum. Did I do the right thing in 'phoning you?" She sounded worried, and I hurried to reassure her.

"You did the precisely right thing, Belinda. In fact, you might have helped solve the case." As soon as the words slipped out, I wished they hadn't. "But be *sure* not to tell anyone about it."

"Well . . . since I don't know anything, I guess I can't, can I?"

"Good point. Thank you, Belinda. I'm going to tell my detective friend right now what you just told me."

"You mean he's there? At your house?" She sounded more titillated than shocked.

Rather repressively, I said, "He was my late husband's best friend. He and my family all went out to dine at Miyaki's tonight."

"Oh, I've heard that's a lovely place."

"It's not only lovely. It's also delicious. I heartily recommend it."

"Thank you, Daisy. I promise I won't say a word. To tell the truth, I'm kind of scared, so I wouldn't dare say anything to anyone else."

Thank God for that! "That's good, Belinda. I'll be in touch if I need to know anything more, or . . . well, nothing, I guess. I'll just be in touch if I learn anything."

"Thanks, Daisy. Sorry for telephoning so late, but I called earlier and no one was at home, so . . ."

"Think nothing of it. I'm glad you called."

"All right. Well . . . good night."

"Good night."

After I hung the receiver on its hook, I stood in the kitchen, pondering the telephone, and wondering if Mr. Eustace Kincaid and the elderly Mr. Millette had been in cahoots for years in the drug trade, and if they'd roped the timid, bland Mr. Grover into the business with them.

Deciding thinking about it did no good, I went back to the living room. Everyone in it looked up at me expectantly. I'd kind of hoped they'd have gone back to reading and playing cards so I could take Sam aside and speak to him privately, but the telephone call at that hour was so unusual, I reckon they were interested. I heaved a small sigh and walked over to Sam. Hauling the piano bench closer to the card table, I sat on the bench.

Deciding there was no use trying to be private now that everyone had taken up staring at the two of us, I just blurted it all out. "That was Belinda Young. She works at the Hastings law firm. She used to be Eddie Hastings' and Mr. Grover's secretary. Now I guess she only works for Mr. Grover."

Sam laid his card hand face down on the table and swiveled to glare at me. It figured. He blamed me for everything, whether it was my fault or not.

I frowned back at him. "It's not my fault she called. She said she was typing a brief—whatever that is—for Mr. Grover today when Mr. Millette and another man came into the firm, went to Mr. Millette's office, and started yelling at each other. She couldn't hear what they said, but she heard the name 'Kincaid' a time or two."

Sam closed his eyes and bowed his head. "Good God."

"Then Mr. Millette must have telephoned Mr. Grover, because he groveled in about twenty minutes later. He was shocked to see Belinda, who doesn't ordinarily work on Saturdays. But she was there because—"

"She had to type a legal brief," said Sam, interrupting me in the annoying way he had.

"Yes," I said, snapping the word out. "Mr. Grover told her to go home, and she doesn't know what happened after that, because she went home."

"And she called you because . . . ?"

"Because she knows I'm interested in Eddie Hastings' murder."

"If it was a murder," said Sam, clearly grouchy now.

"It had to be a murder if he was injected with heroin and no syringe was found," I reminded him.

"My goodness!" cried my mother, who hadn't been privy to all the juicy details of the Hastings case, mainly because I was trying to keep my family out of it. "Daisy, have you been prying into one of Sam's cases again?"

"No!" I cried in my turn, feeling put upon and abused. "There wasn't a case until—uh . . ." There was no way on God's green earth I'd tell my family that the ghost of Eddie Hastings had crashed my séance. I'd already told Pa, and he'd thought I was crazy.

"There's been a change of opinion about the Hastings case," said Sam. "And Daisy is supposed to stay out of it."

"I'm not *in* it! Can I help it if people prefer to talk to me than to the police? Darn it, you're not being fair!"

Pa patted my hand. "There, there, Daisy. I'm sure Sam isn't blaming you for anything."

"Of course I'm not," said Sam, clearly straining to remain calm. "But this information has put an end to our evening, I'm afraid. I'd better get to the station and let the rest of the men in on this latest bit of news provided by Daisy."

"I had nothing to do with it!"

Made no difference. Sam was Sam, and that was that. He did ask me to walk out to his car with him, so I got a sweater from my room and did so, hoping to heaven he wouldn't lecture or scold me.

Oddly enough, he didn't. We both walked to his Hudson in

silence. Then he turned to me and said, "I hope you enjoyed dinner at Miyaki's tonight."

I didn't dare relax quite yet, but I decided his comment had been benign. Heck, it was even nice. "I loved it. Thank you very much, Sam. I think even Ma enjoyed our evening out."

"I'm glad. And I'm sorry I barked at you in there."

I gaped at him for a minute, trying to recall another time Sam had ever apologized to me for anything. Nothing occurred to me, so I just shrugged and said, "That's all right. I'm used to it."

He put his hand on my cheek, surprising the crud out of me. "I don't want you to hate me, Daisy. I just worry when you get involved in cases that might be dangerous to you."

Putting my hand over his—which felt surprisingly warm and good resting on my cheek—I said, "I know that, Sam. But it really isn't my fault that people are inclined to telephone me instead of the police. Most folks don't want to get involved with the police."

He heaved a large-sized sigh. "Don't I know it. Well, thanks for coming out with me tonight. Good night." And darned if he didn't lean over and kiss the cheek his hand wasn't resting on.

I honestly think I'd have kissed him back if he hadn't instantly dropped his hand, turned around as if he were being chased by wild beasts, and climbed into his huge automobile. I stood on the sidewalk, watching as his motor started with a roar and disappeared down Marengo. It occurred to me for the first time to wonder where Sam lived.

CHAPTER TWENTY-THREE

I didn't sleep very well on Saturday night. Maybe the unusual food we'd eaten didn't sit well . . . no. I think I'm avoiding the truth. The truth was that Belinda's telephone call had disturbed me, but what had disturbed me even more was Sam's gentle leave-taking out on the street next to his Hudson.

Sam Rotondo. Being gentle. And me reciprocating. I couldn't be falling for the big lug. That was impossible.

Wasn't it?

Yes. It definitely was. I did appreciate his friendship a whole lot, though, even though he was mean to me an awful darned lot.

After trying to figure it all out for far too long, I finally fell asleep, awaking Sunday morning with a slight headache and a bad mood. I tried to hide my lousy attitude from my family, none of whom would appreciate it. Besides, my rotten frame of mind wasn't anyone's fault but my own.

The choir had practiced "God of the Ages," a pretty, albeit rather martial, hymn with a nice alto part. Lucille Spinks and I were scheduled to sing a duet on the last verse. Our choir director, Mr. Floy Hostetter, had wanted us to sing the third verse, but I always started crying while I sang it (you can probably see why): "From war's alarms, from deadly pestilence; be thy strong arm our ever sure defense; thy true religion in our hearts increase; thy bounteous goodness nourish us in peace." So he'd settled on us singing the last verse instead.

I know that, as a good Christian girl, I was supposed to trust in God and believe there was a reason for Billy's tragic life and death. I was supposed to believe that Billy was in heaven, strumming on a harp—not that he'd been particularly musical in life.

And no, he wasn't an angel. I don't know why everyone thinks that when people die they become angels. They don't. The angels exist in a finite number and were there at the beginning. You can't become one, no matter how perfect a life you've led. One of the original angels, Lucifer, had fallen out of favor with God and had been sent to hell, even. Anyhow, at that point I wasn't sure if I even believed in God any longer. I also know that's a shocking thing to say, but I can't help it. You may judge me if you wish, but if *you* believe in God, you'll leave the judgment part of things to Him. Or Her. My heart had been so battered of late, I didn't care who was in charge of us poor earthlings. Whoever it was seemed to be doing a crummy job of it.

But enough of that. Aunt Vi, as was her wont on Sundays, put a roast in the oven before we all walked to church. When we got there, I veered off to the choir room to don my robe and greet my friends. Lucille appeared particularly happy that morning. When she flashed her left hand in front of my face and I saw the gleam of a solitaire diamond, I understood.

"Lucy! He proposed!"

As I gave her a huge hug, she teared up and said, "Yes. I'm going to be Mrs. Zollinger before the end of the year!"

"I'm so glad for you," I told her. And I was. Really. Just because I thought Mr. Zollinger was too old for her and not particularly attractive didn't mean he and Lucy wouldn't be happy together. I knew for a fact that Lucy had been yearning for marriage and children for a long time. I hoped Mr. Zollinger would be a blessing in her life, and she in his.

See? I'm not totally evil.

The church service went well, and Lucy and I sang our duet with particular fervor, probably because we were both pleased with her new status as an engaged-to-be-married woman. The congregation smiled a lot as we sang, so I guess they liked our duet, too.

When we got home, I changed out of my church clothes and went to the kitchen to set the table as Aunt Vi got Sunday dinner together. She'd made fresh dinner rolls the night before and had put them in the Frigidaire to be popped into the oven the moment we returned home from church. The house smelled heavenly. Does that make up for my earlier comments?

We were just finishing up dessert—apple pie with cheese—when the telephone rang. We all looked at each other. Mind you, the telephone sometimes rang on a Sunday, mainly when my brother or sister decided to call, but such occasions were rare.

Ma said, "It's probably for you, Daisy. You'd better answer it."

"You're probably right," said I, not happy about it.

Nevertheless, I made my way to the kitchen and to the telephone on the wall. I picked up the receiver and gave my usual greeting.

"Daisy, this is Belinda Young. I hope you don't mind, but I'd like to talk to you."

For goodness' sake. Whatever could she want to talk about now? I hoped it wasn't bad, whatever it was.

"I don't mind at all. But let me make sure the line is clear." Two clicks sounded in my ear. I said sternly, "Mrs. Barrow, please hang up your telephone." A second or two passed, and then Belinda and I heard another click. Devious woman. Mrs. Barrow, not Belinda. I wish we could afford a line to ourselves. Ah, well.

"All right. We're private now. What's the matter, Belinda?"

"Nothing's the matter, really. But . . . Oh, Daisy, I don't think I can carry it off!" She sounded mightily distressed.

"Carry what off?" I asked, confused.

"Behaving as though nothing happened at the office yesterday. I'm a secretary, not an actress, and I'm worried that Mr. Millette and Mr. Grover and that other man were arguing about something to do with Eddie Hastings' death. I'm . . . well, I'm afraid."

Oh, dear. Sometimes I forgot that not everyone in the world is as accustomed to trickery as I was.

"Do you think we could meet tomorrow?" she went on. "I'd really like some reassurance. Maybe in Central Park at lunchtime? Would that be hard for you to do? I can bring an extra sandwich for you, so you won't have to miss luncheon."

"Don't worry about the extra sandwich, Belinda. I can always find lunch." Besides, I was spoiled from Aunt Vi's cooking, and I doubted Belinda's mother or aunt could equal Vi's sandwiches. "But I'll be happy to meet you in the park. About noon? Ten past? Or do you take your luncheon break later in the day?"

"I generally take lunch from twelve thirty to one thirty. Central Park is near where I work, so I can easily walk there in five minutes."

"So, let's plan on meeting at twelve thirty-five or so."

"Oh, *thank* you, Daisy. I honestly don't know why I feel so uneasy, but I do. I need this job, so . . . well, I appreciate your willingness to meet with me."

"I understand, Belinda." And, if what I suspected was true, I didn't blame her. I sure wouldn't want to get on the wrong side of Mr. Eustace Kincaid. And if Mr. Millette and Mr. Grover were part of his set, I'd try to steer as clear of them as possible, too. Which, unless she wanted to quit her job, which she didn't, Belinda couldn't do.

The rest of Sunday passed restfully. Spike and I napped after

Ma and I cleaned up the noon dinner dishes. Pa told me he and Sam had made plans to play gin rummy that evening, so I wasn't surprised when Sam showed up about four o'clock. In fact, I took the opportunity to tell him about Belinda's call.

"What do you think she should do, Sam?" I asked as Sam went to the closet under the stairway and retrieved the folding card table.

"Go to work and behave as if she didn't see or hear anything," he said, as if Brenda pretending she hadn't heard Mr. Millette and a stranger arguing in the law office on Saturday would be as easy as pie.

"That would be easier to do if Mr. Grover hadn't seen her there," I said, rather miffed that he sounded so blasé about the matter. "Belinda isn't as good as pretending as I am, anyway, so she's nervous."

Sam didn't speak as he set up the table and Pa got a couple of chairs. Then he dusted off his hands, turned, and glared down at me. "What do you want me to do about it? She didn't see who the man with Millette was, and she didn't hear what they were arguing about. Do you expect me to storm the law office and arrest Millette and Grover because your friend is nervous?"

"Darn you, Sam. Of course I don't want you to do that. But you might post a person to watch out for her or something."

As usual at one of my pertinent suggestions, Sam rolled his eyes. I wanted to kick him, but since I was an adult woman, I didn't.

"We don't have an infinite number of patrol officers on the force, Daisy. Unless someone's threatened her life, I can't post a guard on her."

"Pooh." I stood there, steaming, for a second or two, and then said, "Well, I'm going to meet her in Central Park tomorrow around twelve thirty, so maybe she'll have more information to impart after that meeting."

Shaking his head, Sam said, "I'll never understand how you get yourself mixed up in things like this, Daisy. I suggest you telephone your friend and cancel your meeting. What do you expect to accomplish by it, anyway?"

Furious, I said, "*I* don't know! But Belinda heard the name 'Kincaid' being bandied about yesterday, and that's *got* to mean something, doesn't it? I should think *you'd* want to meet her in the park!"

"Good Lord."

"Don't you 'good Lord' me, Sam Rotondo. If *you* don't care who killed Eddie Hastings, *I* do. And so does Belinda!"

"For God's sake, I care. Believe me, there's a serious investigation into the matter being carried on by the police right this minute. We know what we're doing. You don't. Stay out of it, Daisy. I don't want you to get hurt."

"Oh, pooh. Meeting with Belinda in the park to give her some moral support isn't going to put either one of us in danger. The poor thing's worried, for heaven's sake. What she heard in the office yesterday rattled her nerves."

"All right," Sam said with a heavy sigh. "Give your friend moral support. But don't *you* go anywhere near that law office."

"I've already told you I won't," I barked at him. Then I turned away and went to the sofa, where I picked up *The Adventures of Sally,* by Mr. P. G. Wodehouse. I loved his books because they were very funny and took me away from everything.

Sam and Pa were still playing their stupid rummy game when I took Spike and went to bed. Darn Sam Rotondo, anyway! He drove me nuts. Unfortunately, that wasn't a long drive.

The following day, after Pa and I took Spike for a nice long walk around the neighborhood, I dressed in a fashionable outfit in order to see Mrs. Pinkerton. Never let it be said that Daisy

Gumm Majesty ever looked anything but spiffy while plying her trade, even if it was a spurious one.

I selected from my vast wardrobe a two-piece dress of what the fashion mavens called "Pamico cloth" I'd bought dirt-cheap at Maxime's Fabrics. The skirt was a solid blue, but the top was white, embroidered with blue and pink flowers—by my own talented fingers with embroidery thread bought for a song at Nelson's Five and Dime—above the dropped waist. It had a cunning vest made of the same solid blue material, but with big white pockets with more embroidered blue and pink on them.

I considered not wearing a hat, but hadn't been able to get to the library to look through the *Vogue* magazines yet, so I wore the hat I'd crafted myself out of the same blue Pamico, with an embroidered brim. It was a little loose on me, so I stuck two hat pins in it. Even they were beautiful, having been bought by me at Nash's Department Store when they were getting rid of old inventory. I figured hatpins never go out of style, and these had little fake pearls on their ends and went beautifully with my outfit.

Because I aimed to visit Central Park after I saw Mrs. Pinkerton, I decided to wear my black shoes with lower heels than I'd have worn in the evening, and I took my black handbag with me. It was the same bag I'd used for the past several days, so I only put in a fresh handkerchief, dusted it off a bit, and set out for Mrs. Pinkerton's house. I wasn't looking forward to the visit, but I made sure I had my Ouija board and my tarot cards, just in case Mrs. P didn't care for the advice Rolly aimed to give her and wanted a tarot reading. Which would echo Rolly's advice, whether she liked it or not.

When I arrived at the Pinkerton palace, Featherstone opened the door for me, looking like a stuffed penguin as usual. I adored Featherstone. If ever I decided to hire a butler—not that I ever would—I'd want one precisely like Featherstone.

"Good morning, Featherstone."

"Good morning, Mrs. Majesty."

"Lead me on, please, Featherstone." Not that he needed to, but we've been over that.

"Please follow me," said he, sticking to the script.

So I followed him to the drawing room, where Mrs. Pinkerton, pink and plump and in a dither as usual, awaited Rolly and me. She hurled herself out of the chair she'd been whimpering in.

"Oh, Daisy! I'm so glad to see you! I'm just terrified that Eustace will come after me!"

Before I could think better of it I asked, "Why would he do that?"

"Why? Why? Because . . . Well, I don't know. But why else would he come back to Pasadena?"

I thought I knew a partial answer to that question, but I wasn't going to tell her I thought her husband and Mr. Millette, and perhaps Mr. Grover, were involved in importing illegal drugs, probably from China, where Mr. Millette had contacts. "I'm sure I couldn't say," I told her mildly, in full spiritualist purr. "But I think you needn't worry. If he were in Pasadena to see you, why would he have been arguing in an alleyway with another man?"

My question perplexed her, I reckon, because she said, "Hmm. I hadn't thought of that."

No surprise there. I doubt the woman ever thought at all. I'm sorry. Perhaps I'm being too hard on her. It wasn't her fault she'd been born rich and had never had to do a day's work or think a single thought in her life.

I smiled sweetly. "Would you like to begin with the Ouija board? Remember," I said, knowing it would do no good, but with faint hope, "Rolly can't tell you about Mr. Kincaid's movements or anything like that."

She heaved a sigh almost as big as her bosom. "I know. I do

so wish he could."

"So does he," I said, lying through my teeth.

Fortunately, Mrs. P wasn't in too much of a fuss, so I didn't have to remain at her place for more than an hour and a half or so. I toddled to the kitchen to see Vi before I left the house, and, bless her, Vi gave me lunch. I'm glad I'd told Belinda not to bring me a sandwich.

Then I headed to Central Park.

CHAPTER TWENTY-FOUR

I parked on Del Mar Street, which abutted the park, a beautiful stretch of green speckled with trees and benches right smack in the middle of town. Hence the name Central Park, I imagine. The park sat near the railroad station, and I could hear trains tooting from time to time. Naturally the trains' toots brought back memories of last summer's jaunt to Egypt and Turkey with Harold. With any luck at all, I'd never have to leave home again. Not that I didn't appreciate Harold's thoughtfulness, but . . . well, that trip had been quite stressful. And that's putting it mildly.

Belinda hurried up to me after I'd been waiting for her for about five minutes. I didn't mind the wait, being of good cheer and full of good food. I smiled at her, glad to see she appeared every bit the professional secretary that day as she had when I'd visited the law offices of Hastings and Millette. She didn't smile back; that worried me a bit.

"Are you all right, Belinda?"

"I guess so. But I'm so nervous at work, I can hardly stand it. Mr. Grover has been looking at me strangely all morning long."

"What do you mean by 'strangely'?" I asked, my brow furrowed. I bethought me of the bland Mr. Grover, and thought it would take some doing to detect any kind of expression at all on his face.

Belinda passed a hand across her face, and I could see how agitated she was. I put one of my own hands on her shoulder.

"Come over here to a park bench, and let's sit down." I guided her to the nearest bench, which, fortunately, sat under a spreading oak tree. I saw no other people near us, so that was a good thing. "Did you bring your lunch with you?"

"Lunch?" Belinda glanced around, as if she might find her luncheon box in the park somewhere. "Oh. No, I guess I forgot it."

That made me sorry I hadn't brought some of Vi's delicious luncheon fixings for Belinda to nibble on. "That's not good. You need to eat."

"Oh, I'm too nervous to eat!" she cried.

"Belinda, I'm really sorry you're so worried, but please, tell me why. What's going on that has you in such a state? Has Mr. Grover or Mr. Millette spoken with you about what you heard on Saturday?"

"No, no. They haven't said a word to me. Well, Mr. Millette never speaks to me. I'm too low on the totem pole for him to notice."

"You said Mr. Grover has been looking at you strangely. Can you explain that to me?"

Again, Belinda brushed her forehead with her gloved hand. She dressed impeccably, bless her. "Oh, I don't know. Maybe he's not. All I know is that when I heard the name 'Kincaid' being shouted in Mr. Millette's office, I instantly thought of Eddie's death."

That one stumped me. "Why?"

"Again, I don't know. But Mr. Kincaid was a thief. If he and Mr. Millette knew—know—each other, maybe they're in on something together. If Eddie found out about it . . . well, maybe he said something and they did him in."

Dramatic. But not impossible, unless you were Sam Rotondo. "Hmm. Interesting possibility. Um . . . do you know how Eddie Hastings died, by the way?"

She glanced at me sharply. "Why, no. No one's ever told me. Do you know?"

I nodded. "He died from an overdose of heroin."

Her eyes narrowed, making her look like a very pretty bulldog. "What's heroin? I thought a heroine was a lady hero."

My kind of girl, Belinda. "That's what I thought, too. But heroin, without the *e* on the end, is a kind of drug."

"A drug! Eddie Hastings never took drugs in his life! Are you sure? What kind of drug is it, anyhow?"

"Yes, I'm sure, because Dr. Benjamin read the coroner's report and told me. Heroin is derived from opium, like morphine, but heroin is coming into greater use these days, and the bootleggers are now selling it as well, along with their illegal liquor."

"Eddie Hastings never drank. He hated people who defied the law. And I *know* he didn't take drugs. We used to talk about all the scofflaws who thought it was jolly fun to break the law and go to speakeasies and make bathtub gin and take cocaine and things like that. He was a law-abiding man, and to think anyone *ever* thought he actually killed himself with an illegal drug just . . . well, it makes me sick to think about." She took a hankie out of her handbag and wiped tears from her eyes.

"I agree." Something occurred to me just then—kind of a bolt from the blue, if you know what I mean—and I asked, "Say, Belinda, you said Eddie and his father were on bad terms."

"That's putting it mildly."

"Were they always at each other's throats, or was this a recent thing?"

She took a moment to ponder my question. "Come to think of it, it was recent. I'd say it started about a month or so before Eddie died. They got along all right until then, although I don't think Eddie liked his father much. Nobody does." She shrugged. "But they never fought until that time."

"You know what I think happened?"

"What?"

I deliberated for a minute, trying to sort out my scrambled thoughts. As I pondered, I glanced around the park, not wanting anyone to overhear our conversation. When I'd settled matters to my own liking, I began slowly. "I think perhaps Mr. Millette and Mr. Kincaid were in cahoots."

"Cahoots? What kind of cahoots. Cahoots in what endeavor?" Belinda gazed at me dubiously.

"Hear me out. Mrs. Hastings told me that Mr. Millette and Mr. Hastings were in business together in Hong Kong. There's a huge market for heroin, and a lot of it comes from China. What if those two men were in the drug-smuggling business together?"

"Drug smuggling? Good Lord!"

I held up a hand when she seemed about to protest. "Mrs. Hastings found a note in her home. It was from Mr. Kincaid, and it seemed to have been written from prison. The note said he wanted out of San Quentin, and he aimed to tell on whoever the note was written to if whoever it was didn't aid him in escaping."

"My goodness. Do you really think that's possible? How can anyone help anyone else escape from prison?"

"I have no idea. But somehow or other Mr. Kincaid *did* escape from prison, and Mrs. Pinkerton, who used to be married to him, swears she saw him on the street arguing with another middle-aged man only a couple of days ago. I'll bet you anything that other man was Mr. Millette. And then you heard him and Mr. Millette arguing in the law office."

"But I don't know if the other man was Mr. Kincaid."

"Bet it was. You know Mr. Millette, and Mrs. Pinkerton knows Mr. Kincaid. Put the two men together with that note, and I'm sure they're connected."

"Unfortunately for you, you're absolutely correct," came a deep voice from behind the tree under which we were sitting. Belinda and I both swiveled and glanced wildly around.

A man dressed like a bum came out from behind the tree. In one of his hands he carried a jacket, which was odd for a warm June day. When I peered more closely, I saw the barrel of a gun pointing directly at me. My gaze skittered to the man's face, and my heart plummeted into my low-heeled but fashionable shoes.

Why is it always me in the way of danger? Never mind.

"Wh-who are you?" stammered Belinda.

But I knew who it was. "That, Belinda, is Mr. Eustace Kincaid, escaped felon and, I suspect, drug smuggler in league with Mr. Millette."

"And Grover," said Mr. Kincaid with a sneer. I'd always loathed that man, and my hate was growing by leaps and bounds. "Never forget our dear friend, Mr. Grover." He growled a little louder, "Get out here, Grover. I can't handle the both of them by myself."

"Handle us? What do you mean, handle us?" I demanded, fear growing inside me like a demented mushroom.

"Where's Mr. Grover?" asked Belinda. "He can't be a criminal! He's too . . . bland."

Oh, Lord, I wished she hadn't said that, especially when Mr. Grover minced out from behind the tree, holding a jacket in his hands and frowning at Belinda. Naturally, his jacket hid another gun. I noticed his hand shaking, though, so I knew he didn't want to be doing what he was doing.

"Come along, ladies. It's time for you to get back to work, Miss Young. And you, Mrs. Majesty, will have to come along with us until we figure out what to do with the two of you."

I didn't like the sound of that. "But Mr. Hastings called the police and said he didn't want me anywhere near that building again," I said, sounding whiny.

Belinda grabbed my arm. "Oh, Daisy, please don't desert me now," and I was heartily ashamed of myself.

"I won't," I said. "Of course I won't."

"Damned right, you won't," snarled Mr. Kincaid. "Get moving. Now. Toward that Packard on Del Mar."

He poked the gun in my stomach, and I started moving. Belinda walked beside me, stiff as a hat stand. I'm sure she was frightened as I. "What are you going to do with us?" I demanded.

"I don't know yet. We'll have to chat with Millette about that. Don't worry, though. If we have to get rid of you, it won't hurt a bit."

"It won't hurt? What do you mean?" Then the truth dawned on me. "You mean you'll just kill us with heroin as you did Eddie Hastings."

"No!" cried Belinda.

"Shut that woman up," said Kincaid to Grover.

"Be quiet, Miss Young," said Mr. Grover, his rather high-pitched voice quavery in the sunshine of the park.

"I can't believe you're involved with these criminals, Mr. Grover," said Belinda. "You're too nice a man."

"Don't forget how bland I am," he said, as if her comment had hurt his feelings.

"Wait a minute. We're in a public park, and there are people everywhere. You can't force us to do anything we don't want to do," I said, suddenly feeling feisty. "What are you going to do? Shoot us if we run away?" Not that I wanted to give them ideas. "People would hear the shots, see you, and you'd be caught before you could ever get away."

"Daisy, be careful," Belinda said in a shaky voice.

"Good advice, Miss Young," said Mr. Kincaid.

And that's the last thing I remember. Mr. Kincaid—I think it was he—passed a smelly rag under my nose, and I was out like a light.

I presume he did the same thing to Belinda, because when I woke up, we were both tied with thin rope and huddled somewhere. Wherever we were was dark as night, and my head ached as if someone had bashed me with a bat. A faint sickly odor permeated the air around me, and I recognized it as chloroform. Good Lord, that stuff can kill a person! Instantly I thought about Belinda.

"Belinda!" I whispered urgently. "Are you in here with me?"

No answer came from Belinda. My fear spiked to panic, and I tried to feel around for her. This task was almost impossible, since my hands were tied together. Fortunately, whoever had bound my wrists had not done so behind my back, so I did manage to reach out. All I felt was a wall. That being the case, I fumbled my way to my feet, which were also bound, and sort of scooched sideways, where I almost immediately bumped into a softish object and fell over.

"*Oooff!*" came from the object.

Belinda! Thank God.

"Oh, Belinda, I'm so glad you're here with me. But you'd better whisper. I don't know where we are or if there are other people around."

"Wh-what happened?" she asked, sounding like a line from a bad melodrama.

"Kincaid and Grover chloroformed us and locked us somewhere."

"Oh, my head hurts," she said.

"Mine does, too. Are your hands tied up?"

A second or two passed. I guess she was trying to sort herself out. Then she said, "Yes. Who did that?"

"I suspect Kincaid and Grover again."

"What are they going to do to us, Daisy? I'm afraid!"

"So am I. But let me think. I have a couple of hatpins in my hat." I reached for my head with my bound hands. "If I can just find—Darn it, they took my hat and the pins, the villains!"

"What were you going to do with a couple of hatpins?"

"*I* don't know, but at least they were sharp and could maybe poke someone and hurt him."

"We need more than hatpins," said Belinda, being depressingly honest.

"Well, let's think about this. We're locked in a closet . . . or are we? Let's be quiet and try to figure out where we are before we do anything."

"What can we do when we find out where we are?" she asked. No imagination, Belinda Young.

"I'm not sure yet, but I'll think of something. Just be quiet and we'll try to figure out where we are."

I'd managed to maneuver myself off Belinda, so I felt around for a wall again. Walls were in imminent supply, so again I pushed myself to my feet and moved, very awkwardly, around the space. File cabinets. Bankers' boxes—at least, they felt like bankers' boxes. If we were in the law firm, they were probably deed boxes. The wall met another wall going the other direction, so I did, too. Somebody's coat hanging, I presumed, from a hook. More file cabinets. The place felt like a closet to me.

"I think we're in a closet somewhere. There are file cabinets and boxes, like deed boxes."

"Oh, we use those in the firm," said Belinda, confirming my suspicion. "This place smells familiar, too, if you discount that disgusting sweet smell."

"That's chloroform. They chloroformed us. If we're in Mr. Grover's or Mr. Millette's office, do you know anything about the closets there?"

"I know there should be a light chain somewhere near the door."

From the sounds she made, I presumed she was trying to get to her own feet.

"Let me try to find it," I said.

Easier said than done. I don't know if you've ever tried to walk in a pitch-black closet with your hands and feet bound with rope, but it's not a simple thing to do. However, with the aid of the wall, I managed to ease myself along until a doorknob bumped against my hip bone. Hard. It hurt.

"I found the doorknob."

"The light chain should be close by. The light is directly above the door, and the chain hangs down to about a foot below the top of the door. In the center."

"I'll try to find it."

"Do you think you should? What if someone sees the light from beneath the door?"

Bother. Belinda was undoubtedly a very good secretary. She was clearly detail oriented and thought about the little things.

"Well, I think we're going to have to chance it. If we can get ourselves untied, maybe we can escape. Somehow."

"Why don't we untie each other before we turn on the light— are your hands tied in front of you?"

"Yes, they are. That's a good idea."

So we untied each other's hands; *not* an easy thing to do, since all twenty of our collective fingers were nearly numb by that time. I don't know how long it took us to get untied and then to unbind our feet, but it seemed like hours. We both shook out our hands and wiggled our feet to get the feeling back in them.

"All right," I said at last. "Are you ready for me to try for the light?"

"I guess so," said Belinda. "Although if they see the light, they'll only tie us back up again."

And this time they'd probably tie our hands behind our backs.

But I figured we might as well chance it. Better half a chance at escape than a needle filled with heroin. But wait. I considered something else.

"Is my handbag near you?"

"I don't know. Let me feel around. I think I found it."

It was becoming slightly easier to maneuver in that confined space, now that I was no longer fettered. I took the handbag from Belinda, reached inside, and found the set of chopsticks Keiji Saito had given me. Not much of a weapon, but you never knew what would come in handy when.

Then I managed to find my way to the closet door again, reached for the chain, and pulled.

CHAPTER TWENTY-FIVE

The light went on, making me blink and making my head pound harder. Dang it! I hated Mr. Kincaid with so hot a passion, I'd like to have strangled him with my bare hands. Not that I'd have been able to do that, since he was a good deal larger than I.

I sucked in a breath and held it. When I glanced back—not far back, since the closet was . . . well, a closet and, therefore, a smallish room—I saw Belinda had done the same thing and was now standing stiff as a statue, looking scared and slightly disheveled, squinting and pressing her hands to her undoubtedly aching head. I passed a hand over my own hair, and it was messy, too. Horrid men must have disarranged it when they stole my hat and hatpins.

"So," Belinda whispered, "what do we do now?"

"I'm not sure. Maybe if we look around we can find some kind of weapon."

"In a law office's closet?"

"Well, it can't hurt to look." I was beginning to deplore Belinda's negativity.

And then the door opened outward. Since I still had hold of the doorknob, I went outward too, and nearly crashed right into Mrs. Larkin, who looked as though she'd never seen anything so astounding in her life as Belinda in the closet and me hanging onto the doorknob.

Oh, Lord, what now?

"What in the name of glory are you two doing in my office closet?" she screeched at us.

"Shhh," I said. "Don't make so much noise, for heaven's sake."

"Who are you to be giving me orders, young woman? And Miss Young, what on *earth* were the two of you doing in there?" She glared at Belinda and then at me, as if we'd been stealing all the office paperclips and typewriter ribbons. She hadn't lowered her voice.

"Darn it, be quiet!" I told her in a savage whisper. "Mr. Grover and Mr. Kincaid kidnapped us in the park and dragged us here. Mr. Millette knows all about it."

She stared at me as if I'd told her little pop-eyed men from Mars had swept us up and deposited us on the moon.

"That's the most ridiculous thing I've ever heard. Why, when I tell Mr. Millette about this, you'll be looking for a new job, Miss Young. And *you,* Mrs. Majesty, were told never to darken our doors again."

"Blast it, keep your voice down!"

I heard a heavy tread in the hallway, and my heart started racing like Spike when he ran after his ball. What to do? What to do?

Not a sensible thought entered my head, but I dashed to the door and plastered myself against the wall so that I'd be hidden when the door opened. Belinda still stood in the closet, looking not unlike a frightened deer. You can imagine my surprise when she suddenly lunged at Mrs. Larkin, slung an arm around her, and stuffed her hankie into the old bat's mouth, dragging her into the closet and closing the door behind the both of them.

Which left me to get the heck out of there and fetch help if I could. Oh, joy. Oh, rapture.

Oh, nuts. The doorknob turned, and someone pushed the

door open. Fortunately for me, I was right about the door hiding me.

"Mrs. Larkin? Please come to my room for a moment. I have a letter to dictate."

It had to be Mr. Millette, because it was a voice I hadn't heard before. I discerned a scuttling sound coming from the closet. Probably Mrs. Larkin, being her usual difficult self.

"Mrs. Larkin?" Mr. Millette said again, sounding puzzled. "Are you in the closet? Whatever for?"

He took a step toward the closet, and, thinking fast, I did the only thing I could think to do.

"Don't move or make a sound," I growled, sticking him in the back with both chopsticks, hoping like anything they'd feel like the barrel of a gun. I guess they did, because Mr. Millette slowly lifted his hands.

"What's going on here?" he asked.

"The game's up, Millette. The police will be here any minute to take you, Mr. Grover, and Mr. Kincaid to the clink."

"What the—?"

I guess the chopsticks didn't scare him anywhere near enough, because he lowered one of his arms in a chopping gesture and bashed my wrist. I whirled around and dashed like a bunny out of the room, slamming the door behind me. Then I zoomed across the hall, raced down the stairs, and galloped across the lobby, aiming for the front door.

Pounding after me, Mr. Millette hollered, "Stop that woman! Stop her! Stop, thief!"

Smart man, for a vicious criminal. But not smart enough. Before the poor girl at the reception desk had gathered her startled wits together, I'd made it to the front door. Fortunately for me, I was young and Mr. Millette wasn't. So he couldn't catch me. I raced west down the sidewalk on Colorado Boulevard, heading for Fair Oaks Avenue, which was only half a block away. Scared to death, I kept glancing around as I ran, hoping like mad that neither Mr. Kincaid nor Mr. Grover were lurking about anywhere. All I saw were a whole lot of shocked people looking at me as if I'd lost my mind. They weren't far wrong.

At Fair Oaks, I whipped around the corner and sped north toward City Hall, which was a mere block away, and at the rear of which sat the Pasadena Police Department. I prayed hard the whole way, so I guess that answers the question of whether or not I still believed in God.

By the time I pushed through the double doors to the police station, I was scared out of my wits, exhausted, and ready to drop. But I didn't. I rushed up to the uniformed officer at the desk, who jerked backwards in his chair, and panted, "I need Sam Rotondo. Now!"

He squinted at me, and I wanted to bellow at him to get a move on, but I was too out of breath. "What's the matter, young lady?"

"Darn it, get Sam, will you? Mr. Eustace Kincaid, Mr. Millette, and Mr. Grover have Belinda Young stuffed into a closet at the law firm on Colorado!"

"I beg your pardon?"

"*Damn* it!" I cried, shocking me more than the officer, I'm sure. I don't believe I'd ever used a swear word before. "Just get Sam, will you?"

"Yes, ma'am," he said at last, picking up the telephone receiver, and I wilted some.

When Sam thundered down the staircase, I was still panting. He hurried up to me and grabbed me by the arms. "What's this about? Roger here said Kincaid, Millette, and Grover kidnapped someone."

"Mr. Kincaid and Mr. Grover kidnapped Belinda and me both. They tied us up and stuck us in a closet at the law firm, but I managed to get away. But stop standing there and *do* something, Sam! Mr. Kincaid admitted they killed Eddie Hastings. They threatened to kill us the same way."

A bunch of other policemen, some in uniforms and some in suits, like Sam, entered the lobby as Sam and I stood there. Help. Help was on the way. Thank God, thank God. I sagged against him, and he put his arms around me. "Please hurry. I'm afraid for Belinda." If they'd already done Belinda in, they'd probably also killed Mrs. Larkin, but I didn't care about her, the old cow.

Very well, so I'm not always a good Christian girl.

"Stay here. We're going to the law firm," said Sam, letting me go after a few seconds. When I gazed up at him, he appeared rather red-faced and embarrassed. I guess he didn't ordinarily hug young women who came to him for help.

You've heard about the shootout at the OK Corral? Well, that day there was a shootout at the law offices of Hastings, Millette, and Hastings. It was Mr. Kincaid who wielded the weapon, and who was himself shot for his efforts—not, more's the pity, fatally. Both Mr. Millette and Mr. Grover gave themselves up, Millette grudgingly, and Grover sobbing uncontrollably after the police had scoured the building and found him huddled in yet another closet, this one in the attics of the great building.

After the good guys got him to the police station, he babbled that he'd been forced to aid and abet the two other men, but I doubt that will help him much when it comes to a trial, since he also admitted he'd been the one to use the needle on Eddie Hastings. Evidently Eddie told his father that he suspected Millette and Grover were doing something illegal. Thus, the bad relations between the two men, I reckon.

Belinda was fine after she stopped crying. Mrs. Larkin had an hysterical fit, which laid her low for weeks, which I think served her right.

Did I stay behind in the police station as Sam had advised while the police went to arrest the criminals?

Oddly enough, I did. I considered walking back to the law firm, but I feared Mr. Kincaid and/or Mr. Grover might yet be lurking outside on the streets somewhere. I felt more secure with a bunch of policemen around me.

Sam came to dinner at our house that night.

By the way, I got my hat back, and my hatpins—eventually. Mr. Millette had stuffed both hat and pins into one of his desk drawers. Sam said that was a stupid thing to have done, and that both hat and pins could be considered evidence, so I didn't get them back until after the trial.

"Thanks to Daisy and Miss Young—not to mention the chopsticks Daisy carried in her handbag—we not only arrested the three men for murder, but the drug ring that's been in operation for years and years has also been broken up," Sam said that night at the dinner table. He frowned at me as he spoke, which figured. Never a kind word when I helped him solve a case, drat the man.

"What did the chopsticks have to do with thwarting the criminals?" asked Pa.

"She held them at Millette's back and told him to stick 'em up," Sam said.

"I did not! Well . . . maybe I did, but I couldn't think of any other way to stop him long enough for me to escape that dratted office."

"Mercy sakes," said my mother faintly. "Oh, Daisy, you were in danger. I wish you wouldn't put yourself in such perilous situations."

Not my mother, too? This wasn't fair! "I was at the park with Belinda, Ma. There's nothing perilous about going to a park at lunchtime."

"It's all right, sweetheart. No one's blaming you for what happened," said Pa, bless him.

"I don't know, Joe," said Aunt Vi. "Things do tend to happen around Daisy, don't they?"

"They sure do," growled Sam, cutting into his slab of meat-loaf.

"That's not fair, Sam. I only went to the park to be of some comfort to Belinda. She was scared after what she'd heard on Saturday."

I wished like the devil I hadn't said that when my entire family turned in their chairs and stared at me. Bother.

"What, precisely, happened on Saturday, young woman?" Ma asked, sounding as severe as I'd ever heard her sound.

I heaved a deep and hearty sigh. "You remember that telephone call we received last Saturday night after supper?"

"No, but I suppose it was related to this business." Ma waved her hand over her dinner plate, looking rather like a conjuror, but meaning the business of the criminals captured earlier that day.

"Sort of. Belinda 'phoned me to say she'd heard Mr. Millette and Mr. Kincaid yelling at each other in Mr. Millette's office on Saturday morning."

"Mr. Kincaid?" said Pa, clearly surprised.

"Yes. You know he escaped from prison, right?"

This time my family exchanged glances with each other. "He escaped?" Ma said faintly.

"I guess I didn't tell you, Peggy," said Pa. "Daisy got a call from Mrs. Pinkerton, who told her she was sure her ex-husband had killed Mr. Hastings."

"I thought Mr. Hastings was the head of the law firm." Now Vi sounded as confused as Ma had.

"The head of the law firm—he didn't have anything to do with the murder or the drug smuggling—is Mr. Stephen Hastings. Not that he's a nice man, but at least he didn't kill anybody. His son, Edward, was the poor fellow who was killed."

"I see, I think," said Ma.

"What does the poor boy's murder have to do with the drug trade?" asked Pa, and reasonably, too, I believe.

Deciding I'd already said too much on the subject, I glanced at Sam, who sat across the table from me. He obligingly took over the tale.

"It was Mr. Grover who spilled the beans. He was a nervous wreck when we finally found him. He swore up and down and back and forth that he'd been forced into the dirty business when the young Hastings discovered incriminating evidence against Mr. Millette and asked Grover about it. Grover told Millette, and Millette somehow made arrangements for Kincaid to escape from San Quentin. Instead of heading to Mexico, as Millette had ordered him to do, with the promise of sending him payments from the drug business, he came to Pasadena. This infuriated Millette, of course."

"And frightened his ex-wife," I plunked in.

Sam's eyes paid a brief visit to the ceiling. "Yes. And frightened his ex-wife."

"She called me one day in a tizzy—"

"Typical," muttered Vi.

"—and swore it was Mr. Kincaid who'd murdered Eddie Hastings."

"Which was pure bunkum," said Sam, taking over the narrative once more. "He was still in prison when the Hastings lad was killed. But he was killed by an overdose of heroin, which tied his murder into the drug case the police department has been working on for a long time."

"Heroin?" said Ma. "I thought a heroine was a lady hero."

Sam and I looked at each other, and burst out laughing.

"Well, I don't see what's so funny about that," said Ma, miffed.

I wiped my streaming eyes on my napkin. "It's not funny, Ma. But it's exactly the same thing I said when Dr. Benjamin told me the cause of Eddie Hastings' death. And it's exactly what Belinda Young said to *me* when I told *her* the cause of Eddie's death."

"Hmph. I still don't see what's so funny."

Sam explained all about heroin. "But Kincaid's in real trouble now. He shot at police officers, and that's a serious crime. I doubt he'll be able to live the soft life in the prison library any longer. He's in for hard time."

"Good," I said, feeling vindicated. I despised Mr. Eustace, the fiend, Kincaid. With a sinking heart, I realized I'd have to telephone Mrs. Pinkerton with the news. She'd be thrilled and then go into a frenzy, and I'd have to take myself and Rolly over to her house to give aid and assistance. Crumbs.

Then Sam looked at me, a strange expression on his face. I was instantly on the alert.

"What? Why are you looking at me like that?" I demanded.

"Well . . . don't look now, Daisy, but I think you're in for another commendation from the Pasadena Police Department for your help in solving two unsolved crimes."

My parents, aunt, and I all gaped at each other. I'd received a certificate of commendation from the PPD when I'd helped them smash a bootlegging operation. But my part in that case had been a total accident.

Come to think of it, so was my part in this one.

I set my fork on my plate and bowed my head. "I don't think I can stand it, Sam."

"Buck up, kid," said he with a broad grin. "If you can hold up a man with a pair of chopsticks, you can handle receiving another certificate of commendation."

He was right, of course. I hate when that happens.

Last but not least, I'm pleased to report that not a single spirit has sullied one of my séances since Eddie Hastings made his alarming appearance. I sincerely hope this dearth of death-come-alive will continue forever.

ABOUT THE AUTHOR

Award-winning author **Alice Duncan** lives with a herd of wild dachshunds (enriched from time to time with fosterees from New Mexico Dachshund Rescue) in Roswell, New Mexico. She's not a UFO enthusiast; she's in Roswell because her mother's family settled there fifty years before the aliens crashed. Alice would love to hear from you at alice@aliceduncan .net. And be sure to visit her Web site at http://www.alice duncan.net and her Facebook page at https://www.facebook .com/alice.duncan.925.